Killing a Unicorn

Also by Marjorie Eccles:

Cast a Cold Eye
Death of a Good Woman
Requiem for a Dove
More Deaths Than One
Late of This Parish
The Company She Kept
An Accidental Shroud
A Death of Distinction
A Species of Revenge
Killing Me Softly
The Superintendent's Daughter
A Sunset Touch
Echoes of Silence
Untimely Graves

KILLING A UNICORN

Marjorie Eccles

Thomas Dunne Books St. Martin's Minotaur ♞ New York

THOMAS DUNNE BOOKS.
An imprint of St. Martin's Press.

KILLING A UNICORN. Copyright © 2002 by Marjorie Eccles. All rights reserved. Printed in the United States of America. No part of this book may be used or reproduced in any manner whatsoever without written permission except in the case of brief quotations embodied in critical articles or reviews. For information, address St. Martin's Press, 175 Fifth Avenue, New York, N.Y. 10010.

www.minotaurbooks.com

Library of Congress Cataloging-in-Publication Data

Eccles, Marjorie.
    Killing a unicorn / Marjorie Eccles.—1st U.S. ed.
        p. cm.
    ISBN 0-312-32411-1
    EAN 978-0312-32411-7
    1. Women—Crimes against—Fiction. 2. Architects' spouses—Fiction. 3. Missing children—Fiction. 4. Brothers—Fiction. 5. England—Fiction. I. Title.

PR6055.C33K54 2005
823'.914—dc22   2004051397

First published in Great Britain by Constable,
an imprint of Constable & Robinson Ltd

First U.S. Edition: January 2005

10 9 8 7 6 5 4 3 2 1

Chapter One

London. A stifling early September afternoon, the sun
beating down. Oxford Street and a million shoppers. Sheer
hell.

Overnight bag and briefcase in one hand, handbag over
her shoulder, Fran plunges down into the arguably worse
hell of the Underground at Oxford Circus. Everything
conspires against her, but what's new, when you're in a
hurry? Jostling her way through the shuffling crowds, she
steps on to the down escalator, where a couple of tourists
very nearly cause a major pile-up by stopping dead at the
bottom and opening their map. Squashed between them
and the crowd behind, Fran feels her shoulder-bag slip and
she grabs it just in time. On the teeming platform she's
pushed around between home-going commuters like herself and shoppers weighed down with carrier bags from
Selfridges and Harrods. Plus students of every nationality,
top-heavy with bedrolls and backpacks, a hazard to anyone who isn't adroit enough to dodge their gigantic loads
as they swing round like ungainly camels . . . Why am
I doing this? she asks herself, finally in the tube train,
strap-hanging, in unwanted intimacy with a garlic-scented,
hair-oiled individual who eyes her suggestively, but it's a
rhetorical question.

Clutching the support by the door with one hand, her
grip and briefcase wedged between her feet, the other
hand firmly on her handbag, she closes her eyes and longs
to be able to massage the crease between her brows where
the incipient headache has threatened all day. Staring at

the VDU hasn't helped, trying to co-ordinate the designs so clear in her own mind with the recalcitrant graphics on the screen. O'Sullivan, O'Toole Advertising – O.S.O.T. – in the middle of a prestigious toothpaste account, has been more than the usual madhouse today. If anything could go wrong, it had. Murphy's Law. That's not unusual, either. It's what comes of working for the Irish mob, according to her friend Claire, who is little and neat and deceptively wide-eyed, and sees things very clearly. She's an exceedingly clever lawyer, and would never dream of working for any outfit as wacky as O.S.O.T., though that's hardly the point, as far as Fran's concerned. The point is that there are other factors that make it a good place to work. And however hit and miss it might seem to outsiders, the agency functions well. Saatchi & Saatchi it's not, but they get results.

They'd had supper together last night, she and Claire, and afterwards Fran had stayed in the family's flat, a one-bedroomed pad in Belsize Park, which all the Calverts use as a convenient overnight stopping place on visits to town, or when it's too late to get home. Claire had pressed her to stay on another night and see the latest new release at the Leicester Square Odeon, but Chip has bagged the flat for tonight, and anyway the mere thought of its stuffy claustrophobia, never mind her brother-in-law's large presence and a consequent bed for her on the sofa, was enough to negative the idea. No contest there with the house in the woods, waiting for her, the thought of which is like a long, refreshing draught of cold water.

Home. Even home alone.

Cool and light, set in a wide, open clearing, the windows facing in all the right directions because Mark designed it that way. An award-winning, modernist arrangement of glass cubes, planned for maximum light, wonderful when she's working on the intricate hangings she does in what spare time she can muster, but mainly designed for Mark's working environment. What you can see of it that isn't windows is creamy slabs of Purbeck stone, smooth as marble. No garden, just a large, grassy space beneath the little waterfall and the pool, the backdrop of trees behind it. Shared only with rabbits, squirrels, the odd badger, and the deer who roam the woods and come down to the pool at night to drink. It's what Fran thinks of as part of her inner landscape, or if that isn't too fanciful, the place where, finally, she knows she's meant to be. Not everyone shares her passion for it, much less for the animals. They're a menace in the village gardens, and sometimes the deer herds wander even further out of the woods, up along the bluff behind the house towards Membery and, with no trouble at all, gracefully leap the crumbling six-foot wall enclosing Alyssa's garden, wreaking havoc and bringing out the worst in her. Better to have no roses than no deer, thinks Fran, though Alyssa can hardly be blamed for feeling that way when the garden has become a substantial part of her livelihood. She's gradually having the old wall replaced by a chain-link fence, ten feet high – a less aesthetically pleasing but more affordable deterrent. As and when she has the money. That's the story she's putting about, though it would be more truthful to say when Chip can be persuaded to sanction payment for it.

It doesn't do to take Alyssa too literally. Large and flamboyant, in her mid-sixties but still hanging on in there to the vivid, dark good looks she's passed on to her three sons, exaggeration is as much part of her nature as her flashing eyes, her warm smile and the jewellery she wears with such panache whenever she isn't working in the garden – and sometimes when she is. Unlike most women of her station, she has no inhibitions about appearing vulgar. But then, she wasn't born out of the top drawer. Like Fran, she has only married a Calvert.

The escalator disgorges its passengers into the main-line railway station, Fran makes a run for it across the concourse and by the skin of her teeth manages to catch the commuter train that will bear her home. Miraculously, she finds a seat, collapses into it while she gets her breath back after her sprint and closes her eyes, willing herself to relax.

7

But she can't shut out the vague incipient unease which, like that hint of a headache, has been with her all day in the office, shadow-dancing at the back of her mind.

Why does Mark have to be away on this particular night? She doesn't mind being on her own, as a rule, she's used to it. Only lately she's been a bit jittery – imagining she hears sounds outside, when there's nothing. Hearing someone moving around outside the house during the night, voices, running footsteps, a motorbike revving up and driving away, none of which Mark ever hears, because once his head touches the pillow, he's dead to the world for the next seven hours. Things like that.

In fact she normally enjoys the silence of the forest. The product of divorced parents, she was brought up in the hurly-burly of life with three half-siblings, where there was never enough room, never enough privacy. Then at art college, it was much the same in a way, where not only classes were shared but life outside, the not yet cast off adolescent compulsion to go with the crowd. She'd been determined afterwards to have her own bedsit, but it had come as a shock, a fierce disappointment. She's tried to explain the difference between aloneness and loneliness to Mark . . . has he understood? She isn't sure her powers of interpretation are adequate. Or, as always with Mark, if he's understood only too well.

Meanwhile, the silence surrounding the house is a precious commodity, to be weighed out and savoured in small amounts, alone or, better still, with Mark.

'Look, Fran, you love him, right?' Claire had begun her mini lecture last night, over paella and a bottle of Rioja. 'OK, stupid question! So – isn't it time for some straight talking between you?'

'I've tried that, but he *won't* talk, not really talk, discuss things – and that's so unlike him.' Mark, relaxed, smiling, skilfully changing the subject.

'Then you do the talking, and refuse to stop. He'll have to answer sometime. I wouldn't let Mitch get away with anything like that, and we're not even married yet. Come on, it's not like you, Fran!'

'We-ell . . .'

'Trouble is, you don't know yourself what you want. Am I right or am I right?'

Fran looked down into the bottom of her empty glass, and saw the inescapable truth. 'You're in the wrong job, Claire, you should be working for Relate. All right, when he gets back, I'll give it a try.' For a moment, she'd felt bleak. 'Another try.'

'Don't give up, duckie, you owe it to yourself. Get a life.'

Claire's talking sense. Only, Fran's never been very good at confrontations. If confrontation is the right word.

Hopefully, Mark will be ringing her this evening, though his schedule in Brussels is tight. But she knows really that a brief message on the answerphone is all she can realistically expect. Mark, when working, is totally concentrated – and considering how things have been lately, she can only be glad of it. However, this brings forth aspects of the situation she doesn't want to consider at this precise moment.

Then she remembers that Bibi's coming down later that evening, and hardly knows whether to be pleased or not. It will all depend on what mood she's in. Bibi with all her candles lit is great to be with: she radiates happiness, seeming to dance as she walks, light as a leaf, with her soft hair curving like silver-gilt feathers round her face, unbelievable eyes, a real, gentian blue, complexion so fair and translucent it dazzles. An infectious laugh, when she's pleased, or wanting to please. Totally different from that other self she can assume, as for instance when she goes up to work at the country club: then, she wears severe suits, so unlike her preferred ethnic garments, hair drawn back to reveal the clean modelling of a face beautiful without the need for much make-up, with high, rounded cheekbones and a soft mouth that's belied by a determined chin.

9

But – and that 'but' makes Fran shiver – it isn't outside the bounds of possibility that tonight she'll be in neither persona, but in that faraway, withdrawn mood, where you can never be sure if it's something you've said, or whether any single word you've uttered has actually reached her, never mind that she always answers rationally enough. Indeed, if you didn't know her, you might well think there was nothing wrong, unless you noticed that blank, china-doll stare in those blue eyes, that unnerving, unblinking, inward-looking gaze, as if there was a glass wall between her and the rest of the world. At such times, Fran often wonders whether she'd feel anything if you stuck a pin into her. It's weird. No, it's much more than that, it's frightening, in a way that makes your blood run cold.

Forty minutes later, Fran steps off the train at Felsborough and crosses the car park to where she's left her car the previous morning, slips off her London shoes and ex-changes them for the old flatties under the driving seat, stows her jacket tidily on the back seat – better and better, Fran! – and sets off for home.

Gradually, the tense band around her skull eases as she drives up the wooded hill, one of the ridges of the Chil-terns set high among rolling chalk uplands. Half-way up, the trees begin to close in and it becomes noticeably cooler as she makes the turn for the forest ride that eventually leads to the house. The silence deepens; she winds down the window further and the car is suddenly full of earthy scents and the croo-crooing of wood pigeons and the scrunch of beech-mast beneath the wheels. The forest is considerable, covering four thousand acres of mostly beech and some oak, interspersed here and there by the occa-sional stand of mixed conifers, spreading upwards and outwards across the valley. Jutting forward in the midst of this, cleaving the valley like the prow of a huge ocean liner, is the bluff on which Membery Place stands.

Soon, she drives through the shallow ford that crosses

the road immediately before the point where the drive of The Watersplash appears to the right before whipping diagonally back on itself. The ford has been marked on ancient maps from time immemorial as The Watersplash, and the name settled easily on the new house in the course of its erection without anyone consciously having chosen it.

And there it is, with only a row of slender silver birches to screen it from the forest road, and beyond it the wide green sward of the clearing stretching right up to the front door. It's compelling, totally unexpected in that place, an in-your-face statement, like a lot of Mark's work. All right, a shock it might be – and some of its detractors say it's an outrage, an alien structure in this wood – but its clean geometry of dynamically interlocking glass cubes endows it with a spatial quality that allows it to blend in with its background. Its glass gilded tonight by the evening sun, glimpsed through the birches, it stands at the end of a driveway of ruinously expensive bark chippings that constantly need to be renewed: Mark's poetic vision of this house hasn't entirely encompassed the practicalities of living in a wood. For one thing, a house like this – though not as much at the back end of nowhere as one might think, since a road runs along the ridge of the bluff above and behind the house, past the village of Middleton Thorpe (which has a pub, a church and a school – a shop, even) and then on towards Membery Place, before curling back down the other side – such a house couldn't be built and maintained except at considerable expense and not a little inconvenience. The estimated cost of just laying the services, bringing them down from the road, had almost shipwrecked the enterprise before it was launched. The electricity is unreliable, there are often blips, momentary but enough to cause trouble with all the electronic devices Mark sees as indispensable to life: his PC, fax, video and e-mail, not to mention the microwave, fridge and freezer. Occasionally, however, it fails altogether. The overhead cables are easily brought down by the wind, a falling tree, and once, it's said, by a gnawing squirrel – though how this was known, or what had happened to the squirrel, has not been recorded. Fried, presumably, says Mark. But at least, the lack of a garden poses no problems of maintenance: a scything of the soft, lush grass twice a year, occasional attempts to keep back the encroaching bracken are all that is needed.

Fran drives her car into the area at the back of the house, discreetly screened by a thick holly hedge, and parks it in the double garage, carefully not taking up too much room, although Mark won't be needing his space until next week. She remembers to change her shoes again and leave her flatties in the car. She's learning – though it has to be said that natural tidiness isn't in her nature. She heads for the house.

Its lovely, spicy cedar smell welcomes her as she enters. The muted light filtering through the blinds burnishes the pale wood floor to gold, the white walls to a warm apricot. Interlocking spaces rather than rooms meet her, a suspended staircase and a mezzanine floor. Height and light and, flanking the front windows, the lavish, seemingly never-ending curtains of shimmering ivory watered silk that stretch through two floors to the upstairs ceiling (God knows how many metres – a second mortgage) and are never drawn. There are holland blinds, necessary to shut out the sun when it's too intrusive. Or for privacy. Fran insists on drawing them in the evening against the blank-black night outside, when Mark would leave them undrawn, secure and unperturbed in his lighted glass cube.

The decor Mark chose is minimalist, hi-tech, with transparent tables, cool, neutral colours, tubular furniture. Some of Fran's own brilliant-hued wall hangings provide the only splash of colour. And, on a table, a pile of oranges heaped in the huge black basalt bowl she'd once guiltily splurged a fortune on. She frowns.

They look gorgeous, a black and orange composition on the smoked glass table, but she doesn't remember putting them there, she prefers oranges cold from the fridge, juicy and almost lemon sharp. She cannot abide eating their flesh when it's warm. But there's no denying the evidence of her own eyes, she must have put them there and forgotten. She pauses, then shrugs. Well, yes, perhaps. She's found herself, regrettably, doing this sort of thing before. Subconsciously copying that habit of Mark's, that clever way he has of meticulously arranging groups of *objets trouvés*. Perhaps hoping to please him. Forgetting his habit of sometimes removing her vases of flowers because they don't fit in with his overall perception of what the house should look like. Annoyed with herself, ignoring the thought of what construction Claire would put on such a lapse, she puts the fruit back in the fridge. She's teaching herself to live with perfection, artistic perfection, but it isn't always easy.

She sighs. Most women would give their eye teeth for a husband who never leaves his dirty socks under the bed, who wipes the washbasin, *and* puts the cap back on the toothpaste, without even a conscious effort. Picks her things up, too, as well as his own, and not in any spirit of criticism – he's relaxed and easy, just never thinks about it, it's how he's made. Either that or his training has made him so. She reminds herself that architects need to be meticulous. Mind you, he isn't above letting her change the vacuum cleaner bag, or iron his shirts or struggle to put the fresh cover on the duvet. Wifely things he never thinks of doing.

It cuts both ways, though, doesn't it? He keeps an eye on her car and stops her from forgetting to make out her tax forms. He's wonderful when she has flu. And he's more fun to be with than anyone else she's ever known.

Kicking off her shoes to protect the floor, she pads around. No red, blinking light flashing from the answering machine, but loads of post. More bills than she wants to see, half a rain forest in junk mail, a folded slip of paper that turns out to be a note from Bibi: 'Sorry darling, couldn't make it tonight after all. I'll ring you and we'll fix another time.' Typewritten, but at least she's signed it in her distinctive violet ink, and with her full name, too: Bianca, in rounded, schoolgirl handwriting, and with the tail of the final 'a' curling backwards and round to encircle the whole signature with a great stylish flourish.

Fran goes into the kitchen, pours herself a glass of iced water and drinks it down in one, not entirely sorry Bibi won't be here tonight. It might be her ankle that's bothering her: she broke it a few weeks ago, and though she says it isn't actually painful now, it's still irksome. She's obliged to hobble, even with the aid of a stick. She must have persuaded the boy who works for Alyssa in the gardens to deliver the note on his way home. She isn't able to drive yet and being dependent on others to get about irritates her. She doesn't like everyone to know her business – where she's going and who she's been with. In her own way, she's a very independent person. Stubborn and secretive, more like, according to Mark. Mulish, at times. Yet, when she'd rung Fran that afternoon to say she'd be dropping in, she'd sounded . . . well, almost pleading. She'd insisted it was urgent that they should talk. Perhaps she's been casting her own horoscope again. Maybe there is malevolence in Saturn, or whatever else it is that makes the planets inauspicious. Bibi's actions, her life even, are ruled by her belief in this sort of mumbo-jumbo, but you'd be very brave if you tried to laugh her out of it. She's deadly serious.

It was Chip, the eldest of the Calvert brothers, who brought Bibi to Membery Place, a couple of years ago. Chip, a prep school nickname for Crispin, which stuck and has been accepted ever since with the good humour that's typical of him. Chip, of all people, who might have been expected to settle down eventually with some county gel with a loud laugh, a shiny-haired bob and a way with horses. And, hopefully, money. But no, it was Bibi. About as far from that as you could get.

Fran first met the three Calverts at Henley, where she'd been taken by Connor O'Sullivan, then her boss at the

O'Sullivan, O'Toole agency, now her fellow director. As a stand-in for his wife, who'd decided an invitation to join friends at their villa in Tuscany was a better prospect than the occasional few seconds' fleeting excitement offered by the passing of two racing boats. Blink, and you missed them. Though Fran had seen at once that for anyone other than enthusiasts, the racing wasn't by any means the only point of the Regatta.

Happily sipping her fruity Pimms, she'd gazed across the sea of pretty hats and frocks, blazers and panamas, and immediately noticed the three seriously gorgeous young men in white flannels and striped blazers, Leander pink socks and ties. Who wouldn't have? After the two college boats they'd been vociferously cheering had sped by, followed by the umpire boat, and were lost, they'd turned away simultaneously from leaning over the rail in the stand. Coolly surveying the crowd, standing shoulder to shoulder, they could only have been brothers, or at any rate closely related, sharing the dark, family attractiveness that had a good deal to do with that particular brand of assurance that comes only from a privileged background. Something else shared, too – an obvious solidarity, three against all comers. One for all and all for one.

Chip, of course, had been the first to notice Fran, to make a beeline for Connor's group, and get himself introduced to her, closely followed by Jonathan, himself never averse to a new prospect. But it had been Mark her attention had fixed on: then, and ever thereafter. And for Mark, too, it had been the same. Mark and Fran. Even Chip had acknowledged that before the end of the day, and backed off, showing a sensitivity one wouldn't have expected from him. Fran had found herself holding on to this memory lately, like a good-luck talisman, or perhaps a lifeline.

Chip is the eldest of the three brothers, big and glowing with healthy good spirits, laughing brown eyes and a Rugby-trophy broken nose that adds an endearing quirk to his rugged good looks. At that time obsessed with high-performance cars, long-legged girls and having an astonishing capacity for beer. A phase, a rite of passage, they said. The cars, still fast but now sleeker, more conservative and more expensive, are around yet and, Fran suspects but doesn't really know, maybe the girls, too, though kept in the background, for Chip has become more circumspect as he's grown older, and the situation between him and Bibi is equivocal. Defying all previous prognostications, he has turned out to be something successful in the City, and his mother's adviser, having rescued her from disaster after his father died.

Their father was Conrad Calvert, gentleman of leisure, an ex-army man who'd retained his army rank of Captain to boost a stature he never again attained in civilian life. Who, had he been born into a different class, would have been called a layabout. Unremarkable for anything except the amount he could drink, the staggering extent of both his wine cellar and the debts he left behind when he died. How could a man like that have produced three such sons? All of them self-motivated, successful in the widely differing careers they've chosen. Chip, moneywise and self-assured. Jonathan, the youngest by several years, whose passion is his cello, who draws magic from its strings, who buys it an airline ticket and sits next to it on his flights abroad. He has a growing international reputation as a soloist and an increasingly busy life, with little time for personal considerations. Accompanied everywhere by Jilly, pale Jilly, a wisp of a girl who looks after his bookings and trails with him to the four corners of the earth, sitting on the other side of the cello in the aeroplanes, seemingly largely taken for granted by Jonathan.

And Mark.

Oh yes, Mark. Bright, narrow eyes in a thin, sardonic face. Full of beguiling charm, which goes without saying, seeing he's a Calvert. Less obvious than Chip, and effortlessly clever in a way that makes even Jonathan's dedicated, driven talent seem laboured. Confident and self-contained, but basically, Fran has all too often found

16

herself thinking lately, unknowable. Too erratic and unpredictable for most people to feel sure of him and, despite his flashes of brilliance, too individualistic to settle into a well-paid, successful architectural partnership, which he has consistently refused to do.

He's never been a person you could hold on to, even less so recently. There are times when he seems to slip away from her altogether. More than that, the house suddenly seems to be getting on his nerves. She has a sinking feeling that he has caught the architect's disease and is already growing tired of it: architects don't need to live with the imperfections of their own creations, they can always move on to the next. This suspicion chills her with a kind of foreboding that isn't only to do with fears of losing the house itself, though this is certainly part of it. But he veers away from talking about it, just as he skilfully slides away from what is fast becoming her major preoccupation, the need to talk about their having a child.

Fran's experience of family life has been happy, if crowded and noisy, and she has never envisaged a life without children of her own. But Mark shrugs it off lately, every time she tries to open a discussion. Plenty of time, he says, aren't we happy as we are? Yes, of course they are. They have a loving, trusting relationship, they've built a satisfying life together, but it isn't complete. You can be a couple, but without children, you can't be a family. She tries to be patient, but her patience is growing thin. It isn't that Mark doesn't like children, per se, look how good he is with Jasie, who adores him. Which makes his indifference to having children of their own all the more baffling.

What is it about the Calvert men that makes them so anxious to steer clear of commitments? Understandable where Jonathan and Jilly are concerned: it's hard to see them as a staid married couple, their sort of life precludes it, and anyway, are they an item, in that way? Neither give away anything of their private life. By nature, Jilly plays her cards close to her chest: Jonathan isn't one for explaining much, either. When they come to Membery, they don't share a room, but that might be out of consideration for his mother's feelings. For all her outward unconventionality, there's a strong streak of prudery in Alyssa. And perhaps in Jonathan, too.

But what about Chip and Bibi? No signs of marriage there, either, though it's just as likely to be Bibi who doesn't want permanence. Her previous relationship, which has resulted in Jasie, poor little scrap, has presumably not been an unqualified success.

Poor little scrap, indeed! No way can Jasie be called that. He's an ordinary, outgoing little boy, a cheerful little soul, mischievous – a fiend at times, like all children – but engaging and with nothing at all in him of his mother's feyness. Fran can't help smiling, thinking of him, but her smile is a little forced. She is thirty-seven, and the biological clock is ticking over.

She orders herself to stop mooning around and go upstairs and change out of her city clothes, but as she turns into the one dim corner of the house, at the bottom of the cantilevered staircase, she takes an involuntary step backwards, stifling a scream. Her heart leaps into her throat. In front of her, right opposite the front door, hovers a ghostly shadow. A white owl, wings outspread. It hangs motionless, and for a moment Fran can't move either. It stays there while her heart resumes its normal beat, and a rational explanation presents itself: an owl must have flown straight through the open door into the mirror on the end wall, directly opposite the front door, the impact imprinting the dust from its soft feathers into an uncanny impression of itself, its outspread wings, its large head and short neck, even – oh, shoot! – its eye sockets.

It isn't an unusual occurrence for birds to fly into the windows, deceived by the wide expanse of glass into thinking they're flying into open space. In an attempt to prevent it, Fran has at various times painted images of sparrowhawks, kestrels and other raptors: jackdaws and jays, crows and magpies, owls too, and hung them inside different windows, and sometimes the fear of these birds of prey has warned the smaller birds off. But it isn't an entirely successful deterrent, sometimes the birds fail to see them – or else they aren't fooled. The larger birds arc mostly just momentarily stunned by the impact and fly woozily away, as presumably the owl had done, since there are no other traces of it, but finding the small broken-necked bodies of thrushes, robins and finches distresses Fran, a reminder that the house is the intruder here, pushing itself into the habitat of these wild creatures.

So far, however, none of the birds has ever flown right into the house.

She fetches a duster and wipes the mirror clean of the cerie image, repelled by the ashy, almost greasy residue, by the faintly foetid smell, and is surprised to find her hands trembling, to see her own frightened face behind the image, pale and wide-eyed with shock, her soft, difficult to manage brown hair lank as string with the heat.

It was only an owl, she tells herself. The woods abound with them, their unnerving shrieks echo through the trees at night, it isn't unknown for one to swoop silently, intent on its prey, straight across the car windscreen when you're returning home late.

But it's still there in her mind as she showers, lathering her hair and turning up the power to concentrate the sharp needles of water on her shoulders, letting the warm water sluice over her head and body, taking away the tensions with it. Her hair still slightly damp, she combs it through, slips into a loose shift, then bundles every sweaty stitch she's worn that day into the washing machine. Feeling better, she fixes a hefty gin and tonic while she makes herself a salad in the under-used stainless steel, state-of-the-art kitchen, where you could comfortably cook for an army with every gadget known to man, most of them unused, since she rarely has the time, or need, to cook imaginatively.

But all the while she's wondering how the imprint of the owl could have been left on the mirror, when the house has been locked up for two days. It wasn't there before she left, of that she is certain. She couldn't have failed to see it as she came down the stairs. She'd locked the doors before leaving and Mark had left before her, business in London first, then on to Brussels. And she has come into the house that night by the back door, closing it behind her.

They said owls were bad luck.

It's too hot for supper to have much appeal, but she dutifully eats as much of her salad as she can stomach, which isn't a lot. In the end, she gives up and scrapes the rest into the bin. But she finishes off the second glass of cold white burgundy she's poured, watching the early evening news while she drinks it: television, the solitary person's refuge.

The thought is outrageous, and suddenly she feels a great need for air and a release from thoughts about herself, and the need to move, the feeling she should, perhaps, go up to Membery and see if Bibi is all right.

The heat of the day is still held in the clearing, the dying sun is flickering through the trees with the effect of a shuttered camera. Honeysuckle reaches for the light through a thicket of blackthorn, breathing out its warm and heady scent, mingling with the earthy, woodsy smell under the trees. Further into the woods stinkhorn grow, but their pervasive, disgusting odour thankfully doesn't reach so far. Walking across the grass, feeling it cool against her bare toes, between the straps of her open sandals, she is conscious of unseen eyes watching her from the shadowed depths beyond the trees. She listens to the silence, broken only by the sounds of the forest beginning to settle for the evening, the cool splash of the waterfall into the pool.

It isn't much of a waterfall, to tell the truth, little more than a pretty cascade, not a straight fall, but flowing in three stages for about forty feet from a large slab of rock across the watercourse above, which originates in an underground spring, somewhere beyond Membery. But forty feet is enough to turn the glassy water, sliding like mercury over the lip, into a creaming froth at the bottom, before it gradually disperses into the still water beyond, fringed with ferns and foxgloves. At its far end, the pool narrows again and continues through the clearing and the watersplash to the other side of the road. The water is deep just below the fall, though nowhere is it suitable for serious swimming – not without the major upheaval of removing some of the big rocks at the edges, a job Mark refuses to consider paying for.

Years ago, someone built a rustic bridge over the lip, to make it possible to return along the right-hand side of the stream after taking a stroll along its left. The bridge isn't used now, it's rotten and unsafe. There are planks missing, the railings have grown lichens and moss, just lean on them and they'd give way – but anyway the right-hand path is now invisible beneath its overgrowth of nettles, thistles and cow parsley. The one at this side is hardly any better, being used only as a short cut for the comings and goings between Membery and The Watersplash, ending in a scramble down the rocks alongside the waterfall. The rocks are steep, but hold no terrors for the younger members of the family, who have learned to negotiate them from childhood.

Fran pauses and sits there for a while, as near to the edge of the pool as she can get, on one of the boulders, most of which are green and slippery in wet weather, and even now are embedded in velvety moss. She slips off her sandals and trails her toes in the water, always deliciously cold. She sits for several minutes before she notices the white shape eddying around in the curdling foam at the foot of the waterfall.

At first she thinks, ridiculously, it's another owl, another white shadow. Until she realizes it's larger, much larger, that it has an arm, and a leg, human form.

Chapter Two

Membery Place stood behind closed gates, marked Strictly Private, thirty yards further along the road from the gate leading to the gardens, which were open to visitors on Wednesdays to Sundays, inclusive.

It was too dark tonight to read the sign by the public entrance as they passed, but Jonathan, at least, knew its pronouncements by heart – the opening and closing times, and the entrance fee, two pounds fifty, no concessions. Do not park on the grass verges outside the gates, there is ample parking within the grounds. We regret that we cannot allow dogs (except for guide dogs), no children under five, and wheelchair access is limited, on account of the steep steps. Picnicking within the grounds is strictly forbidden.

He'd often wondered how they ever raised any visitors at all, but Alyssa's assertion that her rules didn't seem to have affected the garden's success couldn't be argued with. His mother had worked wonders, at Chip's suggestion, after their father died, changing and enlarging the gardens from what she'd created to please herself into what would attract others to look around, and spend their money in. A place where they could initially marvel at the immense Kiftsgate rose that cascaded over the great plum tree in the former stable yard, then amble between the long herbaceous borders to the spot where seats were strategically placed to take advantage of the wide view of the valley, the rolling chalk hills and the forest spread below. At this point, where the flat part of the garden ended, the more venturesome might climb down the steeply sloping rocky bluff and then back again, admiring on the way the wonderful collection of rare and unusual rock plants – a subliminal persuasion to buy, on the way out, highly priced propagations of those same plants, raised in the nurseries. After which they could depart, well pleased, fortified by a cup of tea and a home-made scone in the Old Stables.

The taxi turned in through the gates towards the house. Asymmetrical, with long, horizontal lines, sweeping roofs and gables, tall brick chimneys, narrow bands of mullioned windows and deep bays. A great front door and beside it a tall, narrow window, awkwardly placed over two adjacent, oddly angled gables, and carried up two storeys, similar in a way to that of The Watersplash. But this house had been built long before that, on the cusp of the nineteenth and twentieth centuries. Thought to be very advanced at the time of its erection, designed by a disciple of Voysey, in the Arts and Crafts manner, it had been built for Great-grandfather Calvert, a long dead judge of some notoriety. Its roughcast walls, though evidently in dire need of repainting at closer quarters, in this light stood out like a dazzling plaster carving against the background frieze of dark trees, the summer moon shedding a warm radiance over it.

The first thing Jonathan noticed as the taxi cruised up to the front door was that, unusually, every light in the house blazed out into the darkness. For a moment he wondered, with wild speculation, if this was a welcome home after his well-received concert in Vienna yesterday. It was the sort of gesture Alyssa used to make, though the habit had fallen off lately. She'd implied, flatteringly, that his successes were becoming so routine it was no longer necessary to mark them out specially. But she was very superstitious, nearly as much as Bibi, and he thought the more likely reason was that she was afraid of tempting fate. He scoffed at the idea, but wasn't going to argue with her – no success could be that assured. Jilly, too, had surreptitiously crossed her fingers.

As the taxi neared the front door, he noticed that, despite the lights, there was no discernible movement behind the downstairs windows, and almost simultaneously, he saw the police car parked outside.

'What the –?' The taxi braked noisily on the gravel, and he prepared to jump out.

'Oh, Jon,' Jilly breathed, 'you don't think –?'

'Of course not,' he said shortly, with a swift glance at the taxi driver. 'The police wouldn't be bothering themselves with a missing suitcase.' She gave him a quick, odd look.

He spoke more sharply than he had intended, for Jilly had been on the verge of tears all the way from the airport and he was terrified of them starting up again, for whatever reason. He'd never seen her cry before, and had he thought about it, he might seriously have doubted if she ever could. She was so self-contained she could go all day without even speaking unless she was spoken to – not sulking, a condition unknown to Jilly, or miserable, the occasional smile in his direction indicating she was happy enough. Not that she was always so quiet, far from it! When the occasion demanded, Jilly could talk for England. And never had he had need to question her loyalty. Remembering that instantly dispersed his irritation with her. But . . . Bibi! Why had that casual mention of her set her off? He was still baffled by her outburst.

The taxi driver went round to the boot and Jonathan took care of his cello, shrouded in canvas over its case, and deposited it on the front steps. By the time he'd finished, the driver and Jilly had dealt with the rest of the luggage. He gave the man a large tip and slammed the taxi door decisively, sketching a salute to send him on his way and to discourage any more speculative glances towards the police car.

Jilly bent to breathe in the waves of violet-scented heliotrope coming from the giant lead urns either side of the front door, great masses of dark purple blossoms standing above a trailing froth of pink verbena. Jonathan raised his hand to the iron knocker, shaped like a Celtic cross, but Alyssa was in the hall by then and had flung open the door. She stood, framed in the aperture, her arms stretched wide, before enveloping him in a vast hug. 'Jonathan, my darling boy, how late you are! In all this, it had almost slipped my mind we were still waiting for you, it's all so dreadful! But thank God you are here, at last!' At once deflating him and wrapping him in her warm love. His mother, ever the same, wearing black, as she invariably did in the evenings. She was heavily made up and a lot of gold jewellery decorated her person. Over the top, as usual, but he was so used to this that it barely registered.

With slightly less enthusiasm, she planted an air kiss in the region of Jilly's pale cheek. 'Jilly!'

'Sorry we're so late,' Jilly said politely. 'We've had the most appalling things happen.'

'You, too?'

They had stepped directly into the huge hall that was carried up two storeys. Despite the long window, stretching upwards and disappearing into the darkness above, and several more horizontal ones, oddly placed and too small to be of much use other than as decorative elements, it was a dim place, even in daylight, with a great deal of stonework and wooden panelling, unpredictable corners and a huge, inglenooked fireplace at its far end. Seen from the outside, the house had presence, and inside it was replete with the fine, aesthetic ideals fashionable at the time of its building, when medieval simplicity was being extolled above the excesses of the Victorians. Untouched by ill-conceived restoration as the house and its interior were, it was sometimes visited by architectural historians.

Mementoes of Judge Calvert were everywhere, notably in a dark and forbidding portrait dominating the wall above the fireplace, with below it a Biblical quotation, writ large in Gothic lettering across the width of the wide chimney breast: 'GOD IS A RIGHTEOUS JUDGE, STRONG AND PATIENT.' God in this case, presumably, being His Honour, the family had long ago decided. His robes and wig were displayed in a glass case set into an alcove next to a passage that led eventually to a downstairs cloakroom, but since Conrad's death Alyssa had had the alcove screened by a heavy tapestry curtain. She said she could manage to ignore the portrait from her chair by the fire, since it was placed so high, but she didn't want to be reminded of the old tyrant every time she went to the loo. The judge's unforgiving spirit brooded over everything, so no one had ever dared to remove the portrait, and most of his original furniture remained, too – enormously heavy, plain oak tables and straight-backed, wooden bench-seats set in draughty alcoves. The windows were curtainless. Architectural gem though it might be, it wasn't a comfortable house to live in.

'What's wrong, Ma?' asked Jonathan immediately. 'What's going on?'

'Oh come in, come in, it's just too terrible! I can't even bear to think of it. Jane will tell you, won't you, Jane?'

He heard what sounded suspiciously like a shake in his mother's voice and looked more carefully at her. Under the make-up, under all the bravura, he saw her suddenly as she was, an elderly woman who'd had all the stuffing knocked out of her, looking her age, rather tatty round the edges, it had to be said. There was surely more grey in her black hair than he remembered. When he'd kissed her, her skin had felt soft, powdery, yielding, like the marshmallows he'd hated as a child. Against her too-bright lipstick, her teeth appeared yellow. Her shoulders sagged, she looked as if some vital spark within her had been extinguished, and for the first time in his life he had the prescience that one day she would not be there. He touched her hand gently and, as if sensing his thoughts, she smiled shakily, and almost visibly made an effort to pull herself together. But it was Jane Arrow who spoke.

'Well, I suppose someone will have to tell them,' she answered Alyssa in clipped tones and, with her usual

26

directness, came straight to the point. 'Jonathan, it's Bibi. There's been an accident, and I'm afraid she's dead.'

She stood in Alyssa's shadow, five foot nothing, a drab little wren beside a large black crow, a diminutive figure in a Liberty print blouse and a beige cotton skirt, her straight pepper-and-salt hair drawn back unbecomingly at either side by tortoiseshell slides, showing no emotion other than to press her lips firmly together, whether in sorrow or disapproval of Bibi's unseemly act it wasn't possible to tell.

Jilly gave a huge, choking gasp, and subsided on to a window seat as if her legs wouldn't hold her. Jonathan didn't feel too good, either. Every drop of blood felt to be pumping away from his heart. He lowered himself down beside her and a long, slow look passed between them. He put his arm round her shoulder. 'Those damn sleeping pills?' he asked his mother, slowly and with a great effort.

Bibi. Dead? It wasn't possible. Not Bibi. He felt a heavy weight of guilt, as if that stupid, pointless quarrel about her, erupting out of nowhere, had been somehow to blame. But then, beneath the guilt, something lifted.

'No, no, not sleeping pills,' Miss Arrow said softly, 'I'm afraid she drowned.'

'Drowned?' This was so totally unexpected he had difficulty in taking it in. Jilly stiffened beside him. 'How? Where?' His voice sounded as dry and gravelly as it felt.

He noticed Jane Arrow's face working. He'd always had the impression that there wasn't much love lost between her and Bibi, and he was surprised at what he took to be this belated show of emotion, until she put her finger to her lips and he realized his mistake. He saw that she was trying to tell him something. Almost before he grasped that she was attempting to warn him of the presence of someone else in the room, that someone had risen from one of the two high-backed settles by the great fireplace, the one with its back to the door, and turned to face the newcomers.

27

He was a big, unsmiling man with grizzled dark hair, dark-complexioned, a shave-twice-a-day man to judge by the shadow across his jaw. He came forward and extended a large hand with dark hairs springing from the back. 'DI Crouch, I'm in charge of the investigation. And Sergeant Colville,' he added as an afterthought, in an accent that originated somewhere south of the Thames, indicating with a jerk of the head a young woman with a frizz of dark hair who had also come forward. 'You are . . .?'

'This is my youngest son, Jonathan Calvert,' Alyssa announced proudly.

The name brought no flicker of recognition. The detective merely nodded brusquely. Either he was no music lover, or he'd made the connection earlier and decided not to be impressed. 'Forgive me for being obtuse,' said Jonathan, 'but you did say investigation?'

'Any unexplained death always has to be looked into.' This time it was the sergeant who answered. She was thin and sallow, wearing a dark grey trouser suit whose colour did nothing for her. But her tone was coolly sympathetic, in a detached, official way, which was more than Jonathan would have been willing to say for the other officer.

'Even if it was an accident?'

'We-ell –' she began.

'Just a minute, Sergeant, let me deal with this,' the inspector interrupted officiously. 'Ms Morgan was found in the pool at the bottom of the waterfall, near your brother's house, The Watersplash,' he went on, irritating Jonathan with that euphemistic Ms so that he almost missed the implications of what had been said. A combination of last night's concert – any concert invariably wired him up so that he couldn't sleep and was left feeling drained the next day – plus a sweltering journey during which Jilly's normally efficient travelling arrangements had met with nothing but frustrations and delays, including a suitcase failing to turn up on the carousel at Heathrow, had not conspired to leave his brain at its most lucid.

'What happened? Did she slip on those rocks, then?'

'That's what it looks like. Seemed at first she might've fallen from that rickety bridge, but we can't detect any signs of recent damage. Very unsafe, though, something like that.'

The knot in Jonathan's guts was tightening, as though he'd eaten something bad. Ignoring the disapproval, he said, 'So why the investigation?'

The DI didn't seem to feel the repeated question worthy of an answer. He had small grey eyes, opaque as clay marbles, and his hard stare deliberately gave nothing away, as if to project the image of the hard-nosed copper who'd seen it all before. Jonathan tried to dismiss this as play-acting, a need to intimidate and overwhelm, but he couldn't help feeling that behind it all lurked the sense of a very real aggression. The inspector was, at a guess, just the wrong side of fifty, retirement looming, and making the most of the nearest thing to drama the local force could have had in years. The acme of excitement in Felsborough nick must be rounding up drunk and disorderlies. 'As my sergeant said,' he replied at last, 'we have to make sure that's how it happened. There are certain things that need to be explained.'

'Such as?'

'Well, it was a bit careless, at the least unwise, wouldn't you say, taking a dangerous path like that one down by the waterfall, if she was going down to your brother's house at The Watersplash, as it seems likely? She'd recently broken her ankle, hadn't she? Couldn't walk easily yet, not even with her walking stick?'

'That wouldn't necessarily have stopped Bibi! Anyway, dangerous is relative. If you know the path, as she did, there's nothing to it. It's not Mount Everest. And with her dodgy ankle, it's more likely the stick would've helped, rather than hindered.'

'Maybe so.' He paused to look Jonathan up and down. 'We haven't found the stick yet, by the way, but we shall.'

29

'I should hope so! I said you should never have allowed her to use it, Alyssa!'

Crouch's gaze swivelled towards Miss Arrow. His eyes narrowed, perhaps not yet able to place her in the scheme of things. Jonathan thought he'd better not make the mistake of thinking her diminutive size bore any relation to her effectiveness. 'That was the Judge's walking stick, you know!' she declared. Jane was a fiercer defendant of all that appertained to the Judge than any of the family were. Given her own predilections, she probably admired his authoritarianism.

'Oh? Which judge was that?' asked Crouch, ill-advisedly, earning himself a severe look from Jane.

'Judge Calvert, of course! It was his malacca cane, with a silver knob and an inscribed band, which they gave him when he retired from the circuit and was appointed to the High Court,' she said, nodding, almost genuflecting, towards the forbidding portrait of the man over the fireplace. Crouch followed her gaze with a sardonic amusement he didn't trouble to hide. He had obviously met judges like that before. Clearly, he thought the walking stick had been given in gratitude for seeing the end of him.

Jonathan couldn't quite see the cane's importance to the police, but he could imagine the fuss Jane would make if it were to be permanently lost, though that seemed unlikely. If it hadn't turned up anywhere along the edge of the pool, it shouldn't be beyond the resources of the police to dredge for it. But maybe Bibi had fallen in higher up, and been carried down into the depths of the pool – and then the stream itself would be the obvious place to look – something like a walking stick would surely have got itself wedged into the bank or among the pudding stones on the bed, but he thought it wiser not to suggest this. He didn't think Crouch was the type to appreciate being told how to do his job.

'You mentioned sleeping pills, just now,' Crouch was going on, putting Jane's comments aside and watching

Jonathan narrowly. 'Why did you immediately assume Ms Morgan's death was due to an overdose?'

'Overdose? Did I say that? I don't recall.' Jonathan spoke sharply before he caught a dangerous gleam in the inspector's eye and decided he'd better not push too far. He shrugged. 'It's just that those pills of hers were knockout tablets – instant drowsiness. I know my brother made her promise she'd never take any unless he was around. He always thought she could easily forget she'd taken one and swallow another.' *Especially if she'd had a few drinks.* 'She used to be like a zombie the next day, anyone will tell you.' In fact, he had a strong notion that Chip had removed the pills altogether.

Sergeant Colville was writing something carefully in her notebook. Though she had lapsed into silence again after her rebuff from the inspector, he was aware of her complete concentration. The word 'overdose' still hung in the air. He realized, locating the sense of his unease, that the inspector's other questions had been leading in the same direction. 'What is this?' he asked, keeping his voice down with an effort. 'What are you suggesting? If you're thinking Bibi took her own life, forget it. She just wasn't the type.'

That's what they all say, said the inspector's expression. And in fairness, could that ever be stated, with complete conviction, of anyone, and especially of Bibi, who had never been a person you could pigeonhole? Jonathan's eyes automatically sought out Jane Arrow and he sensed straight away that she'd read his thoughts, and that they probably coincided with her own. She was sharp, Jane. Maybe that was why it was always she who seemed to take charge of situations in this house – not Alyssa, with her outspoken opinions and her emotions all on the surface. Jane, as the daughter of a naval officer, had a background of inherited pragmatism. Just what her position was in the household never seemed to have been defined . . . for years she had ridden daily, sitting uncompromisingly upright on her old-fashioned bicycle, from her house in Middleton Thorpe village to Membery Place, where she performed many of the duties normally associated with a housekeeper, as well as acting as companion, friend, adviser, occasional helper in the nurseries – all without, as far as Jonathan was aware, being paid a penny. He'd always assumed she had independent means, but he sometimes wondered about her motives.

'Where is everyone?' he asked her. 'Where's Chip?'

'He's in London, supposed to be at some function – but we haven't been able to locate his secretary to find out where. And Mark's in Brussels, Francine hasn't been able to get hold of him, either –'

'Where's she, then? Where's Fran?'

'She insisted on going back home,' Alyssa said. 'I wanted her to sleep here, but she wouldn't, she thought Mark might ring. She shouldn't be on her own after a shock like that. Poor Fran!'

There was some subtext here that he hadn't yet read. He looked once more at Jane Arrow for enlightenment.

'It was Francine who found her, Jonathan. After she had put Jasie to bed, Bibi looked in, excusing herself from supper, as she had one of her headaches coming on. She was going outside for a breath of air, and then to bed. That, I'm afraid, was the last we saw of her.'

Alyssa said, 'Oh dear. We were waiting for you, wondering where on earth you'd got to. We watched television for a bit, had a little aperitif. I – er, I think we may have dozed a little, we'd had a busy day and you know how it is, at our age.' Jane raised her eyebrows. 'Well, Jane, we *both* of us jumped sky high when the telephone rang! But it wasn't you, Jonathan, it was Fran, in an awful state, the dear girl, to say she'd found Bibi in the waterfall pool.'

'Jesus.' Jane pressed her lips together at the profanity and, automatically, as if he were still a boy, Jonathan followed up with an apology.

But for Fran to have come across Bibi, drowned, there, of all places: in the pool with its mossy rocks, the place Fran so dearly loved! It was where he and she had sat together that memorable evening, years ago, when he'd arrived home from Budapest, full of his first major success. He'd gone down to The Watersplash, ostensibly to see the new house, then almost finished, taking a bottle to drink to its completion, though perhaps that hadn't been his only objective. He'd also been bursting to talk about his concert. Praise was sweet music indeed, in those early days.

Mark hadn't been there however, only Fran. She'd had food that she'd brought with her for her supper and they'd sat by the pool, sharing a funny, impromptu meal. Peanut butter sandwiches and half an apple each. And afterwards, they'd drunk the golden Tokay he'd splashed out on in the euphoric aftermath of the concert, by then deliciously cool from being suspended in the depths of the pool. A fine, sweet wine that wasn't as innocuous as it seemed, and had loosened their tongues, especially his, since he had learned not to make a habit of drinking too much. Previously, he and Fran had never really had the opportunity to get properly acquainted, but that evening had established an immediate rapport between them that had continued ever since, an easy comradeship that was like being with the sister he'd never had. It had been an evening very much like this had been, still glowing with the heat of the day, and they'd sat there peacefully until the sun went down and the trees cast their shadows, watching the reflections die from the water. He found it impossible to think of the place now. 'I'll go and fetch her, bring her back here,' he said immediately.

'She won't come,' Alyssa said. 'She's already said so and you know what Fran's like.'

'I'll go, all the same.'

'I've no objection,' the inspector remarked as he jumped up, though it hadn't even occurred to Jonathan that he might be expected to ask for permission. 'We have all the relevant details. I don't think I need waste any more of your time at present,' he added, throwing open the remark to the room in general, glancing at his watch. 'There doesn't seem to be any point in waiting for the other Mr Calvert to arrive. I'll see him tomorrow.'

'But why do you need to see Chip at all?' Alyssa asked. 'He can't tell you any more than we have done.'

The big inspector stared at her with cold grey eyes. He spoke loudly and slowly, as if addressing someone slightly deaf. 'He'll be needed to make a formal identification of the body. You do realize that, I suppose? He can come down and do it tomorrow.'

'Come down where? And what do you mean, identification? Fran's already told you it's Bibi. Anyway, why can't he do it here, if it's necessary?'

'She's already been taken away, Mrs Calvert.' The young policewoman spoke gently, risking another snub from the inspector by her intervention.

'Away where? We haven't been in touch with the funeral directors yet. Oh! Oh, my dear Lord . . . I suppose you mean – the mortuary,' she finished faintly. 'But – but is that necessary?'

'I'm sorry, yes, in the circumstances.'

'No need to hurry over contacting the undertaker,' said Crouch brusquely. 'There'll have to be an autopsy before there can be any funeral.'

'A what?' Alyssa was horrified.

'An autopsy – a post-mortem. Just to make sure . . .' He paused and looked round at the circle of stricken faces. '. . . that everything's just as it should be.' His tone was unsympathetic, just on the edge of insolence.

He wasn't always that odious, Kate Colville reminded herself as they drove away, just a man who couldn't ever forget that he'd had what he thought of as a rotten deal. To be fair, most other people thought the same – most of the men in the squad, anyway. Demotion wasn't something any man took easily, it was what they all dreaded, especially someone as macho as Dave Crouch. And today hadn't been one of the good ones. Its ending seemed all of a piece.

Every man and woman in the Division knew his history by now. There was a lot of 'there but for the grace of God' in the way they regarded him and, for the moment at any rate, they put up with his rotten attitudes, excusing him. He'd screwed up his career with the Met and got himself transferred here to lick his wounds. No one blamed him for what had happened, he was just bloody unlucky, that he'd been the one out of the two-man armed response unit to go and shoot the robber toting a gun which, it turned out, had been nothing more than a replica pistol. But hell, you didn't stop to ask questions when you were at the wrong end of what looked like a .22 handgun in the hands of a known and dangerous villain.

Nevertheless, somebody had to take the rap, the top brass had to go through the motions, justice had to be seen to be done. Disciplinary questions were asked, measures taken. But you couldn't expect a man like Dave Crouch to accept the inevitable so easily. No one had reason to know that better than Kate. Apart from anything else, there was the loss of face such censure implied. He had other problems, too, of a personal nature, that he carried with him from much further back in the past.

'When did Logie say he'd be doing the PM?' she asked as the police car sped through Middleton Thorpe village. It was barely more than a hamlet, all of two minutes from the pub at the beginning to the church at the end, less if you disregarded the signs requesting the lowering of the speed limit, as Crouch had done. But he always drove too fast, a legacy from his former days, when a speedy response had been a necessity. She knew better than to remonstrate, or to complain about the way he'd treated her during the interview, either. *My sergeant!* she remembered, smarting. It would just give him another handle to start a row, and that was something she tried to avoid unless it became absolutely necessary.

He seemed unaware of her tension and answered her

question calmly enough. 'He's set it up for early tomorrow morning, first thing. He's off on a lecture tour or some other jolly abroad, Barbados or wherever the international forensic pathologists are gathering for their fun, but he's decided to fit it in before he goes, he's anxious to know the result. Interested enough to change his flight reservation for a later one.' He brooded on this for a while. 'Whatever the result, I'll lay money it's going to shake the gentry up there at the Big House out of their bloody complacency.' He spoke in sneering capitals. The chip on his shoulder – working-class boy pulled up by his own bootstraps – was almost visible.

'You could've put it to them less brutally.' She knew he hardly realized how boorish he was being, sometimes. 'And we don't know for sure, not yet, Dave.'

'If Doc Anderson and Logie both think so, that's good enough for me.'

The sharp-eyed police doctor, Anderson, first on the scene, had voiced his doubts about whether Bibi Morgan's death was, in fact, due to drowning, and when Logie, the pathologist, had been called in, they had together formed the opinion she must have been dead before she entered the water – although, cautious Scot that Logie was, he was not prepared to commit himself until he'd examined her under proper conditions, since there were no immediately obvious signs of deliberately applied violence to the body. The stream that ran through the grounds at Membery was swift, it ran downhill and the bed was full of sharp-cornered flints, which would have accounted for the many cuts and bruises the body had sustained and could have obscured the real cause of death. Rivers and streams, of course, were the ideal way of getting rid of forensic evidence, washing away blood and contact traces and, with luck, removing it from the actual spot where the crime had occurred. Which, if Logie's initial opinion was proved correct, implied somebody who knew what they were doing – somebody with nous enough to appreciate that fact, or even a professional. The bonus in this case, mused

36

Crouch, mulling it over and speaking his thoughts aloud, was that the corpse couldn't have travelled any appreciable distance, so there was reason to believe there might still be signs of any scuffle that had taken place at the spot where she'd been tipped, or pushed, in – if, indeed, she had been. Anyone seeking to obliterate such signs completely was on to a hiding to nothing – there'd be something, trampled grass, broken plants, even damage to the bank itself.

'I'll have a team out there first light. That walking stick, for one thing – I want it, though it won't be anywhere near the water, I'm bloody sure. No killer's going to be stupid enough to lead us right to the spot where she was done in.'

'Isn't it more likely she did just fall into the pool and drown?'

'If she did, she wouldn't have had all those scratches, darlin',' he answered witheringly. 'She was tumbled down that stream, take it from me. And I'll lay my pension she didn't drown. You know me. I've a nose for this sort of thing. I can smell it a mile off.'

Construct a theory and then find facts to buttress it, more like, thought Kate, and if you can't find evidence, manufacture it. Dave Crouch's biggest failing. He'd always walked on the windy side of what was permissible, relishing the danger, enjoying the rush of adrenalin, the buzz it gave him, and wasn't going to change, even now. That was something she'd learned to accept, if not condone. She sighed and said, 'Even Logie won't commit himself a hundred per cent, yet. What makes you so certain it's murder?'

If it is, nothing would please you more, she thought. I know that, because I know how much it would mean to you. How much you need an important case to soothe your wounded self-esteem and raise your standing. But, remembering the bereaved people they'd just left behind – and oh God, there was a child, wasn't there? – she knew not even Crouch would wish that. 'You don't half like to think of yourself as a bastard, Dave Crouch.'

He grinned as if she'd paid him a compliment. 'Don't underestimate me. I don't only think it, Katie darlin', I am one. It's a special gift I have.'

She said nothing more. It was always the best way. Keep him happy if you didn't want a row. Then he surprised her by saying, suddenly serious, 'It stinks, Kate. Not just to me. Old Logie wouldn't be interrupting his hols if he didn't think there was something fishy. It was no fall, I'm sure of that. Think about it. There she is, unsteady on her feet, says she's going out for some air, and goes to find it by walking by the side of the stream, of all places. It ain't easy, that path, not even with two good legs and in bright sunlight. It's narrow, and slippery, and broken away in places – and as for that so-called track down by the water-fall, it's like the north face of the bloody Eiger. Dangerous at any time, I should think, and it's darkish under the trees even in broad daylight. At that time, with the sun going down, it must have been pretty murky, to say the least.'

'Why d'you think she did go down there, then?'

'To meet someone? If she was deliberately killed, it's a stretch to think it was mere chance that the killer just happened to be around.'

It was frustrating, but there was nothing to be gained by mounting a search in the dark, even in the moonlight. Nor, until the post-mortem proved that she hadn't died by accident, was there any justification for commandeering the resources necessary.

'Sleep on it, that's the only thing to do.' He put a thick, hairy hand on her knee and gave her his special leer. 'What's for supper, darlin'?'

Chapter Three

It took all he had to drive carefully, to keep well within the speed limit, suppressing every instinct that urged him to put his foot down, roar up the motorway and to hell with the consequences. But innate caution warned Chip not to do it. The last thing he needed was to be stopped by the police, and his new, silver Lexus coupé was inclined to attract notice at the best of times. In his monkey suit, no doubt still reeking of wine and brandy fumes, he'd be fair game for any gung-ho traffic police waiting to pounce with a breathalyser. He wouldn't stand a cat in hell's chance of getting away with it. The truth was, he shouldn't be driving at all, though the unexpected sound of the telephone, shrilling through the empty flat as he opened the door, his mother's voice when he answered, and the unbelievable news she'd given him, had immediately shocked him into a sense of stone-cold sobriety.

Twenty minutes earlier, he'd been feeling mellow and expansive after a leisurely dinner at one of the City livery halls. The wine had been as good as it always was, and he'd sunk a fair amount, secure in the knowledge that he'd be taking a taxi back to the flat, where he was to stay the night. It had been an agreeable evening, one way and another. Chip was a clubbable man and happy in the company of other like-minded men, networking – or furthering his own ends – whichever mode of expression you chose. Tonight had had the added attraction of being a ladies' evening. He'd found himself seated next to the Master's wife, a middle-aged woman of few words, and he'd politely done his duty by her, keeping up a pleasant, platitudinous conversation when necessary and in between turning with relief to the witty and attractive woman, a financial analyst, on his other side. She'd made him laugh with some rather scandalous stories about people they both knew, and there had been more than a hint of flirtation in the exchanges. Their eyes had met over the rim of the loving cup as it was customarily passed around. Holding it by its two handles while she drank, he'd sensed a promise that this wouldn't be their last meeting.

The curve of the motorway, on a slight rise, stretched out in front of him, the flare path of yellow sodium lights signalled the intersection, and his turn-off ahead. A myriad insects whirled in his headlights, their mashed bodies and tiny specks of blood and body fluids blurring the windscreen. He switched on the washers and a smell of the detergent Bibi had disliked so much filled the car, mingling with the scent of soft leather and new carpets.

She would have been here with him tonight if it hadn't been for her broken ankle. She'd taken to accompanying him to this type of function more and more lately, encouraging him to think – why not, after all? A woman like her and a man like him – they were meant to make a go of it, she was beginning to see that, at last. Too late now, too bloody late. He slammed his fist on the steering wheel.

Disbelief at what he'd been told had been followed by anger. What the hell had she been doing, clambering down the waterfall path, with her still-wonky ankle? If she'd wanted to visit Fran at The Watersplash, Humphrey would have driven her down with pleasure. But Humphrey, he remembered, was away, visiting his daughter in Cornwall. Even so, someone would have taken her down.

A worm of suspicion began to burrow insidiously into his consciousness: that perhaps it hadn't been an accident.

No, she wouldn't!

He tried to believe himself, but no one knew better than

he that yes, she could, thinking back to the time when it had very nearly happened. He'd been proud of himself then, how he'd risen to the occasion and coped, taking her and young Jasie away from everything that had gone on and installing them at Membery. Using patience with her, moreover, not something that came to him naturally or easily, so that gradually, she'd become a woman no longer so terrified that she'd seen suicide as the only way out. He'd persuaded himself that she'd put her past behind her. She and her child had been accepted, without question, into the bosom of his gregarious family. She'd lost her fear and rediscovered her confidence. She'd even managed to start working again, albeit in what he considered a menial capacity, a job which he'd been hoping he could soon persuade her to change for something more appropriate. They'd all rubbed along together quite happily. But now he wondered uneasily how much of that was true, how much he'd been deceiving himself.

Chip wasn't a deep-thinking or introspective man, he took things and people pretty much as they came, but the doubts had started, and wouldn't go away. When he'd brought her to Membery, he'd promised her no questions would be asked, and as far as he knew, none had been. He'd warned everyone that she'd had a rotten time and couldn't bear to talk about it, had asked that her privacy be respected. No one had bothered her, not even Alyssa, who was notorious for asking the things other people wanted to know but hadn't the brass neck to ask. Nor had he himself probed, beyond what he already knew. He'd agreed, albeit reluctantly, to a no-strings relationship. Bloody lucky for him he had, as it turned out. If he'd had to rely on Bibi these last two years, well . . . Enough said.

Together with Jasie, the three of them had occupied the several converted rooms in a wing of the house, formerly the servants' quarters, which Chip had moved into some years before. For all its discomforts, he'd never been able to envisage living anywhere else but Membery, his family home: at the same time, he couldn't live continually under his mother's all-seeing eye. The set of rooms had been ideal when Bibi came to live with him. Better so. Away from prying eyes, save him embarrassment.

Jasie. They hadn't told him yet, Alyssa had said. Poor little sod, lying peacefully asleep, unaware of what the next day would bring. Panic gripped Chip at the thought of having to be the one to tell the child his mother was dead. Must it be him? A woman would be bound to do it better. Alyssa? On reflection, no. His mother's brand of sympathy wasn't the sort calculated to help in this situation. She'd overwhelm the boy with tears, terrify him with her own sorrow. Although she would certainly be a comfort later, letting him cry in her arms, she wouldn't do at all to break the news. Jane? Stalwart Jane, to whom they'd all taken their troubles, as children, and beyond. You never got a shoulder to cry on, that was for sure, yet somehow you went away feeling better. Perhaps sympathy wasn't always what was needed. This time, however, it was, in spades. No, then, not Jane. Which left only Fran . . .

He pulled himself together. Not Fran, either. It came down to himself, no getting away from it. The lessons taught at school, never to shirk unpleasantness, to face it like a man, were deeply ingrained. He saw there wasn't really any alternative but to tell Jasie, himself. He owed him that, at least. He was a first class little chap, he had guts. He'd bear up. Look how plucky he'd been when he'd had to have that cut in his wrist stitched, after tripping up with a lemonade bottle in his hand. Seven stitches, and never a tear. Physical courage was something Chip could recognize, understand and admire.

And then another unwelcome thought struck him. Acting the role of father-figure to a child whose mother was always there, in the background, was a totally different concept from having to assume sole parental responsibility, from now into the future. Yet there was no one else. His heart sank. Fond as he was of Jasie, he felt bowed down with the weight of something he knew he couldn't begin to cope with.

His headlights picked out the sign for his turn-off. He peeled off at the slip road, negotiated the roundabout then reached for the music switch. Quadraphonic sound drifted from all corners of the car: his brother's latest recording, the deep, plangent notes from the Elgar cello concerto. Bibi must have put the cassette in, it wasn't at all Chip's music of choice, way above his head to be honest. More of a jazz man, himself. He dimly remembered Bibi reading out from the newspaper, when this particular recording came out, what some critic had written: 'How can anyone comment on any recording of this piece without failing to compare it with the Jacqueline du Pré version? Yet Jonathan Calvert manages to extract another dimension, blah, blah, blah . . .'

He'd almost forgotten old Jonners would be home when he arrived. He'd never been as close to Chip as Mark, piggy in the middle, had been to either of them, there was ten years in age and a whole cultural divide between them. He was fond of him, naturally, as family, as his kid brother – but cello playing as a career, good God! That was going too far by half for Chip, especially when he remembered the caterwauling they'd all had to endure when the young Jonathan was practising. You had to allow his success, though – music scholarship to Cambridge and now – amazing, really, how many people one knew who'd heard of him. Deep down, Chip was quite proud of the relationship, and not a little impressed, while trying not to stand in awe of his brother's achievements by remembering him as the snotty-nosed little sprog he'd once been. In actual fact, he was much prouder of the thing which had redeemed him for ever in his eyes, almost made him able to forgive Jonathan for the cello: that century he'd knocked up when batting for the school eleven in his last year.

All in all, though, he was glad to think he'd be there, at Membery. He wasn't Mark, but he could be relied upon to be supportive of Chip who had – so natural to him he never thought about it, or even realized he had it – a sense of responsibility to those close to him: he'd done his best to act like a father to Jonathan after Conrad had died.

Yes, it would be good to have him there, Chip reflected. At least, he wasn't going to find himself the sole male in a house full of women, and that included Humphrey, if he was back.

Alyssa had murmured something horrified about the police requiring identification, an inquest. Another thing he'd have to face. Christ, this business could drag on for ever! While he had affairs waiting to be dealt with, things that couldn't be left to his subordinates – or rather, things that he wouldn't leave, wasn't prepared to chance, in particular one certain risky operation that was at a crucial stage. He was as sure as he could be that everything in that direction was sewn up as tight as a nun's knickers – all the same, he was uneasy, as he increasingly was when something like that was brewing.

And suddenly, without warning, he broke out into another of those cold sweats that had lately been coming over him, all his hidden doubts and fears coalescing and refusing to be ignored. All too often recently, usually in the wee small hours, it had occurred to him that he might not be cut out for this lark. Without doubt, he enjoyed the rewards that a bit of fancy footwork brought in, but he was dimly beginning to see that he wasn't made to live permanently on the edge, he didn't relish danger as some of his acquaintances obviously did, even though he put a good face on it, pretended he did, tried to speak the same language. But maybe it wasn't in him to feel truly easy while keeping a dozen irons in the fire all at once, trying to live as though his right hand didn't know what his left was doing. He would wake up trembling, in a mucksweat that he'd be found out, and exposed. He tried to tell himself there was no disgrace in what he was doing, half the Establishment was at it – the disgrace was in being found out, a cardinal sin that would never be forgiven.

Only the truth was, he was mortally afraid this last

44

eventuality might well be possible. He wasn't a nit-picker, never had been, the fine print was something you paid the lawyers to read for you, but all the same, there'd been too many times for comfort when he'd discovered in himself an alarming capacity for overlooking essential details, and a feeling that one day this would be his downfall.

Bloody fool, he told himself, able to be honest for once, shaken by the realization forced upon him that if the unthinkable could happen, if Bibi could die, just about anything was conceivable. Should've known himself better, realized he wasn't a natural risk-taker, even when Membery was at stake, the main reason he'd got himself into this hole. Well, it wasn't too late, even yet, he wasn't in so deep he couldn't dig himself out, he thought, the more sober side of his nature beginning to assert itself.

Try to be too clever and you got yourself right up the spout. 'Sailing a bit too close to the wind, aren't you, old lad?' Mark had commented only the other day, when he'd hinted that he could put him on to something big.

Damn Mark. He saw too much, always had. And why the hell did he have to be away now – of all times? They'd had wild times together when they were younger, though Mark had always seemed to stand one pace back, viewed events sardonically from the sidelines, so to speak, even when he was included. And then, after he'd met Fran, the laddish times had ceased altogether. All the same, without any doubt, Chip knew that Mark would instinctively know how to take charge of a situation like this. Clever bugger, he's always pipped me to the post, Chip reflected ruefully, without rancour. Except in one thing. And now, even that had been taken away from him.

Chapter Four

Bibi used to claim she could see people's auras, and kept on saying she was worried about how much dimmer Fran's had become of late. She'd advised her to get free of negative influences. She'd talked about Indian head massage, feng shui analysis, positive energies, destinies. Maybe she really had believed it all. It was a dreadful thought that maybe she had actually been able to sense that terrible events were overshadowing her own life.

Certainly Fran has felt at odds with herself recently, but that's nothing to how she feels now, positively weighed down with a heavy sadness. She's restless and strung up, unable to settle, and she knows sleep will be impossible tonight. She pokes the remote control at the television, zaps from channel to channel but chat shows and soaps, or anything else for that matter, are unlikely to hold her attention. She wanders around the house like a lost soul, and finally ends up in her workroom. Without thinking, she begins sorting out the contents of a battered old toffee tin, once green and gold, a receptacle for old buttons, unwanted keys and other oddments that she'd bought last week at the village jumble sale. It's something to do. Even so, she finds that although she can will her hands to perform mechanical tasks, she can't stop her mind from squirrelling around, or remove the sense that she's plunging permanently, ever deeper, into an abyss.

Compared with the rest of this orderly house, her workroom is a mess. Or ordered confusion, depending on your point of view. In fact, she knows just where to find anything she needs – wools of different colours, skeins of silk, bits of fabric, in any of the dozens of baskets or the random boxes and drawers filled with scraps of anything she's picked up and found interesting. Mark raises his eyebrows, but all the same, he encourages what Alyssa, without any intention of being condescending, refers to as 'Fran's little hobby', or sometimes 'her labours of love'. Labours they certainly are, in a very literal sense. Depending on the size, they can be heavy, and physically tiring to work with as well as being mentally taxing. This one, for instance, a sort of moonscape for want of anything better to call it, is two metres by one and a half, and hangs on the wall the better to work on it. Sometimes she needs to perch on a stool, sometimes she kneels on the floor, sometimes she has to use a stepladder. Either way, making it has been no picnic. She'll finish it, now she's got so far with it, but will she ever do any more?

Alyssa is wrong about Fran doing these hangings simply for love, since she has no idea what they fetch when they're sold. Not a fortune, admittedly, but a respectable price. She'd find it difficult to believe if she *was* told – they were only bits and bobs melded together on a background of beautiful or interesting fabric after all, weren't they? Interspersed with the embroidery Fran has found, to her own bemusement, she can do easily and well. This last takes some accepting, even by her. Fran, the girl in the needlework class at school with ten thumbs, doing old-lady embroidery!

All the same, she can see Alyssa's point of view: even to her, it's inexplicable what people will shell out for something like this, and Alyssa's opinion of them pretty much coincides with Fran's own, anyway. Their appeal has to be transitory, she tells herself, nothing more than a fad of the moment, a craze that won't last, but still, if people are well off enough – or mad enough – to throw their money away, there seems no reason why she shouldn't get what she can for them while the mood lasts. Mark disagrees, he thinks they're worth their price and says he's shocked by her cynicism, but is it all that far removed from the way he regards his own work, she asks, rather sharply? So far, he's sidestepped that issue.

There had, however, once been a time when she'd seriously considered giving up her work at O.S.O.T. and making a full-time job of this sort of work; she'd thought it could prove to be a useful income supplement when she eventually did have a family. But since the subject of children has become an issue – or non-issue – between her and Mark, she's dropped the idea, convincing herself it wasn't a very practical suggestion in the first place. She hadn't taken into account the fact that the hangings take her ages to do. Despite what they're sold for, if she were paid by the hour, she'd soon be into penalty time. And for another – the hassle of travelling up to the city every day is a bind, sure, something she could turn her back on without regret, but abandon her regular job? The truth is, she loves her work at the agency, and she's achieved a satisfying status, as Art Director. It's what she's become, what she's made of herself, what she wants to be. Her job is, moreover, well paid, and she likes the people she works with, the easy-going, larky atmosphere, the Irish bull. And if she did resign from the agency, gave them the push, how would they live? Precariously, is the answer. Mark's income is an uncertain, wavering concept at the best of times, dependent upon the haphazard arrival of commissions which he might, or might not, feel disposed to accept.

'Of course, you wouldn't *have* to face all that commuting if we found ourselves somewhere to live in London,' he'd thrown out a couple of weeks ago. The thin end of the wedge? He loves cities, the bustle, all life being there. Fran loves them too, but more moderately. For the present, working in London, living here, is like having your cake and eating it.

This moonscape she is currently working on is unlike her usual vibrant, glowing work. It's all silvery, neutral colours, with pearl beads sewn in and pieces of mirror glass and lengths of decorative silver chain incorporated into it, stitched on to a background of gunmetal tussore silk, backed by canvas. And too gloomy by half, she thinks, inspecting it critically. In the jumble sale tin, she's found treasure trove: some antique, iridescent buttons, shimmering like opalescent Lalique glass, which might lighten it somewhat. They run through her fingers like rain, and one falls into the saucer of French chalk she uses to pounce designs through pinpricked holes on to dark cloth. Picking it out, she feels the chalk's slightly greasy texture, like that of the residue the owl left on the looking glass. With a shudder, she drops the button, rubs her fingers and pushes back her chair, goes to the window. The glass as she rests her forehead against it is cool. She pushes it open wider and leans out into the warm evening. The sky is dark and starlit, the moonlight soft and mellow as a pear.

Jonathan is there, hurrying across the clearing. He must have come down from Membery directly through the woods, where there's no proper path, slithering and sliding, picking his way through the brambled undergrowth, bypassing the route by the waterfall, which the police have cordoned off with blue and white tape. She's struck by his physical resemblance to Mark, although he's not so tall and loose-limbed. He walks more deliberately, without Mark's lank, casual grace. In character they're not at all alike. None of the brothers are, their make-up is totally different, almost as though they possess different sets of character genes. Her initial glimpse of them, that day when she'd first seen them together at Henley, that certain facial similarity, gave her the wrong idea entirely.

Jonathan wasn't normally very demonstrative, but he threw his arms wide now as she opened the door for him and hugged her close, and for a moment or two she allowed herself to stay there, cocooned in his brotherly comfort. 'I guessed you wouldn't have obeyed doctor's

49

orders and be in bed. Couldn't sleep, eh? No wonder. Was it very terrible?'

'Well, it wasn't exactly a birthday treat!' she said, disengaging herself, speaking in the sharp, often too sharp, way she had. Words she was invariably sorry for having spoken, as she was now, when she saw his immediately chastened face, plus a secret look that slid over it and was immediately wiped off. 'I'm sorry, that sounded . . . I know what you meant.' She squeezed his arm. 'It was pretty ghastly, Jon, but I'd rather not talk about it, for now.'

Would she ever forget it, though? The slow recognition that the thing circling round and round under the waterfall, the draperies lifting and sinking from the water, the hair floating like pondweed, was human, was a woman, was *Bibi*? That it was already, by a long chalk, too late to save her? Even if there had been the remotest possibility that Fran, by herself, could have manoeuvred her up out of the water and over the rocks on to dry land?

Nevertheless, she'd tried to, oh heavens, how she'd tried! She'd lain down on the rocks and stretched desperate hands down to grasp – anything, the floating dress, the sodden hair, before admitting the impossibility, nearly falling into the water herself in the process. She'd stumbled back to the house to dial 999 and told the calm voice at the other end what had happened. After what seemed like for ever, they arrived, an ambulance, paramedics, a nurse – and a police doctor who told her that Bibi must have been dead for nearly an hour before she'd been found. Still numb with shock, Fran had allowed a police driver to take her up to Membery, to give what support she could. Alyssa had wanted her to stay the night but, certain that Jane would stay with Alyssa until Jonathan and Jilly arrived, she'd managed to put her off by saying she wanted to be at home in case Mark rang. The truth was, she had simply needed to be alone. Alyssa wouldn't have understood her need for solitude, especially after such a shock, but she accepted Mark as an excuse, after making Fran swear to take the pill the doctor had left, and then go straight to bed. Fran hadn't taken the pill, she didn't intend to. She knew the effect sleeping pills had had on Bibi and she didn't want to feel disorientated, the way she'd said she felt, the next day.

Jonathan said, 'Have you had anything to eat? Thought not. I've brought some food.'

He'd raided the kitchen up at Membery and there was a feast: an eclectic mixture of smoked salmon, olives, avocado, watercress, garlic sausage, Parma ham, Brie. Party food, ordered by Alyssa for his homecoming. He sat her down in the kitchen and warmed ciabatta in the oven, put out a little dish of virgin olive oil for dipping the bread into, disregarding her protests that she couldn't eat. She watched his delicate musician's fingers slicing tomatoes, fastidiously fanning out avocado, laying out bread and cheese, all on a huge platter. This was a side to Jonathan she'd never seen before, and she was amazed. He opened a bottle of Beaujolais. She'd already had more than enough alcohol tonight, but perhaps the wine might help her to sleep. She drank obediently and when the food was ready, despite her protests, found she was hungry and ate ravenously.

Jonathan joined her at the kitchen table but said little as they plucked food at random from the platter and ate, and when they'd finished, she did feel better.

The telephone rang. She rushed to answer it, but it was only a wrong number. 'I thought that might have been Mark,' she said dispiritedly, returning to find Jonathan clearing the plates and putting them in the dishwasher, very domesticated. 'I wish I knew where to contact him.'

'Hasn't he left a number?'

'He must have forgotten.' Jonathan raised his eyebrows. Mark wasn't a forgetful, nor an inconsiderate man, as they both knew. 'He left in a hurry,' she added, a little lamely.

Jonathan carried the coffee tray into the big room, put it down on the glass-topped table where the oranges had been and looked around for somewhere comfortable to sit.

'It's as bad as Membery, this place,' he remarked with a shade of irritation. 'Nowhere nice and soft to relax. It's all ideas.'

Fran smiled slightly. It had been said before. 'You'll find that chair's OK. I'll pour.'

She knelt on the Berber rug while he sank into the Swedish leather sling chair which was, contrary to appearances, very comfortable. How long was he here for? she asked, as she handed him his coffee. Theoretically a week, he answered, meant to be a holiday, which he had to take when and where he could. But already he could see it dwindling: he had rehearsals at the Wigmore Hall beginning in a few days' time, for a recital which would take place on Tuesday, when he was to be the guest cellist with a renowned string quartet for a performance of Schubert's Quintet, marvellous but notoriously tricky. After that, Berlin, then Philadelphia, the merry-go-round starting up again.

She sat back and drew her knees up, wrapping her arms around them, studying his tired face. He'd been working in various parts of Central Europe for the last few weeks and his skin was tanned to a dark, coffee brown. He was thinner. He looked tired, his eyes shadowed. 'Thanks for coming down, Jonathan, but I think you should go home, now, I'll be OK. You've had a heck of a day. You look gutted.'

'Forget it. Nothing I'm not used to.'

'Don't you ever get fed up, all this being on the move?'

He shrugged, suddenly cagey. 'Don't have much choice, do I? Goes with the territory. And anyway, I wouldn't want it any other way, it's the life I've chosen, after all. I've no responsibilities,' he added, 'it's not as though I was a family man.'

She watched him as he took a nonchalant swig of coffee. Was that the way the wind was blowing? Could it be that Jilly was pressurizing him to settle down, give up this killing pace and take a nice teaching job somewhere? He was sounding defensive, slightly guilty, as if he'd been through all this before. Don't, Jilly, Fran warned her silently, that wasn't the way to go with Jonathan, any more than it was with Mark. It wasn't an easy life he led – and nor, of course, by extension, was Jilly's – but did he really have any choice, did anyone, with his gifts? What alternative was there to this peripatetic life he had to live, while spreading his shining talent round the world? To deny it would be wilful, shameful. She should talk to Jilly, Fran decided.

'Fran . . .'

Here it came. They'd skirted around the main issue, the reason he was here, for long enough. No way was it possible to avoid talking about what had happened. It was going to dominate all their lives for a long time to come, the ripples of it were going to extend far beyond the present, that she could already see. But no, she still didn't want to talk about it. Before she could head him off, however, he asked, 'Fran, is everything all right between you and Mark?'

'Of course.'

She'd been too quick. He was looking at her steadily, reading her mind. It was a disconcerting habit he had. 'He needs his backside kicking.'

'Most men do, at times.' She stood up, smiled brightly and began to stack the tray. 'You really should be on your way, you know.' She pushed her sleeve up. Damn, she must have left her watch at the office again. The clasp had proved faulty once before, so she'd slipped it off for safety, and then forgotten it. 'What time is it?'

'Never mind the time, and put that tray down,' he ordered, 'there's no rush. I'm not leaving you on your own tonight. I'll doss down on the floor somewhere, save you making up a bed. Someone should be with you, after a shock like that.'

She read into his words the implication, however unfair, that the person with her should have been Mark, but she dismissed this as paranoia, and to her relief, he dropped the subject, having seen, perhaps, the stubbornness on her face. He held up his hands, as if in surrender, and smiled. Mark's smile, Alyssa's smile. And suddenly, to her shame, his kindness broke down her defences, and the tears she hadn't allowed herself until then began to pour down her face. He let her have her cry out, not attempting to touch her, until she'd finally mopped her face with a scrabbled-up handful of tissues from the box he found for her in the bathroom. Only then did he reach out and take her hand.

'Better?'

'I suppose. But Jonathan, how bloody all this is! What could have possessed Bibi to think of climbing down that way to see me? If she'd changed her mind, I would've driven up for her.'

'What do you mean, changed her mind?'

'She rang me at work this afternoon and said she'd something she wanted to talk over urgently with me. I was going to drive round and pick her up. But when I got in, I found a note to say she couldn't make it – perhaps because of her headache coming on.' Bibi's headaches were legendary – migraines, that prostrated her, sometimes for a couple of days.

He thought for a moment. 'So maybe she began to feel better, and decided to come down after all. When she rang you, did she say what it was she wanted to see you about?'

'No.' Fran felt upset, recalling the odd, almost frantic note, in Bibi's voice – which at the time she'd put down to her own imagination or a bad phone line. 'I think she might have been very worried about something though, Jonathan.'

He frowned. 'How did she get the note to you? And why send one, anyway? Why not just ring? Or leave a message on the answerphone?'

'I expect she asked Gary Brooker to drop it in on his way home. I'd probably left the office when she decided not to come and see me, and my mobile would be switched off in the train. Maybe she didn't leave a message because – well, she knows I don't always pick messages up immediately,' she admitted. 'Then after she'd sent the note perhaps she felt better but didn't want to mess me about, fetching her, and thought it wouldn't be a problem, getting down the path.' She stopped. She was sounding garbled, even to her own ears, but she thought he'd know what she meant. 'If only she hadn't tried!'

They were silent, both visualizing Bibi, preoccupied with what was on her mind, not being as careful as she might have been. One false step –

'She couldn't swim, you know,' Fran said, trying to keep her voice steady. 'She was scared of water. Chip wanted to teach her at the same time as he taught Jasie, but she hated the idea, wouldn't hear of it. It might just have saved her life, if she had.'

'You could never tell Bibi what to do, though, could you? She'd smile and nod and then do exactly as she pleased – or as her stars told her, more likely. Jilly's right, behind that beautiful façade she was stubborn as a mule.' He paused. 'Amongst other things.' There was an odd, almost bitter note in his voice.

It was interesting, Fran thought, that he'd used the word 'façade'. Interesting, too, that he and Jilly should have been discussing Bibi. His face had tightened, and she wondered, for a wild moment, if Jilly had had reason to be jealous of Bibi . . . but no, Jonathan, of all people, would never cheat on anyone. Yet – there was always a secretiveness, something deep hidden under the surface, a streak of melancholy in him. Hidden for the most part, but surfacing from time to time.

'But it wasn't just a façade, Jonathan, was it? She *was* lovely – good. Though I think I know what you're getting at.' She didn't want to remember that blank, frightening, glassy look of Bibi's. 'No wonder Chip was in love with her, wouldn't any man be? She was so . . .' Her voice trailed off. 'Why are you looking at me so old-fashioned?'

'Sexy,' he said. 'You thought Bibi was good, too? And *sexy*?'

'Well, yes.' What did he mean by that word 'too'?

'Why is it that women couldn't see it? She might have looked sensational, Fran, but most men, I'd be willing to bet, didn't find her attractive. Not in that way. She was OK, beautiful and all that, but sexy? No way! If it wasn't for Jasie, I'd have sworn – well, think about it.'

Fran digested this for some time, and presently had to concede he might have a point. Thinking of all the women she knew who were generally regarded as being sexy, beauty didn't actually seem to come into it all that much. She said eventually, 'She was a bit of a mystery all round, wasn't she? The way she never spoke about her life before she came here. Nor does Chip talk about it, though I suppose he must know.'

'Which makes it even more of a mystery. Big brother's not exactly one for keeping things to himself.'

Indeed not. Chip was transparent as the day, naïve in a way. Not cut out for secrecy – or that's what one might have said before the advent of Bibi. But it had become obvious, of late, that he had been covering something up – at least that was what Mark thought, saying he had his suspicions as to what sort of thing that might be. All that money he'd been throwing around lately, his talk of speculations, Chip had better be careful. But if Mark was right, what could that have had to do with Bibi? Money had had less meaning for her than anyone else Fran could think of.

Chapter Five

Alyssa, deeply asleep in her big downy bed, is dreaming she is young again. Stepping out down the promenade at Brighton, arm-in-arm with her father, who wears a light-coloured suit, a jaunty hat and brown and white co-respondent shoes. She has on her New Look outfit, cherry-red, with a long, full skirt and a peplum on the jacket, high-heeled black suede shoes, and a little feathered slip of a hat which curves round on to her cheek. Her hair is short, gamine-cut like Audrey Hepburn's. Her skirts swirl as she swings along in a cloud of Coty L'Aimant. She thinks she's the bee's knees.

Oh, but they're a handsome couple! Tall and dark, making heads of both sexes turn, she with her youth and vitality, and he with his mature, devil-may-care charm.

No wonder they're smiling. She is, in fact, blazing with happiness, and he's happy because she is. They are on their way to meet her soldier boy, returned to be demobilized after finishing his tour of duty in Cyprus, and whom she is to marry in six weeks' time and live with happily ever after.

It's not her soldier boy whom they meet when they get to the hotel, however, but his adjutant, Captain Conrad Calvert, who tells them that Lieutenant Crabtree, waiting to board the tender at Limassol which would ferry him across to the troopship bound for home, has been killed in a stupid accident with a runaway trolley on the dockside. It is, in fact, Captain Calvert whom she marries – but later, several years later. And as for living happily ever after . . .

Her eyes flew open, and she found herself bathed in sweat, her heart thumping with some unremembered dread. The night had been hot and sticky and the moonlight was lying across her face because she'd failed to draw the curtains before she went to sleep last night – Lord, no, this morning! After two it had been, what with Chip's late arrival. That's why she'd been dreaming, the moonlight on your face does that. She used to leave the curtains open deliberately, before she was married, so that she could dream of Stephen Crabtree, but it never worked. She had to wait many years to dream of him, until the disappointment of her life with Conrad really came home to her.

In the moon's radiance the room looked haunted, the gauzy curtains stirring at the open window were transformed into grey wraiths, here and there were dull, wicked gleams of silver and cut-glass. The dressing-table mirror reflected the room in a long, unfamiliar perspective, making it look even larger than it was, and its shadowed corners deeper, as though they held secrets and impressions of all the people, long dead, who had occupied this room, this very bed.

The lovely dream, and whatever dread had come to break it, had dispersed and separated into the shadows like curdled cream. But darkness lay on the edge of her consciousness, clamouring to be recognized. She kept it there, she wasn't ready for it, whatever it was, not yet.

Instead, she tried to hold on to the cheerful image of her father that the dream had left her with, he was there in the room with her, large as life, exactly as in that old photo she still kept, the one the street photographer took of them walking towards him arm-in-arm, so confidently smiling, on that bright, doom-filled June day.

A silly dream, with no sense to it, as dreams often are. To begin with, her father had never owned a loud suit like that, hardly ever wore a hat, and certainly not those vulgar co-respondent shoes, which must in any case have been out of fashion for donkey's years by then. But – a strangled laugh escaped her – he might have wanted to wear them, or he might even have done so in his youth. Like the Duke of Windsor, he was always a natty dresser. Though never quite the gentleman.

He'd always had aspirations towards her becoming a lady, however, which was why he had – well, yes – bought Conrad for her. No getting away from it, that's what it was, another of his transactions, an exchange, buying and selling like any other commodity – his name, and an introduction to the county set, for her father's money. Conrad hadn't taken much persuading – and to be fair, her father had had no idea what Conrad was like then, any more than she had. They'd both been taken in by his good looks and easy manners, and what they'd seen as thought-fulness in delivering personally that terrible news about Stephen Crabtree. She later came to realize that was Conrad all over – he'd been going to Brighton, anyway, and it had been less trouble than writing a letter. But at the time, she'd been deceived by the good impression he made, the charm he could exert in spades when he wished, her father by his plausibility. Sharp and acute in business, never missing a trick, Jack Rathbone could be very naïve in matters of personal relationships.

Her mother had died when she was a very small child, and Jack had been mother, father and friend to her while she was growing up. She could hardly bear the sorrow when he died of a stroke, shortly after her marriage, and she'd continued to miss him most dreadfully ever since. He was the man she'd loved more than any other man in her life, more even than any of her sons, which was saying a very great deal, certainly more than Conrad Calvert, who'd done his best to squander every penny made, how-ever questionably, by his wife's father. The day he'd been found at the foot of the stairs, having fallen down, dead drunk, if not the happiest day of her life, was the beginning of another, richer one.

It was no use, she was wide awake now and there was no chance of dropping off to sleep again. She rose and pulled on her old yellow Jap silk kimono, its embroidery snagged and rubbed through years of wear, padded about the room in her soft slippers, boiling her small electric kettle for a cup of strong tea. When it was ready she took it to the walnut table in the wide bay window and sank into the velvet armchair, pulling up a footrest and settling a soft cushion behind her back. The older she grew, the more she appreciated small comforts, daily routines.

The hot tea brought her to life, and as the day lightened and her dreams faded, she was forced to let her mind open to what had happened last night. Nothing short of calamity, coming out of the blue, totally unexpected. Chip, she thought, oh my poor boy! How was he going to cope with this terrible thing? She tried to reassure herself: her first-born had much in him of his grandfather – his optimism, his cheerful outlook on life, a lot of courage. He wasn't great on ideas, you always had to tell him what to do (which had made his firmness about Bibi, his ordering everyone to let her be, all the more astonishing) but he was blessed with luck, again like Jack, who'd had the Midas touch, being able to make money without ever having a steady, recognizable occupation. Even if it had sometimes been, Alyssa had discovered as she grew older, perhaps not always in ways that were quite above board. Too old to fight in the war, he'd dabbled in the black market and made his pile, regardless of any illegality. But people winked at it, they had a sneaking admiration for barefaced cheek, getting one up on the authorities, and nearly everyone had bought the odd thing or two illegally during the war years, and afterwards, too, when the shortages were somehow harder to bear.

But poor Chip, she thought again, hardly able to bear the remembrance of his unhappiness last night. Even her sympathy couldn't reach him, he'd shut her out for the first time in his life, he who'd always been the easy one of her three to comfort, his childish despairs soon forgotten. And of course, one mustn't forget poor, poor little Jasie. And only then was it 'poor Bibi'. But then she was, after all, beyond sympathy now.

Alyssa had known from the first, when Chip brought Bibi home, that her arrival signalled some sort of disaster, though as time went by, and nothing happened, her fears were allayed a little. Bibi was gentle, and sweet, if also frustrating. Moody and elusive. Fey was the word that came to mind, a true Pisces.

There, she was doing it too, thinking in that silly way! Just like Bibi herself, looking for signs, portents, omens. Because of course, one didn't *really* believe all that stuff about stars and planets and birth signs ruling one's life – though it had to be said, Bibi had almost succeeded in convincing her there had to be *something* in it. Apparently, there was a conjunction of planets approaching – Cancer in the Third House or something equally incomprehensible – that made the time auspicious for Alyssa to make decisions about her future. The timing was so uncanny, given how her thoughts had been running recently, she had been impressed despite herself. She decided not to say anything to anyone about her feeling that Bibi herself was worrying over what her own stars foretold.

As far as her own personal affairs went, Bibi had seemed more secretive than ever lately. But then, she never gave anything of herself away. You could neither persuade nor push her. All the same, you had to admire her spirit – like Alyssa before her, she had picked herself up and started over when things had gone against her.

She had never been made privy to what had caused Bibi's marriage to go wrong. An invisible barrier was immediately erected whenever anyone got within a mile of that subject. Jasie might have been able to enlighten her, but her own sense of decency and what was right had prevented Alyssa from quizzing a child, who might well have his own miseries on the subject, simply to satisfy her own curiosity.

Today was one of the days when the garden regularly opened. Alyssa contemplated her course of action and decided, without too much heart-searching, that it would have to remain closed for the time being, if only as a mark of respect. At the back of her mind was a certain relief: she'd be glad of an excuse. The demands the garden made on her were becoming more and more of a burden, despite the help she had, especially from Jane, and dear Humphrey. She took less and less pleasure in it, its necessary commercialism, and its relentless demands. You couldn't afford not to be on your toes all the time when you had visitors walking around looking for signs to enable them to feel superior about their own gardens: every weed must be rooted out, every rose deadheaded, dahlias could not remain unstaked or climbers grow rampant. It must look like a *Gardeners' World* garden every day. Wonderful, simply to garden for her own pleasure! She'd known for a long time that she'd have to give up Membery Place Gardens as a commercial proposition sometime, and she was beginning to think it should be sooner rather than later. It had served its purpose and made her financially secure for the time she had left (never mind that Chip thought it was down to him that she was able to keep it going – it did no harm to boost his ego by letting him think this. He had enough on his plate, helping to maintain the house.). Perhaps Bibi had been right, now was the time. It wouldn't take much persuasion for Alyssa to agree to Humphrey's suggestion that she should marry him and leave Membery. Which wouldn't please Jane Arrow one little bit. She'd been throwing out hints for years that Alyssa was more than welcome to share her own house. Well, there was no question that it would be infinitely more agreeable to share with Humphrey, notwithstanding his stipulations. As she grew older, Jane was becoming very trying. The boys just ignored her when she became too overbearing, and went their own way, but Alyssa couldn't do that. Jane had been with her too long, helped her so much and in so many ways. She couldn't just be snubbed. All the same, she remained a problem to be solved, and the earlier the better. Meanwhile . . . Alyssa sighed. She would need to be strong again now, face this other crisis in the family, see to it that life went on despite the intrusion of death – so untimely, so unfair that one so young should have been taken. She couldn't begin to think how she was going to manage it.

The little silver clock on her bedside table sounded its discreet alarm. Five thirty, the time she normally rose, before everyone else, and started getting things done in the garden. Alyssa didn't move. She sipped her tea and for once let the day begin without her.

'Doc Logie's instincts were right.' Crouch, fresh from the PM, faced the people variously dispersed around the CID room at the police headquarters in Felsborough, generously attributing credit to the pathologist. His own twitching antennae had told him pretty much the same thing, but give him his due, he wasn't gloating. He'd no need for it, confirmation of what his instincts had told him all along would be the case was enough. Now he was simply impatient to get stuck in.

But Detective Superintendent Bob Vincent wasn't a man to be rushed. He was here to satisfy himself that the complex wheels of a murder enquiry were being put in motion properly, that the system being set up would ensure that all aspects were covered logically and thoroughly, and that whatever resources and skills were available would be allocated efficiently. Murder, in a provincial constabulary such as this, apart from the odd domestic as a result of a family barney, wasn't exactly a commonplace, but he intended this enquiry being conducted with no concessions to that. He hitched his backside more comfortably on to the corner of a desk, considering possibilities.

'Bring us up to speed, Dave, for a start,' he said at last,

when the noise level had subsided and he was sure everyone was ready to listen, at the same time keeping a careful
eye on his DI without appearing to do so. Crouch had been
wished on him for political reasons, and he wasn't yet
altogether sure about him, notwithstanding the recom-
mendations on his performances in the Met which had
accompanied his transfer. Vincent felt an instinctive wariness around Crouch, a potential loose cannon if ever he'd
seen one. He'd nothing to support this suspicion, barring
that one lapse of Crouch's, which was his reason for being
here, and though anybody could be forgiven one, it was a
hell of a long way from the dramas of the Met to this quiet
corner of the Chilterns, and Crouch gave every indication
of being the sort to manufacture his own excitement.

He turned off his doubts and listened to what the inspector was saying, glad to see that the chip on his shoulder
had been sloughed off, at least temporarily, allowing his
professionalism to the fore. Everything about him now
said here was what he was good at, his real job, and he
was finally being allowed to do it. He spoke urgently and
his listeners were attentive. Everybody liked him better for
not having time to spare for getting up their noses. 'She
was stabbed in the abdomen,' he was now saying, 'and
with some force, a deep upward thrust that penetrated the
abdominal aorta.'

'Inferring someone she knew?' Vincent led in.

Crouch nodded. 'Such close contact – a knife – any
stabbing – implies that, yes. The possibility of being able to
get near enough to inflict such a wound . . . But – it was
a hot day and she was wearing a thin white skirt and a top
that left her midriff bare, some sort of muslin affair –'

'Cheesecloth,' murmured Kate.

'OK, cheesecloth. If you say so, Sergeant.' He gave her a
glance from under his eyelids. 'And as I was about to say,
there's a double cut in the fabric of the skirt that corres-
ponds with the fatal cut, as if the weapon caught up a fold
of fabric as it was pushed in. Logie has a theory that the
attack came from behind, meaning she wouldn't have seen

her attacker. Think about it. She's secured around the neck by the arm of someone behind her – she'd be struggling, and the skirt could easily have become rucked up by the hand wielding the knife and trying to find its target. That could also account for the fact that she was stabbed lower down than he would have expected – anyone with deliberate intent to murder invariably goes for the area higher up, around the heart, right? And from behind, in that position, it's easier to stab upwards, rather than down.'

'A man, then? Or at least someone strong enough to hold her while he reached round to push the knife in?' queried a young PC.

'Don't underestimate the surprise factor, Hanson. And immobilized as they say she was by her lame ankle, she must have been an easy target for anyone.'

'Sir.' It was Kate, circumspectly polite after that curt reminder they were inspector and sergeant, here at the station, in case anyone thought otherwise. As if. 'The skirt could equally have been caught up by the weapon if the attack had come from the front. And should we be looking for defence scratches on any potential suspect? She was fighting for her life, after all.'

'Maybe not all that hard, Sergeant Colville.' Equally polite, Crouch ran his finger down the autopsy report. 'There appears to have been more than a fair amount of booze in her system, so she'd have been an easy pushover.'

'Enough to make her drunk?'

'No, but she'd have put up a lot less resistance.'

Vincent transferred his gaze from Crouch to Kate, assessing them both. Sensible woman, Colville. All the same, relationships like hers and Crouch's were nothing but a nuisance. What they did with their own lives was their own business, as far as he was concerned, though that wasn't his official line. They'd transferred here at the same time and it suited him at the moment to let them work together, mainly because he believed that Colville, whom he liked, was a steadying influence on Crouch. Though if

65

the truth were told, choice didn't actually feature much in Vincent's decision, since nobody else would have put up with Crouch's attitude for five minutes – certainly no other woman on his strength. Vincent held on to the belief that he would remain in Felsborough only as long as it took for him to find a way back into the job he'd come from. Which would be a relief for everyone, and would possibly save Vincent a lot of bother in the future. In fact, if Crouch hadn't proved himself such a damned good officer in the short time he'd been here, he'd already have been out of it quicker than a dose of Andrews. He only hoped Kate Colville knew what she was doing.

'There was no evidence of skin tissue under her nails,' Crouch was replying. 'But however he did it, he dumped her in the stream, obviously hoping the water would wash away any contact traces. In my opinion, that's a more likely reason than a deliberate attempt to misdirect the evidence from the stab wound amongst all the other cuts and grazes the body would probably suffer. Although it *is* true that her midriff area was unprotected and took most of the punishment from the stones in the bed of the river, so that the cut might have been missed, the killer couldn't guarantee that. Even though the wound was very small, outwardly not much more than another scratch. There might not have been all that much external bleeding, which, ultimately, wouldn't have mattered, because it was very evident at the PM, Logie says, that what she died of was a massive internal haemorrhage, caused by the stab wound.'

'What sort of knife are we looking for?' asked Hanson.

'Tapering, narrow, double-edged, thin, very sharp. Something very like one of his own scalpels, in fact, but wider. More like this.' He turned and drew the shape on the whiteboard fastened to the wall behind him.

'Odd shape, that weapon,' Logie had said. 'Very narrow at the point, long enough to penetrate ten centimetres, at which point it was four and a half centimetres wide. Unless it was buried up to the hilt, it would probably have widened further towards its base. Like one of those cook's chopping knives, but not shaped like a right-angled triangle, as they are, blunt on one side and with the handle continuous with the straight edge. Remember your geometry? An isosceles triangle – one with two sides of equal length? But in this case not quite equal. You're looking for a weapon with that sort of blade, sharp on either side.'

Easier said than done. Crouch could foresee problems in identifying something like that.

'A pointing trowel, sir, sharpened?' suggested Hanson brightly.

Hanson was young and keen, he bounced up whenever the opportunity arose, often with way out ideas, but this wasn't a bad supposition. Encouraged by a nod from Vincent, whose policy was always to let everyone have their say, he took it further. 'If he came equipped with something like that, it doesn't look like a spur of the moment killing.'

He was warming to the idea when a woman constable from the uniformed branch chipped in, a curvaceous little blonde, bouncy and pneumatic in her uniform shirt. She had a reputation for eating tender young officers like Hanson as hors d'oeuvres. 'Not necessarily. She might simply have surprised someone who'd no right to be there – somebody up to no good. Some yobbo, intent on breaking in. There's no telling what sort of weapon somebody like that might not have handy.'

Hanson stood his ground. 'All the same, Susie, killing her would be a pretty violent reaction.'

'Panic?'

Someone else put in, 'The gardens were open yesterday, the perp could have hidden there when they were closed, waiting his opportunity.'

'They could, but there's no need. You can get into the private part from practically anywhere in that wood. Forget that. What I want this morning are a few hard facts, never mind speculations. We'll begin with everyone at Membery Place, gardens and house. I'll be talking to the

Calverts myself,' he said, as if relishing the idea. 'Ms Morgan's husband, or partner, the one they call Chip. I've already seen his mother, Mrs Alyssa Calvert, his brother Jonathan, and the sister-in-law who found her. And I'll have another word with Miss Jane Arrow, family friend. There's also an old boy, another friend of the family, name of Humphrey Oliver, who gives a hand, but he's been in Cornwall for the last few days, not back yet so we needn't bother with him for the time being. That leaves the staff at the garden centre. Get the foreman, George Froby, to round 'em all up. See if anyone noticed anything or anyone. One of them might even have a motive.'

This last was put forward without any real belief that it would be so. He had a gut feeling that the solution to this murder lay within the Calvert family, that it was a simple domestic, backed up by statistics which said most murders were: the sort where the culprit was fairly obvious and would either give himself up or be easily tracked down. A random killing, someone unknown to the victim, he was willing to dismiss as being too way out to consider.

He was damn sure he was right, that it was one of those Calverts, never mind that Vincent didn't want to think it, primarily because, if it was, the Calverts being who they were around here, it would spell trouble in a big way.

Vincent was a big, slow-moving man, with a country-man's fresh complexion. He thought, sometimes for a long time, before he spoke. A bit of an old woman, in Crouch's opinion, and though he'd learned that his assessment of people and situations was shrewd and generally accurate, his patient methods grated on Crouch's more gung-ho inclinations. As did his cautious approach to anything that might disturb the status quo. He wasn't about to let his superior know that's what he thought, though.

Vincent, however, had a good idea what Crouch was thinking, the heartless bastard. However, getting the facts straight without letting emotion intrude was what a mur-der investigation was all about, and so perhaps he might do after all.

Chapter Six

Fran, after a heavy, sedative-induced sleep, wakes to another wonderful day. A shining, first morning of the world sort of day, clear, cool and sharp, but promising to be yet another scorcher. Its beauty is heartbreaking, and death an obscenity. Bibi's death has altered everything, while nature remains unchanged, uncaring.

She closes the door behind her and begins walking across the grass. The sun has burnt the dew off by now, taking with it all traces of the footprints of fox and badger, rabbit and deer which have crossed and recrossed in the night. Long shadows lie across the clearing, the water in the pool sparkles, the foxgloves at its brink stand purple, pink and white. But summer is imperceptibly drawing to its close. Already, the phallic spadices of the lords and ladies growing on the shady banks have been replaced by spikes of scarlet berries, looking poisonous and sinister within hooded dark green spathes. Some of the beeches are wearing their first yellow leaves. The earthy scent of mushrooms is in the air.

She leaves the police behind at the The Watersplash, swarming around the pool and the waterfall, desecrating the pristine morning with their presence and their equipment, setting up their search, they say. What search? Do they always go to such lengths when investigating an accident? And she feels again that plunging sense of disaster that has been haunting her these last few days. The worst has already happened – so what else can befall? Maybe – and despite the warmth of the air all around her, she shivers – maybe she's been wrong to laugh at Bibi's belief in auguries and portents.

She clambers up towards Membery, taking the same scrubby track Jonathan used last night to come down to The Watersplash, dodging round the brambles. If this weather goes on, the blackberries will be ready for picking within a week, luscious and black, but now the red fruits, waiting for the touch of the sun to ripen them properly, look horribly like bright blood dripping from the ends of those wicked shoots. She's promised Jasie she'll help him to pick them when they're ready and taking her at her word he's already shown her a young fallen branch he's found, conveniently angled at the end, to reach down the thorny branches.

How can one face a child with the death of his mother? Fran's heart fails her at the thought. It's school holidays, but then, he'd hardly have been going today, anyway. So at least she can maybe arrange to take him out today, when she gets up to Membery. She'll have to find something that might help to take his mind off the sheer awfulness of what has happened, and lift its black cloud, if only temporarily. Children are easily distracted, they live in the moment. Perhaps she can drive him over to Whipsnade. It seems a trite idea on the face of it, and she isn't enamoured of zoos, but Jasie adores them, and anything will surely be better than hanging around Membery. He's kept asking Fran if she'll take him to see the animals again. What he's hoping, she thinks with a smothered laugh, is that they'll be lucky enough to see the African white rhino uninhibitedly shedding the copious gallons of water its massive body daily consumes, the sight of which doubled up Jasie and all the other delighted, giggling children the last time they'd paid the zoo a visit, but which tedious, repetitive subject Jasie has been forbidden to mention ever again.

Up at Membery, the dreadful day had begun in earnest for Alyssa, in a way more terrible than even her worst imaginings could have conjured up. She had, in spite of herself, dropped off again after drinking the tea she'd made at dawn, sitting in the chair by the window. She'd gone deep down, as one can after a late and restless night, and to her dismay and annoyance hadn't wakened until nearly nine, cross, stiff and cramped in her chair.

She dressed hurriedly, dismissing the idea of her usual workday gear of trousers and shirt, choosing instead a safari-style, sludgy-coloured cotton dress which she'd worn only once before and for some reason hadn't thrown away. Never mind that it was a big mistake (the colour made her look like putty and the bunchy style like a box), she only had black otherwise, and that, she felt, would be crass in the circumstances. She had just reached the bottom of the stairs, deciding she must make up for a bad start by having a sensible breakfast to sustain her through whatever the day might bring, no matter that she felt not at all like eating, when Jilly whistled along the passage between the main body of the house and Chip's self-contained part, and dashed in through the connecting door.

Jilly? Rushing? Never had Alyssa seen her do other than tread softly about the place, as if afraid that the very sound of her footsteps might disturb others. She followed. As she neared Bibi's kitchen door, she could hear a great commotion going on behind it. Why did people always gather in kitchens in times of stress? The telephone rang, voices talked over each other. She heard sobbing. Her heart turned over. It wasn't Jasie's childish sobs, however. It was Rene Brooker, who came in each day from the village to help out with the chores.

'What's all this?' Alyssa demanded, stepping through the door into a temporary silence, where Chip was listening on the end of the wall-mounted telephone. Everything in this bright kitchen matched, all yellows and creams and shining copper, unlike the original old kitchen she herself still used, whose inadequacies she never noticed, since she didn't spend any more time there than she had to. But Bibi had loved to cook. Vegetarian meals, brown rice and beans and something Alyssa preferred not to know about, apparently called tofu.

'Oh, oh, the poor lamb!' Rene's sobs, regardless of Chip's impatient hand-shushings, were beginning all over again.

'Now, now, that's going to help no one, least of all poor little Jasie,' Alyssa asserted, assuming Rene had just been told about the tragedy and was bewailing the little boy's loss. She spoke briskly, admonishingly, which she'd always found to be the best course with those who went to pieces in a crisis. She didn't want to admit that she might start weeping in sympathy if she allowed herself to dwell on Jasie's plight.

Though the room was full of people, Jasie himself was not in evidence. Chip, his back to her, was now speaking into the telephone, and presently hung up. She couldn't see why Jilly had been rushing: all she was doing now was staring out of the window at the rows of cabbages and peas in the kitchen garden, her hands twisted together behind her back. As Alyssa spoke, however, she turned and filled the kettle, began to slice bread. It was Jonathan who came to Alyssa and put his hands on her shoulders. 'Mother, sit down and prepare yourself for a shock. We can't find Jasie.'

'Why don't you look in the tree house? He always rushes out there before breakfast to see if the squirrels have taken his conkers.'

He was keeping a dozen of them, still wearing their prickly green overcoats, in the private hide-out Humphrey had constructed for him in the fork of an ancient oak, hoping his secret hoard would ripen and harden before the squirrels stripped all the horse chestnuts bare.

'No, he's not in the tree house. He doesn't seem to be anywhere.'

She looked at the clock and realized it was nearly half-past nine. Jasie was always awake before seven, ravenous for his breakfast, making enough noise for three and cheerfully talking the hind legs off a donkey. She felt the tension in the room and sat down heavily. Her heart began to thump uncomfortably. She thought, I'm not up to all this. She wished desperately that Humphrey were here.

'His bed doesn't seem to have been slept in.'

'Nonsense! Bibi put him to bed herself last night before – before she went out.'

'The duvet isn't even rumpled.' As if this wasn't conclusive – any bed that Jasie occupied for more than five minutes looked like an earthquake disaster – he added, 'We can't find any trace of him.'

Chip sat down at the table. 'The police say someone will be here very shortly.' He looked grey and haggard. Last night, Alyssa had been proud of him and the stoical way he'd accepted Bibi's death, but this morning his courage seemed to have deserted him. He looked utterly shattered by this second blow.

'Police?' Her heart jerked painfully. 'Surely there's no need –'

'We've already looked everywhere,' Jonathan said, throwing a quizzical glance in his brother's direction. How was it that Chip had been so immediately and absolutely certain that something untoward had happened to the child, rather than naturally assuming he'd just wandered off? The grounds, if you included the gardens, were, after all, pretty extensive and offered plenty of scope for an adventurous small boy to hide himself mischievously, or perhaps to fall and hurt himself. Plenty of trees to climb and fall off, a stream to fall into . . .

But that had been the first place they'd all looked, Jilly as well, scouring the undergrowth along both banks, calling his name. Even, with mounting reluctance, but at Chip's insistence, following it as far as the pool and the blue and white police tape. After finding nothing there, one look at his brother's face had told Jonathan he'd given up all expectations that Jasie would be found anywhere within the grounds of Membery. But outside, there were still acres and acres of forest woodland . . .

Jilly brought tea things and a plate with two pieces of

freshly buttered toast over to the table where Alyssa sat. 'You'll feel better after this,' she said quietly, pouring a cup of tea. It was thick and strong, just as Alyssa liked it.

'How kind,' she said absently, patting Jilly's hand. 'Hasn't Jane arrived yet?'

As if on cue, Jane Arrow walked in at the door, looking as neat and fresh as a daisy, though she hadn't cycled home until well after one, refusing offers to put her up for the night. She had on a pale blue blouse, a flowered print skirt and a beige cotton sun-hat with a deep crown, which she wore as she'd worn her school hat, and all her hats ever since, well pulled down on her head and with the brim turned up at the back. She was rather flushed. 'I'm so sorry to be late,' she began. She made a point of always arriving by nine, as if she were a paid employee who might have her wages docked if she didn't. 'But the police came to see me, which of course held me up. They've now gone down to The Watersplash again, for some reason. They said they'll be up here to see you, Chip, later.'

'That was quick!' Chip said. Jane looked mystified. Her sharp, enquiring glance passed from one to the other as Chip added, 'Impossible, in fact. I've only just finished speaking to them. They said they'd come straight away, but it'll take them at least half an hour to get here from Felsborough.'

'But they're already here! They only left my house ten minutes since. After asking me a lot of impertinent questions – which I chose not to answer, I might say! I find that perfectly dreadful inspector person no more appealing this morning than I did last night.'

'Why on earth did they want to see you again, Jane?' asked Alyssa, momentarily diverted.

'Only they know why! I couldn't tell them anything more. They asked what exactly I'd been doing up here last evening, why I hadn't gone home. It wasn't any of their business, but it should have been fairly obvious that I was staying to have supper with you – and to see Jonathan, when he arrived.' She shot Jonathan a bright, meaningful

74

glance. Jonathan cowered. No doubt her obsessive interest in his performances was kindly meant, but it did him no favours. She herself was no mean performer on the viola, and demanded a note-by-note discussion of every piece he played. Thread to the needle, that was Jane Arrow, practically every semi-quaver to be worked over. It was even worse if his concert had been recorded on Radio 3 and she'd been listening. 'They want to see all of you again, too,' she informed everyone.

'I think we're talking at cross-purposes,' Jonathan said. 'If these police are the same people who were here last night, they weren't the ones Chip's been speaking to in Felsborough.' Explanations followed.

Jane stood like a pillar of salt in the middle of the room, a miniature Olive, Lady Baden-Powell in her Girl Guide hat, shocked but doughty and unassailable, saying absolutely nothing, and thereby effectively silencing everyone else. It wasn't so much that she didn't speak, however, as her utter stillness, though Jane was rarely silent and never still. She was quick as a bird, forever pecking out staccato conversation in sharp, starling-like little bursts, in the spiked, admonitory way they were all so accustomed to that they scarcely noticed. 'Jasie?' she said at last. '*Jasie?*' and then began demanding the how and why. Always quick on the uptake, she had no difficulty in absorbing the necessary facts, and thereafter wasted no more time in expressions of shock, or horror. Whatever she felt was hidden, though for a moment back there, it had seemed as though her tough old heart might have been breached. A course of action was already forming in her mind, everyone could see. She was an organizer by nature (possibly an inheritance from her father, the Commander) and was in her element in any sort of crisis, stemming from her time as a nurse during the war.

There was no denying that everyone in the house had been glad of this at some time or other, but now there was a concerted, hasty movement, everyone suddenly busy: Chip looked at his watch, murmuring something about going outside to wait for the police. Jonathan said abruptly, 'I've already seen the police once, if they want me again, they'll find me with Fran. I managed to persuade her to take the sleeping pill the doctor left with her and she was still out to the world when I came back up here this morning. No sign of her being up and about when Chip and I went down to The Watersplash looking for Jasie, either.'

'Oh yes, do go and bring her back here!' implored Alyssa. 'She'll surely come when she knows what's happened!' The thought of Fran was like the strong shot of brandy Alyssa would have preferred in the circumstances, even at this time in the morning, to the tea Jilly had made for her, welcome though that had been. The person Alyssa really wanted, however, was Humphrey. He'd said he wouldn't be back until eleven at the earliest, he didn't like to push the old girl – meaning his ancient and beloved bull-nosed Morris Minor, into which he folded his long stork's legs like an Anglepoise lamp, and drove sitting bolt upright with his Sherlock Holmes hat on. Alyssa always felt she ought to be wearing a motoring veil whenever she sat next to him. 'Tell Fran I desperately want to see her, Jonathan – and when she speaks to Mark, ask her to tell him to come home immediately. I'm sure whatever it is he's doing in Antwerp can wait. At times like this, it's the family that counts.'

'Brussels,' corrected Jonathan. 'OK, I'll ask her, but he won't just be able to drop everything, you know.' He reached for the door handle. 'Coming, Jilly?' he asked, as an afterthought.

'Better not. I should start doing something about that suitcase.'

With luck, it might have turned up by now. It might, on the other hand, still be languishing in Schipol airport, a notorious place for luggage going astray; where they'd had to change flights, due to a missed connection. The time taken to try and trace the case could conceivably extend to fill the day, but she was glad to have something to occupy

76

her that would help to span this terrible hiatus. She wouldn't be missed, anyway, she thought wryly. They all wanted Fran, and that was of course understandable, Fran being part of the family.

When Jonathan had rung her from The Watersplash last night and told her he'd be staying there, Jilly had reasonably agreed that it was the best thing. It wouldn't have made any difference if she hadn't, she supposed, though to argue wouldn't have occurred to her, or to get herself in a twist about Fran. Not in the same way she'd once got worked up about Bibi. Fran was too wrapped up in Mark to look in other directions. In any case, Jilly shared Jonathan's liking for her . . . she was the only one around here who treated her with genuine, unselfconscious friendliness. She was warm and funny and really nice – if a bit sharp on occasions – and yet with such sad eyes sometimes.

It wasn't, Jilly admitted with a sigh, as if she herself wasn't welcome at Membery. Everyone was invariably polite and agreeable, but it would be nice if someone occasionally gave a second thought to throwing a little affection in her direction, too. Jilly often had the weird feeling that she was invisible to them all here, an appendage of Jonathan's, of rather less importance than his cello. Alyssa, for instance, was never less than amiable, even if she sometimes looked surprised to find Jilly there, throwing those absent, brilliant smiles in her direction whenever she remembered, meaning to be kind, Jilly supposed.

It was disconcerting to see how like Jonathan's those smiles were.

At that moment, the doorbell rang. Jilly took herself off to answer it and came back to say the police were here, and wanted to speak with Chip.

Three people were waiting for him, a woman and two men, the younger of whom was staring round the lofty spaces of the big hall as though he'd never seen anything like it in his life before, as no doubt he hadn't. It was a not unusual reaction from first-time visitors.

Chip's gaze, too, skimmed round the old familiar place, at a glance taking in what the young man was looking at, seeing it all at once through his eyes, right down to the sunlight coming through the long window in dusty motes and showing up all the grubby corners that would have been better kept hidden. However strong the will to keep it spotless, the house defeated most efforts. It had been built on the assumption that the days of hordes of available and affordable servants would go on for ever, and Rene Brooker, even when supervised by Jane Arrow, and with occasional help from one or two women in the village, didn't have a hope. It was very obvious for instance, with the sun streaming through it, that the inside of the big window hadn't seen the attentions of a shammy leather in recent, or even distant, times, but who was there to mount a ladder and do it? As for the outside of the window, which needed a double ladder and a man with the agility of a monkey to get to it, it hadn't been washed in living memory. Any cleaning that was needed out there was left to the rain.

Membery soaked up money like a thirsty drunk. A bit of new guttering here and there, a few roof-tiles replaced and chimneys pointed, it seemed like nothing – but all too often there were nasty surprises in the way of bigger, necessary repairs. Added up, on an old building of architectural interest like this, it came to a great deal. The demands were endless. Chip had so far been quite prepared to fork out when necessary, without bothering either of his brothers, because there wasn't much doubt that ultimately Membery would be his, whatever the terms of his father's will – but that was only as long as there was money there to spend, which might not be for much longer.

He felt the same deep, inward plunge of despair he'd felt last night, coming home in the car. He'd never questioned his feelings for Membery, he'd simply regarded it with the fierce sense of possession of those who are born with tradition in their veins but not much imagination, and when the opportunities to make money to revamp the house and keep it going had been put before him, he'd seen it as an easy way out of his obligations. But now it was as though, his other hopes having died with Bibi, for the first time he saw his speculations for what they were. How had he ever imagined he had the nerve to be a successful gambler? He was an amateur at the game. The risks he was taking had appeared enormous to him, but, let's face it, they were too small to make the gamble worthwhile. It was no good simply dipping a toe in the water, it had to be a plunge from the high-diving board. He saw himself facing ruin. He might even – good God! – be forced to sell the new Lexus! Bibi had been right. The house was an albatross around his neck.

All this flashed through his mind with lightning speed, as a drowning man sees his past life, in less time than it took to walk forward and greet the police. He came back to the present to hear Inspector Crouch introducing himself and Sergeant Colville, expressing polite sorrow about Bibi. He hesitated. 'And of course there's the little boy, too. We had word over the radio that he can't be found for the moment, and it seems sensible to run the two enquiries together until he turns up. What we need just now are a few more details, what he looks like, what he might be wearing and so on, before we begin the search proper. DC Hanson here will find that out from the others, while you give me a few minutes of your time, Mr Calvert, if you please.'

'Leave it with me, sir. Soon have it sorted.' Chip glanced at the blond, smooth-cheeked DC who was answering the inspector with a super-confident smile, and hoped he wasn't over-estimating himself. He looked more like a school-leaver on work experience than a competent police officer.

'This way,' he said. He took them all through what had once been the green baize door, the demarcation line, beyond which had lain the servants' quarters, now his own set of rooms. Once through, he decanted DC Hanson off into the kitchen to get on with questioning the rest of the family. After which he led the woman sergeant and the big, hirsute inspector with the blue chin further, into a room which still bore a decorative plaque on its door, matching the ornate door furniture: 'Mrs Heatherfield, House-keeper', it still said, in Gothic letters, gold on black.

If the kitchen had been modernized, thought Kate, who had glimpsed easy-clean working surfaces and pale painted units through the door, nothing appeared to have been done to this room since it had been appropriated for use as a study, save to install a few shelves for files and a big, modern desk to hold computer equipment. A hooded stonework chimneypiece with blue and green de Morgan tiles decorating the fire surround dominated the room, skirting boards were eighteen inches deep and there was a heavy cornice and frieze above the 'greenery-yallery, Grosvenor gallery' William Morris wallpaper. A big bay window with its leaded lights wide open saved the room from dreariness, however, and its outlook over a part of the garden Kate recognized as being open to the public showed perhaps why Chip Calvert had chosen it as his study. Only a few weeks ago, she'd paid her two pounds fifty for entrance and walked along that flagged path between the yew hedges, breathing in the delicious fragrance of the old roses beyond. Since moving here from London, she'd visited Membery Place Gardens along with other notable local spots, as part of a self-imposed duty, getting to know her area. Kate was like that, she would have done it anyway, but in this case pleasure had outweighed duty.

'Please sit down,' Chip said absently, indicating two sagging armchairs, before taking his own seat at the chair in front of the desk, swivelling it round to face them. The cruel light from the uncurtained window, the sun climbing high in the sky, fell directly on to his face, telling all too clearly the story of a man who hadn't slept well. All the same, thought Kate. Wouldn't mind going into the long grass with him, as a game old aunt of hers had been wont to say. A real Alpha male, and no mistake, obviously the owner of the big silver status-symbol car parked outside. Tall and athletic, craggy profile, attractive smile, roguish brown eyes, the lot. He even had a romantic scar down one side of his face, reminiscent of a duelling scar. She took a firm hold on herself. Chip Calvert, apart from all of this and despite the smile, which she began to sense was automatic, she could see was a deeply disturbed and worried man, and with every good reason, she thought, her sympathy chiming with her returning common sense. She was very much afraid he was going to be even more upset when he heard what she had to say.

The fact of Bibi Morgan's murder had been made all the worse by this latest happening, the child going missing just at this crucial time. Contrary to how untypically soothing his initial remarks had sounded, she knew that Crouch was worried by it. He'd immediately dismissed the idea that the boy's disappearance was nothing to do with his mother's murder, that he'd wandered off on some childish prank. The child hadn't slept in his bed, they'd been told, although his mother had reportedly said she'd put him to bed before slipping outside, so clearly fears for his safety couldn't be lightly discounted. They'd both seen too many cases of missing children not to be concerned about the possible outcome; there was every possibility that they might find the same terrible thing had happened to him as to his mother.

At the front door, while they had been waiting to be admitted, Kate had suddenly taken the initiative. 'Leave this to me, Dave, OK? Telling him, I mean.'

He'd considered her. 'All right,' he'd agreed, after a moment, acknowledging there were some things she was better equipped to deal with than he was. Dave Crouch was the first to admit he didn't have a bedside manner, or anything approaching one. If anyone had anything unpleasant to say to him, he preferred them to give it him

81

straight, wham, no pussyfooting around, but over the years he'd been reluctantly forced to admit that not everyone felt the same about the way bad news was imparted. And on top of that, this was a case that was turning out to be one of Crouch's worst nightmares, touching on his one soft spot. Case-hardened and prejudiced as he was in more ways than he was ever likely to admit, and however tough the carapace he'd grown around any sensitivities he might have had, here was the one thing likely to penetrate it. His fuse was notoriously short in any event, but anything involving harm to children, and he was liable to explode without warning. In his opinion, such perverts were lower than a snake's belly. These sort of investigations rarely, however, came his way, he couldn't think why. It was just as well, though – he knew, and thought no one else knew, that he couldn't have held himself responsible for the consequences if he'd had the chance to lay his hands on the perpetrator of such crimes. Deep down inside him, never openly stated because it was definitely not a politically correct point of view, was the belief that vigilante groups had a lot going for them. He kept these opinions to himself, however, especially from Kate, who knew that his first wife had left him, taking their child with her; that every time there was a case involving a child, it brought back the pain and loss of his own child. She met his eye now and he gave her the nod to start.

It would be easy to try and reassure with platitudes, that children don't think, they lose track of time, he's sure to turn up, and so on, but Kate wasn't going to say that unless she had to. Privately she agreed with Crouch that such a contingency was unlikely in the extreme. She merely said that they had initiated a thorough search in the grounds. There'd be time later to voice the other fears that must be in everyone's mind – snatching by some sexual deviant, or taken as a hostage by some nutter who wanted a favour in exchange. Or even kidnapping for ransom money . . . Membery was the local Big House, the Calverts were known to be not exactly on the breadline, though rich was relative: certainly, whatever family money there still was didn't appear to be spent on the house, its past splendours were by now definitely shabby. But you might view things differently if you were desperate for what they might still regard as petty cash – if you were homeless and hungry, on the dole or, even more likely, with an expensive habit that needed feeding.

'You won't find him,' Chip was saying, 'we've already looked.'

Not professionally, Kate thought, and held her breath, hoping Crouch would have the sense not to voice the grumbles he'd made to her on their way here: Bloody amateurs, trampling down the evidence, any hopes of finding anything to do with Bibi Morgan's murder now gone for a burton. Why the hell couldn't they have waited until we got here? But Crouch was being unusually silent, leaving her to get on with it.

'I expect you've been told that later on we shall need you to come and identify Ms Morgan's body – when we've finished here, that is. I'm sorry, it's a rotten thing to have to do, but I'm afraid it's necessary.' He accepted this with a nod, without raising his head. His feet planted squarely on the ground, leaning forward slightly, hands on knees, he was apparently absorbed in tracing, with the toe of a well-polished loafer, the complicated geometrical pattern on the oriental rug, its predominant burnt oranges and peacock blues still bright and glowing, ancient and threadbare though it was. 'What I have to say now may come as rather a shock, Mr Calvert,' she ploughed on. 'We've already conducted a post-mortem, it was pushed forward to accommodate the pathologist, who had to catch a flight abroad. I'm afraid he came to a rather disturbing conclusion.'

'Are you saying it wasn't an accident?' he asked quickly, glancing up. There was an odd, strained note in his voice. 'You mean that she . . .?' He resumed his study of the rug again. 'Well, I didn't imagine it would be straightforward.'

Kate didn't look at Crouch, but she could feel his interest sharpening. He was stroking his chin with his big, hairy hand, and she distinctly heard the faint rasp of bristles. She addressed the bereaved man gently. 'No, Ms Morgan didn't take her own life. But it was no accident, either. I'm sorry, Mr Calvert.'

The silence became acute. Chip met her gaze fully at last, but straight away she saw that even this news wasn't as much of a shock as one might have expected it would be. She didn't pursue the line that opened up, just filed his reaction away for future reference. 'That leaves only one other possibility, then, doesn't it?' His voice was harsh. 'How?'

'She was stabbed before being thrown into the stream. The current apparently took her down to the waterfall pool.'

'It's always been strong. We used to try rafting there, when we were boys, but we always came to grief long before we ever got as far as the bridge, too many rocks and sharp flints on the stream bed . . . Stabbed? Oh, God.'

That, at least, had surprised him. It wasn't, Crouch thought, watching him carefully, what he'd expected to hear. 'Mr Calvert, if you've any reason to think of someone with a motive to have killed her, please say so.'

'For God's sake, it could have been anyone! The grounds here cover thirty acres, all told, including the gardens and woodland, and not everywhere's barbed-wire fenced, you know, anyone can get in via the woods. Anyway, does there have to be a motive these days? Someone they've let out from the loony-bin, no doubt –'

Crouch interrupted. 'Random killings are much rarer than you'd think. Most murders occur within the circle of people known to the victim.'

'What are you suggesting?'

'Simply that we shall have to question everyone. The family, the people she worked with. All those she might have been in contact with over the last few days, someone she might have met recently – she worked at the country club, didn't she?'

'Yes, she did. But she'd only been going in for an occasional few hours lately, because of her ankle and the standing about it involved. They'd asked her if she'd help them out, very busy time of year for them, but she wasn't there yesterday. Anyway, as far as I'm aware, she hadn't met anyone new recently.'

'New people must come and go all the time, place like the country club.'

'Not all that many, actually. Too far off the beaten track for that. Most of them are regulars, people she's known ever since she went to work there.'

'We'll see what they have to say, all the same.'

He shrugged, looking almost bored with the idea. 'You'd be wasting your time.'

Crouch said, watching him closely, 'Tell us about you and your wife, Mr Calvert. Did you and she have any problems?'

'My partner. We weren't married. And what the hell do you mean, problems?'

'Sorry, I meant were you and Ms Morgan getting on well lately?'

'Why don't you just call her Bibi?' Chip said wearily. Jonathan wasn't alone in disliking the euphemism. 'Of course we didn't have any bloody problems! Bibi wasn't the sort to have problems with. Not with anyone. Ask them, anyone will tell you that.'

Somebody that perfect had problems to begin with, thought Crouch. He said, 'I believe she came to live with you here about two years ago.'

'So?'

'And before that?'

Pause. 'She lived in a village near York.'

'Near York? Tell me how you met.'

'What the bloody hell does that matter?' He stared at Crouch, then shrugged. 'We met when I went up there for a few days' racing. Accommodation's always hard to find during the season, but I'd been told of this hotel – fair way out of York, nearly half-way back to Leeds to tell the truth, but worth the drive. Country pub that's been tarted up and got itself a good reputation for food. Quiet, but it was OK. It was Bibi's mother's place. Bibi helped run it.'

'So you met her there and brought her back here to live with you?'

'Not then. That was years ago – when we first met. It was only when I went back several years later that we –' He broke off and his gaze wandered to a point somewhere above their heads and remained fixed while he presumably fought for control. Only somehow it didn't seem like that. That some inner struggle might indeed be going on was indicated by the concentrated swivelling of his desk chair, ever so slowly in perfect forty-five degree arcs, back and forth, back and forth, but Crouch was beginning to doubt it – it seemed to him the man's mind had detached itself from the proceedings and was off on some other tack. He felt like giving him a prod, waking him to the realization of just how bloody serious the situation was. Clearly, Chip Calvert wasn't a deep thinker, or a quick one, but what the hell? His wife – OK, his partner, then – had just been *offed*! Surely, that ought to have roused him to some protestations of anger, disbelief, any of the usual emotions shown by the nearest and dearest of those who'd been untimely killed. But – nothing. You might almost have said he had expected it.

Chip was indeed wandering. He was far away, in a strange country, the country of the mind, one he didn't inhabit any longer than he had to. But the lump of misery which had been inside him ever since they'd first missed Jasie, when he didn't arrive for breakfast as usual, prattling happily away, ready to tuck into his bowl of Coco Pops, was now expanding like a balloon and threatening to choke him. He was mortally afraid he might be going to blub, in front of this gorilla of a detective. Up to now, he'd had no trouble in accepting with his mind that Bibi was dead, perhaps because he'd always subconsciously been

86

aware that this was likely to happen – but it was only now he felt the reality of it, like an actual, physical pain, somewhere in the region of his breastbone. He felt his blood beating. Perhaps he was going to have a stroke, like his grandfather, Jack Rathbone. 'She was so beautiful,' he said, out of nowhere.

Above his head, the glances of the two detectives met – a crack at last – but Chip didn't notice.

He was seeing Bibi as he'd first seen her. Dazzlingly fair. Sweet and so – yes, you had to believe it, so innocent, standing behind the hotel desk, a modern angel in a navy suit and white blouse, her name tag, Bianca, on her lapel. Truly an angel. And just as unattainable.

And then another picture superimposed itself – the burnt-out house, the child screaming at the window, the fire brigade. He scraped his chair back and pushed it aside so violently that it went spinning several feet on the polished boards. He strode to the cupboard in the corner and lifted out a bottle of Glenmorangie. He held it up, but both police officers shook their heads. 'Don't mind if I do, then?' he muttered, pouring a generous portion into a heavy glass whisky tumbler. Sun not over the yardarm by a long chalk, but what the hell?

He went back to the desk and took a deep swig of the spirit, then swung round to the desk and put the glass down carefully. Suddenly, his back to them, he put his head in his hands.

Crouch allowed the man time to pull himself together then said, 'Would you mind coming to sit over here, sir?'

'What?' Chip swung round to face them again, his face ravaged.

'Over here.' Crouch moved to sit on the window seat and indicated Chip take the armchair he'd vacated. It was lower than the window seat, which would give him an advantage over the other man. 'I can't talk to you when you're on the go like a blasted yo-yo,' he said, forgetting his morning's resolve to be polite. Despite the open window, the room was hot and he was tired. It wasn't yet much after ten and he'd been up since dawn, he'd already worked five hours, one of them in compulsory attendance at the PM Logie had called for six, and his never very elastic patience was being stretched to its limits. And it was going to be a long day, with most of it still to go.

Chip, to his surprise, obeyed without demur, his show of emotion apparently having spent itself. If Crouch had hoped to shake him out of his lethargy with his brusqueness, he hadn't succeeded. He sank back into the armchair and his shoulders sagged. He fingered the scar on his cheek.

'Right, then, what is it you haven't been telling us?' Crouch asked suddenly. Chip's head jerked up.

Watch it, Dave! Kate apostrophized silently. She could read the warning signs, the temper flecks in his eyes. (And you watch it, Kate, too. Not your problem, how he conducts his interviews. Oh, but it is, answered a silent voice inside, how could it be other?) And then, as if she'd spoken aloud, Crouch almost visibly took control of his rising anger, his mouth relaxed. He said quietly, 'If we don't have all the facts, we shan't have much chance of finding out who killed her.'

'Oh, for God's sake, I know who killed her!'

Crouch stared at him levelly for some time. 'Perhaps, then, you'd be so good as to share that knowledge with us.'

The heavy-handed sarcasm went unnoticed. 'It has to be that bloody stalker! The one sending her the threatening letters . . . as I said, some nutter from the loony-bin.'

'Well,' said Crouch carefully, 'and how long has this been going on?'

Chapter Seven

Fran lets herself in through a side door when she arrives at Membery, just in time to see Chip disappearing into his study with the same two detectives who were directing operations last night. They'd said they would very likely want to see her again, and she's steeled herself for another interrogation. She's ready for it, but she hasn't prepared herself for the shock that's waiting for her when she at last finds Alyssa, sitting in Bibi's kitchen with a barely touched plate of toast on the table in front of her.

'But Jasie wouldn't ever have gone off, on his own, just like that!' she repeats for the umpteenth time, later, after she's prised Alyssa away from Rene Brooker's lamentations, though even as she says it she isn't sure whether that's reassurance or not, imagining the alternatives. It's a large, well-shaped hand she's holding, brown and tough as old shoe leather, the nails filed short, with rough cuticles due to gardening that no amount of hand-cream can soften. What a capable hand, but how cold it is! As if realizing this, Alyssa withdraws it gently before standing up and beginning to pace about again. She seems incapable of sitting still. Somehow, they've found themselves in the hall, which is stuffy, but even so the coolest place in the house to be, apart from the old library, on a day fast becoming hotter than yesterday. Even though the garden's closed, Jane Arrow is over in the office, coping with the activities that go on behind the scenes. Life must go on, her every action says. The police have politely indicated they would prefer the family not to be further involved in the search for Jasie, but they should make themselves available to answer questions. Jonathan has vented his frustration at this by taking refuge in his inexorable, sustaining practice routine, and Jilly has disappeared to deal with the missing suitcase, then with schedules and bookings, a chore which can't be put off, no matter what. Inspector Crouch and his sergeant are still closeted with Chip.

'Shouldn't you be at work, Fran?' Alyssa looks at her as though it's only just struck her that this, despite everything, is an ordinary workday for everyone else.

'Don't worry about that. I rang and told them I wouldn't be in.'

Fran had felt warmed by the immediate support she received from O.S.O.T., the reassurances that all would be taken care of until she felt she could come back into work. She'd told them she would have to look after Jasie, at least temporarily – she couldn't leave that to the two old women, willing as they both were, nor, she felt, to Chip, who was fine with Jasie in a blokeish sort of way, but no good with the routines involved in looking after a child, much less the emotional issues that would have to be faced. 'You stay until you're sure everything's OK,' Connor had reassured her. 'We'll cope.'

'A day or two,' she'd promised. Until things here resumed something like normality – though how that could ever be again, she simply couldn't imagine at that moment. 'Probably only until Monday. I'll have a word with Kath now, if you'll put me through.'

Kath is nominally her assistant, intelligent, middle-aged and unflappable – nominally, because she is the one who really runs the office. 'Sure you must stay and see to the little boy,' she said immediately. 'What's an account with Colgate compared with that?'

Fran had never imagined then, only an hour ago, that Jasie wouldn't be here, at Membery, to be looked after. She once more reassures Alyssa, as she begins worrying again, that he'll be found soon, has to be, there must be some simple explanation.

Yet even as she utters the comforting platitudes, she knows with dull certainty that there'll be no such thing, that Jasie isn't just playing truant, misbehaving, or anything so simple. He's never been a specially disobedient child, usually doing what his mother told him, perhaps sensing, as children do, how she worried about him, and hadn't yet rebelled against this over-protectiveness – apart from refusing to let her hold his hand on the way to school.

He attends the village school. Chip had wanted him put through the system, to be processed in the same way he and his brothers had been, he thought his name should have been put down for Marlborough, but Bibi had held out against it. She preferred to have him under her eye, and the village school has a good reputation. It's small, but it has a ratio of three teachers, plus the headmistress, to about fifty pupils. She used to insist on Jasie being walked or driven there each morning, and met in the afternoon. She couldn't always do this herself because of the shifts she worked at the country club, but someone else has always been there as a stand-in, mostly but not always Humphrey, who looks on Jasie as an honorary grandchild. 'It's only half a mile,' Chip would say, clamorously backed up by Jasie, 'he can go himself. Don't namby-pamby the boy.'

But Bibi wouldn't hear of it. 'Apart from anything else, you haven't seen it, it's like Piccadilly Circus down there, especially in the mornings.' Which may be an exaggeration, but everyone knew what she meant. Being a country school, it has a large catchment area, and the mothers, arriving with one minute to spare before school starts, dishevelled and distracted with the morning battle of getting husbands off and the children ready for the school run, park all over the place and don't look where they're going, jockeying for position on the village street in their 4x4s to decant their loads of children before heading home for that blessedly peaceful cup of coffee. 'Anyway,' she would add, making sure Jasie wasn't listening, 'it's not safe for children anywhere, these days. Nobody lets their children go to school alone.'

It made sense and, their eyes meeting, Chip had given in. But everyone else thought he also had a point, she *was* over-protective of the child. It doesn't, however, seem to have done him any harm, as yet. He loves the village school, where his friends call him Jasie, instead of James, a name he'd immediately decided everyone else should adopt.

A sudden memory comes to Fran, of walking to school with him one morning, reaching old Walter Grysdale's house, where he and the black dog with the plumed tail live. As usual, the dog was loose, dashing out to terrify passers-by with his hysterical barking and his bared teeth, dancing around their legs and snapping at their heels. He's all noise, but Fran has always been wary of dogs, especially those of uncertain temper, she's never managed to get over being knocked to the ground by a large one, as a child. Pathetic, really, too sad for words. She can laugh at herself but she's very much ashamed of the weakness and tries to pretend the black dog doesn't scare her.

On that particular day, Jasie must have sensed her shrinking. He took hold of her hand and said, kindly, 'Don't be frightened, Fran, I'll look after you.' At the memory of that, now, she's in danger of becoming unravelled.

At that moment, Chip and the police officers emerge from his study, and Chip, with a starched face, disappears, accompanied by the young constable, to undergo the ordeal of formally identifying Bibi, and what the woman sergeant presently tells them shocks Fran beyond tears.

She says that a post-mortem has been performed on Bibi and that, without possibility of doubt, she was killed before she was put into the stream. With a sharp instrument, she says, in the jargon of their tribe, police-speak for knife, Fran supposes. She adds that in the circumstances, Jasie's disappearance is being regarded as a cause of major concern, and there are grave fears for the little boy, but

Inspector Crouch has taken over both investigations and they can rest assured no stone will be left unturned. She goes on to say that if any of them can remember anything out of the ordinary that has happened recently, or if they know of anyone with a grudge against Bibi, they should say so.

It's crazy, to think of anyone hating Bibi enough to kill her – hating her at all, in fact. As crazy, for that matter, as to believe that some unknown maniac has been hanging around the garden, waiting his chance to pounce on her, before turning his attentions to Jasie. Fran finds difficulty in taking such a bizarre notion on board, and stares at the policewoman in disbelief. She's a colourless sort of person, but she's reached the rank of sergeant, so presumably there's more to her than meets the eye. Her name's Kate Colville, and she has a mop of frizzy hair, which Fran thinks she really ought to wear in a less unattractive style. Her clothes are nothing to speak of, either. Perhaps she's trying to be anonymous. If so, she's succeeded. But she's being kind to Alyssa, who isn't bearing up over this as well as she normally weathers the *Sturms und Drangs* of life. This last blow has been especially cruel to her: she adores Jasie, encourages him to call her Grandma and spoils him as much as she is allowed. His disappearance, even more than Bibi's death, has simply flattened her. She looks old and worn, and her weather-beaten face is devoid of its usual make-up. The whites of her brown eyes have a jaundiced look. And why is she wearing that terrible dress?

Well, since we're criticizing everyone else's clothes, Fran thinks, I could have done better than these tatty shorts and this old sports shirt of Mark's, myself – though she'd hardly noticed it was his when she snatched it from where it was folded over a chair in the bedroom, only seeing it as short-sleeved and light enough for a hot day. Wearing his clothes is maybe another of those subliminal acts, in this case a need for comfort and reassurance. She still hasn't heard from him, and beneath the surface of all the other

93

happenings, feelings of anxiety and fury at him for not leaving a contact number are warring inside her.

Footsteps sound on the oak floorboards of the passage from the rear of the house, the measured steps of a man who plants his feet firmly on the ground in every sense, heavy footsteps for such a thin man. 'Humphrey!' declares Alyssa, springing up, quite transformed. Fran, too, feels an enormous relief.

Outside in the grounds, a policeman gives a shout. He's found a child's shoe, but on closer inspection, the excitement dies down. It can't be one Jasie had been wearing. For one thing, it's too small, but more importantly, it has clearly been there for months, if not years. The leather is rotting and the upper parting from the sole.

Down at the mortuary in Felsborough, a policeman draws back the sheet that covers the face of a female corpse and asks Chip Calvert if this is Bianca Morgan. He looks down at the pale, bluish white oval, and the hair, once shining gilt and now stiff and dried like straw. She looks, not asleep, but as though she's no longer there, and she's no longer beautiful.

'Yes,' he says and licks his lips. 'That was her.'

Humphrey Oliver came in through the door, and he and Alyssa met in the middle of the long hall. He muttered something unintelligible, red-faced, looking as though he would like to embrace her but wouldn't, since there were strangers in the room and this would offend his sense of propriety, but Alyssa had no such inhibitions. He submitted to her embrace and planted a chaste kiss on her forehead from his great height. They'd had a sweet, old-fashioned romance going ever since Conrad succumbed to the bottle, but anything more than that was never openly acknowledged, especially by Humphrey, who would have felt a fool admitting such a thing at their age. He wouldn't agree to their living together in his house at the far end of Middleton Thorpe unless they were married, and this Alyssa had so far refused to go along with, saying more or less jokingly that her experience of one marriage hadn't led her to seek another. Nonsense, of course. Humphrey loved her with all his heart and would have put himself on the rack rather than see her harmed, or even upset, in any way.

He'd carved himself a little niche, here at Membery, rather like Jane Arrow, in a way, except that he didn't insist on being indispensable, as she did. All the same, he helped a good deal, in an unobtrusive way. He enjoyed outwitting the house's ancient heating system, and also spent a lot of time in the gardens, supervising the ordering of supplies and so on, a task Alyssa found boring, but he kept himself pretty much out of the way, otherwise. He was always welcome in the house at any time, though he was rarely seen there unless invited, except on Thursdays. This was when he went along to the out-of-town hypermarket and stocked up with groceries, covering the distances around the aisles at speed with his long stride, negotiating the tots who were being a pest with their miniature shopping trolleys while their mums gossiped and blocked access to the shelves. 'Excuse me, madam,' he would say politely, touching the brim of his tweed hat, and they would part like the Red Sea, leaving him to consult his list and stack things in an orderly manner into his trolley, checking the prices and buying everything at best value, all in record time. 'Nothing to it!' he averred when he got back, unpacking tea and detergent and three boxes of cornflakes for the price of two, stowing it all away tidily into the kitchen cupboards. He'd once been a quantity surveyor, and commodities and logistics were child's play to him.

For such a self-effacing man, he was like the Rock of Gibraltar here at Membery, and the oppressive gloom lifted visibly with his arrival. 'Oh, Humph, such a tale to tell!' cried Alyssa, her eyes brimming, leading him to the settle. Fran disappeared to make coffee for everyone and when she came back he'd been told everything.

His rosy face was very grave. He sought for words to comfort, and finally got out, 'Bad business. One hardly knows what to say. Not to worry, though, bound to come right in the wash.' But he agreed, absolutely and utterly, with Fran's assertion that Jasie would never have disappeared of his own accord. 'Why, bless my soul, he wouldn't do a thing like that!' He considered. 'Though he might just have taken it into his head to go exploring and got lost. Enterprising little feller.' Which wasn't quite as comforting as it should have been.

And now the inspector was asking what they could tell him about some letters Bibi had apparently been receiving, from someone who, it seemed, had been stalking her. The glances that passed from one to the other were thunderstruck. Letters? Stalking?

'What are you talking about? You must be mistaken – she never said anything about any letters!' Alyssa declared, but then her eyes widened, as if she was remembering something. She said nothing more, however, and looked down at her shoes. Equally mystified, Fran shook her head. Humphrey's jaw dropped.

'We have it on good authority – from your son, Chip,' said the inspector to Alyssa.

'But neither of them ever breathed a word about it!'

'Are you sure about that? She didn't she confide in any of you?' He searched Alyssa's face, glanced at Fran. 'Women don't usually keep something so upsetting to themselves.'

'She told Chip.' Alyssa was annoyed equally at the generalization, and that she should be disbelieved.

The detective said drily, 'But apparently didn't let him actually see them.' He regarded them all with ill-concealed scepticism. He had big, rather well-shaped hands, with black hairs springing off the backs. Men with hairy hands always made Fran think of bears, this one more than most, perhaps because she had rarely found anyone before so entirely overpowering and unpleasant. What right did he have to assume they were all lying? Didn't they give them any training in public relations?

'You didn't know Bibi,' she said shortly, which had the effect of turning his interest directly on her. 'She was inclined to keep things to herself.' Which, had he but known it, was the ultimate understatement.

'How well did you know her, Ms er – oh yes, Mrs Mark Calvert, isn't it?' he asked, consulting his notes as if to remind himself who this woman was, though this was ridiculous, since he knew perfectly well from last night, or should have done, since he was the one who'd spoken to her after she'd found Bibi.

'Francine Calvert, Mrs if you wish,' she said woodenly. She wasn't going to let this man rile her. 'Bibi and I were good friends, but she never mentioned that she'd been getting anything like that. Although . . .'

'Yes?'

'When she rang me yesterday to arrange for us to meet, I did have the impression, looking back, that she might have something on her mind.' Alyssa looked up quickly and gave a slight nod, as if this confirmed what she'd been thinking. 'That was mainly why I decided to walk up here to see her.'

'Despite the note you said you received, cancelling her visit?'

'Despite the note I received, yes.' With an effort, she kept her voice level.

'Didn't it occur to you that might have been because she had another appointment?'

'Yes, it did, but I thought . . . I suppose I thought it wouldn't do any harm to come up here . . . oh, I don't know, I just wanted to see if she was all right.'

It was the truth, but it sounded lame, even to her own ears. She thought dully, every word we speak from now on is going to have to be weighed. This, then, was what it was really like, being in the middle of a murder investigation.

Feeling guilty, even if you weren't, an associated guilt because someone you loved was so horribly dead, and you were alive. Looking sideways at even your nearest and dearest, wondering if they were telling the truth, wondering if anything you said was implicating someone else. These were depressing thoughts – it was even preferable to believe that there really was some lunatic who'd been stalking Bibi and had ended up by murdering her.

All right, then, supposing they had? It might be credible – just – but where did Jasie come into it? Who could have wished to harm the little boy, as well as Bibi? The simple hopes of an accident or hiding himself away were fading rapidly as the police combed the grounds and came up with nothing. The waiting was growing intolerable. Fearing the worst – that some poor devil of a policeman might stumble across a small, mutilated or molested body. Hoping against hope for the best – that some communication would be received, demanding ransom in exchange for his safe return. Not even thinking of other alternatives.

She came back to the present to hear Crouch saying disapprovingly, 'Hmm. It's a pity you destroyed this note she wrote, but what's done's done. How do you think she got it to you?'

'It's only a guess, but I think probably the boy who works in the garden may have delivered it on his way home. Gary Brooker.'

The inspector exchanged a significant look with Sergeant Colville and there was a small silence. Distantly, the mournful sound of Jonathan on his cello floated into the room. He'd been playing the same passage, over and over again, for the last half-hour. The music room was well away and was insulated for sound, but the windows would be wide open today because of the heat. Crouch looked pained, but it wasn't clear whether this was disapproval of the sort of noise he didn't call music assaulting his ears or at the name of Gary Brooker, Gaz to his mates, well known to him and every other officer at Felsborough police station. 'So the bad lad's actually got down to working, has he? Well, well, wonders never cease. But he's not everybody's choice of employee,' he warned, addressing Alyssa. 'Keep your eye on him, ma'am, that's all I can say.'

'I make my own judgements about those I employ,' Alyssa said frostily, drawing on the authority she could always summon up when necessary. 'Everyone is redeemable, or so I find. Besides . . .'

'Besides what, Mrs Calvert?'

But Alyssa had thought better of it and closed up. It was an art, the inspector's knack of putting people's backs up, Fran thought. He'd offended Alyssa and now she was leaving him to draw his own conclusions. She'd almost certainly been going to say that it couldn't have been Gary who wrote the letters, he was barely literate. Anything he attempted to write would have given away his identity immediately. Unlettered though he might be, however, Gary was anything but stupid. But the police weren't thick, either, they'd be the first to recognize this.

'I simply meant,' Alyssa said, relenting slightly, though still in grande-dame mode, 'it's ridiculous to think of Gary stalking her. And anyway, if she'd thought he was the culprit, she would never have kept such a thing secret from the rest of us,' she added, though clearly with more hope than conviction.

'Oh, I don't know,' put in Humphrey unexpectedly. 'Kept herself to herself, didn't she, as Fran says? That stare of hers – put you off your dinner, it would. Sometimes used to wonder if she wasn't all there, in fact.'

'Humphrey!' Alyssa was mortified. Dear, sweet old Humphrey, for such a well-meaning man, his speech was often tactless in the extreme. Nevertheless, he'd voiced what they were all thinking, they knew what he meant, except for the two detectives, who were looking for an explanation, which no one seemed prepared to give.

'Sorry, m'dear,' answered Humphrey, 'but that way she had . . . looked right through you. As if you weren't there.

Unnerving, you must admit.' He broke off. 'Oh Lord, not doing very well, am I?'

'No,' said Alyssa.

'It was just a habit,' Fran said. But she thought, Well, it wasn't just my imagination being over-active about Bibi, then. When even Humphrey had noticed it.

The repetitive music had stopped, leaving an oddly breathless vacuum, and Humphrey, too, almost relapsed into silence under Alyssa's accusing look, but then, plainly needing to justify himself, he harrumphed and spoke again. 'Blame it all on that mumbo-jumbo about looking into the future, myself. Didn't do her a lot of good in the end, did it, all that crystal gazing?'

Crouch looked alert. 'Crystal gazing?'

'Oh, Humph!' What on earth had got into him? Alyssa wondered distractedly. If she didn't stop him, he was going to say something everyone would later regret. 'It wasn't crystal gazing, or anything like that. She was just very interested in the stars.'

'What do you mean?' said Crouch. 'Telescopes and things?'

Fran threw him a look, knowing he'd deliberately mis-understood. 'No, the movements of the stars and planets and how they affect our lives,' she said shortly.

'Just another habit, eh? I see,' he replied, meeting her glance and coming back at her with her own words.

And then he suddenly seemed inclined to leave it at that, though he managed to convey the impression that he didn't think much of all this family solidarity, and that the matter wasn't by any means finished with. He stood up, and the sergeant closed her notebook, in which she had been carefully writing down everything that had been said. Fran met her eyes and she smiled, and Fran thought, she's nice, but there probably wasn't much she missed. She decided to risk Crouch's scorn again and voice the worry-ing thought that had been buzzing around in her head like a nasty little wasp: 'You don't suppose – you don't sup-pose Jasie could have been taken away because he saw what had happened to his mother?' *Or that Bibi was murdered because she saw what happened to Jasie?* But she put a hand to her mouth as if that unspoken fear might leap out without her volition.

She knew Crouch had read it though, and could only be thankful for his surprisingly mild reply. Something seemed to happen to him whenever he spoke of Jasie. He didn't entirely lose his abrasiveness, that was probably as much a part of him as his blue chin and his hairy hands, but he was noticeably kinder. 'We haven't dismissed that possibility, no. But we'll concentrate on looking for him before we start thinking about whether he was abducted – and why.'

'Well now,' Alyssa announced into the silence the police left behind them, and with a reproachful glance at Humphrey went to see about sandwiches.

'Made rather a hash of that, didn't I?' remarked Humphrey unhappily to her departing back. 'Foot and mouth disease, always been my problem.'

Fran smiled a little, as she was meant to. But it had to be said that Humphrey, with his awkward silences, like many another frequently inarticulate person, did have an unfortunate propensity for screwing things up when he finally found himself able to speak.

'Poor woman's dead, after all, what does it matter what I thought of her antics?' he said, not noticeably improving matters.

'Don't look so upset,' Fran consoled him. 'You only spoke the truth. I don't suppose it matters in the least.'

The Judge looked heavily down from his frame above the mantel, as if he could tell them a thing or two about such half-baked attitudes, which no doubt he would if he were still alive.

'I see what they meant now,' remarked Crouch after the

first dazed impact, looking round the bedroom Bibi Morgan had occupied. 'Well, I suppose it takes all sorts!'

The weird effect of the room was enhanced because, despite it being broad daylight outside, here the curtains had been drawn and the centre light left burning. Instructions had been given for the room not to be touched, and they'd been literally adhered to. It was just as its occupant had left it before she went out for the last time. It was on that side of the house which didn't get the sun until late afternoon and early evening, the time when she had presumably drawn the heavy, dark blue chenille curtains against it, and then left, forgetting to switch off the light.

It hung low from the ceiling, a pendant light-fitting with a deep fringe, directly over a table on which were several lumps of what Kate thought might be New Age crystals – rose quartz love stones, some crystal palm stones, clear quartz for energy and focus. On various chairs around the room were throws decorated with the signs of the zodiac, more zodiac signs on the velvet cushions, a mandela on the wall above the bed.

'What's that smell?'

Kate sniffed. 'Joss sticks, incense? Scented candles?'

Crouch rolled his eyes, then swivelled his gaze round the room, coming to rest on the narrow bed, three foot wide at the most. His eyebrows rose. 'Can that be the matrimonial bed?'

'Maybe they liked to cosy up.'

'Very cosy it must have been, with a bloke Chip Calvert's size.' He flung open the wardrobe door and rattled a few hangers, then walked into the tiny, adjoining bathroom, where he could be heard opening and closing cabinet doors. 'They didn't share a room,' he announced as he came back. 'Nothing of his anywhere. What d'you make of that?'

'There might be all sorts of explanations.'

'There might. Give me one or two.'

'We – ell . . .'

'You ever come across a young couple that age – and

calling themselves partners, mind – occupying separate bedrooms? I've yet to see it. Can't imagine Chip Calvert tiptoeing from one room to another every time he wanted a bit of how's-your-father, either. But maybe I've come across a platonic relationship for the first time in my life, who knows?'

The bed in question was adorned with a crushed black velvet bedspread with a central embroidery in gold silk in the form of a cross with a loop at the top. 'She was wearing a cross like that on a silver chain round her neck, wasn't she?' said Kate. 'Isn't it an ankh, supposed to symbolize eternal life?'

'Like the old codger out there said, didn't do her much good then.' He thought for a moment, scratching behind his ear. 'She was wearing *two* chains, one with some other fancy doodah on it.'

'Yes.' The other chain had had two crossed fishes threaded on to it. 'I think that was an astrological sign – Pisces, the Fish.' There were fish signs, all around the room. 'Must've been a Pisces.'

'How come you know all this stuff?'

'Just interested. And I read What the Stars Foretell in the Sunday paper, so I can see what sort of week I'm likely to have, of course,' Kate answered.

'You are joking?'

'What woman doesn't? And plenty of men, too. Even you know your birth sign.'

'Yeah, they tell me I'm a Virgo. But you, Kate, horoscopes . . .! And I thought I knew everything about you!'

'That's a dangerous thing to think about anyone, Dave.'

Suddenly, the banter had gone.

'Well, come on, let's have a bit more light on the subject,' he said brusquely, after an awkward moment. 'Pull the curtains back.' She was standing near the window and he switched off the light before she had a chance to comply. For the moment the room was in complete darkness.

Kate pointed to the ceiling. Above them, what appeared to be a midnight sky was liberally sprinkled with constellations of luminous stars, crescent moons, shooting stars, long-tailed comets and orbiting planets, the whole panoply of the heavens filling the entire ceiling.

'Jesus,' said Crouch, taking some time to realize they were phosphorescent stickers, activated by the light to glow for a while in the dark. 'Somebody had an interesting time putting that lot up there!'

'Glow stickers. My sister's children have them on their bedroom ceilings.' But they, she thought, were adolescents. She drew back the curtains. The heavenly bodies faded and, turning round, she decided the room actually looked better in the dark. The daylight that now flooded in showed its accoutrements to be tawdry. The crushed black velvet bedspread was balding and slightly dusty-looking, the fringes on the lamps tatty, the throws creased. There was something out of kilter with the room. It had a claustrophobic atmosphere that felt to grip you by the throat.

Crouch was looking at a long shelf filled with knick-knacks, a pack of tarot cards and some books, almost all of them devoted to astrology, alternative lifestyles and the occult. He perked up and began to look interested, but on closer inspection, the books didn't reveal any indications that Bibi Morgan had been into black magic, or devil-worship, or anything sinister that might have provided a different insight into her death. He leafed through them but they appeared innocent enough, if incomprehensible. No Aleister Crowley. An ephemeris. Titles such as *The Goddess Pathway, Cosmic Connections, Balancing your Chakra, How to Live your Life with Astrology, Feng Shui, I Ching.*

He picked up one from the end of the row and after looking at it, handed it to Kate. Bound in suede, with thick pages, illustrations between sheets of tissue, glowing like medieval illuminations in stained glass colours, touched with gold. It was simply entitled *Myths and Legends*, by someone called C. de Verrender D'arcy, and appeared to

104

have been privately printed. It looked old, and valuable, and though well used, had been taken care of.

Leaving the books, they began a more systematic search, though they'd only know what were looking for when they found it. More of those threatening letters, perhaps – a faint hope which wasn't realized.

'But here's a photo,' she said later, extracting it from one of the drawers.

They'd already been given a rather blurred snapshot of the boy which could, in the absence of any other, be used to circulate his description if necessary. Chip had promised to look for a better one, and Kate had been hoping there might have been one amongst his mother's possessions. But the one she'd picked up now was a coloured studio portrait of Bibi herself, taken when she was younger . . . or maybe it was just that someone had recently done a good job with the airbrush and made her look about eighteen again. As if Bibi Morgan, of all people, had needed help to make her look startlingly attractive. Even in death, her face battered and scratched, it had been possible to see that she must have been an exceedingly beautiful woman in life, and this photograph confirmed it. It wasn't conventional beauty alone that immediately caught your interest, however, but something more elusive, and even Crouch stared at it for a long time, wondering what it was.

It was rare to see such dazzling, almost Nordic fairness. The hair, yes, anything could come from a bottle nowadays, but not that complexion. Or the intense, almost gentian-blue eyes, which saved the face from vapidity – that and a bone structure revealing high rounded cheekbones and a firm chin. She was looking upwards, from under her lids, with a glance that might have been coquettish, yet Crouch knew, without recognizing what he knew, that this would be the wrong thing to believe.

Kate was also puzzled as she looked at the face, but this was because she knew she hadn't yet got a handle on the murdered woman, she didn't know what had made her tick, what her relationships were with other people. There had to be a lot more behind that lovely, blank face than met the eye. Unnaturally blank. Kate was reminded of Humphrey Oliver's words and would have smiled, except that at the same time she was immediately convinced of something else – that this was, indeed, the face of a pre-destined victim.

Chapter Eight

Jonathan stopped playing when Jane Arrow came into the music room a couple of hours later, though she motioned him to go on. 'It's all right, I've done enough for the time being, I'm due for a break,' he told her, pulling the spike from his cello and resting the instrument across a chair, though she knew as well as he did that he was capable of carrying on with several hours' hard practice without even thinking of pausing. But he felt he'd been punishing himself for long enough. What was happening outside, the disruption and chaos of it all, this wound-up feeling, expecting the worst, had played hell with his concentration. He'd been too emotional to detach himself, as he normally could with ease, totally unable to relax and slip into the single-minded application that normally never failed him. The long session had been counter-productive; he'd played like a cack-handed polar bear, and gained nothing except an aching right arm.

'I've brought you some tea.' She set the tray down, complete with cups and saucers – no mugs for Jane – and some of his favourite chocolate chip biscuits, and began to pour.

'No milk, please.'

'Did you think I'd forget?'

He finished wiping the sweat off his hands, his brow and the back of his neck with a paper towel, and smiled at her as he took the cup and began nibbling at a biscuit. No, she never forgot things like that. The reminder was automatic, because back here in England, people invariably assumed that tea meant milk.

She sighed deeply as she took a first sip of her tea. 'It's wonderful to have you here, Jonathan, especially with Mark away. Chip's not up to this sort of thing, he never was any good in a crisis.'

'A fat lot of good I am at the moment, aren't I?' he grumbled. 'Reduced to practising scales while the macho mob get on with looking for Jasie!'

'Of course you're a help, just being here. You do yourself an injustice, but then, you always did.'

That was a surprise, coming from Jane, one didn't normally think of her as a perceptive person, nor did she dish out compliments easily, though in actual fact she had him dead wrong there. He never underrated himself. Belief in what you did was an integral part of being a world-class musician, of being creative in any way, come to that. Not arrogance, but a very necessary feeling of self-worth, and knowing that what you did mattered. But perhaps that wasn't quite what she'd meant. She looked old, he thought. Tired, and old. That was twice in the last two days he'd had that thought. First his mother, then Jane. You never thought of Jane being old although, come to that, she was probably a year or two ahead of Alyssa. She'd looked the same ever since he could remember, with her trim skirts and blouses, her neat little figure and sensible shoes, only now her hair was liberally threaded with grey, more grey than brown, he noticed, and fine lines had cracked her skin, like old porcelain. The determined set of her mouth had dragged down the corners permanently, so that when she smiled, as she did now, it was always a delightful surprise.

He suddenly felt very sorry for her. She was a bit of a family joke, old Jane, but despite what they all thought of as her rather bossy self-righteousness, she took on so many burdens and nobody ever seemed grateful, or admitted she might have feelings of her own.

'What would we do without you, Jane? You're always so unruffled.'

'Oh, I don't know about that.' She flushed with surprise, and perhaps pleasure. 'Certainly not now, anyway. I'm all to pieces.'

She put her teacup down with care, tidily gathered together a scatter of fallen, copper-coloured rose petals from around the pewter bowl on the polished table. 'Jiminy Cricket, never keeps his petals long after he's been cut.' Suddenly she fished for a handkerchief, and dabbed her eyes, blew her nose. 'Oh, dear,' she said shakily, 'I'm sorry.'

'It'll be all right, Jane.'

'Yes. Please God he'll be safe.'

'He will be. He has to be.'

She stuffed the handkerchief back into her skirt pocket, lifted her chin and stared out of the window, unseeing. 'He reminds me so much of you at that age, Jonathan. You were such a lovely little boy.'

'There are still traces, if you look hard enough!'

He knew, of course, that he'd always been Jane's favourite, right from a baby. He could always get what he wanted out of her, though sometimes it was a responsibility, a burden he could have done without, being so favoured, having to live up to it. But he had a lot to be grateful for: years ago, he might well have contented himself with being a talented amateur had it not been for her relentless pressure to practise and yes, encouragement to go that bit further, to stretch his talent as far as it would go. Easy-going Alyssa would never have pushed him in the same way.

'Oh, why did this have to happen to us?' she burst out suddenly, and then, no longer able to keep what she was thinking to herself: 'What's going to happen to Jasie now? Who's going to look after him? Two old women like us. I'm no good with children –' Not necessarily true, he thought, '– and heaven knows, your mother's wonderful, but she's showing her age. I know she works hard in the garden, but it's what keeps her going, all the same, despite Bibi harping on about the portents and omens being right for her to give it up. Really, what rubbish, trying to make people believe they have no control over their lives, that it's all down to the stars! Take the garden away from Alyssa, and she'll be finished.'

She stopped abruptly. It had been a long and curiously incoherent speech, for Jane.

'If it's any consolation, I agree with you entirely. But it doesn't have to be the garden at Membery, you know. She'd be happy anywhere she could put spade to soil.'

That had been the wrong thing to say, though Jonathan was blessed if he could see why she'd suddenly closed up. Her devotion, though, had always been as much to Alyssa as to her three sons: perhaps the one followed the other. He wondered why he hadn't appreciated this before.

'Well, we'll have to do what we must. That's all any of us can ever hope to do. We must sort things out some way.' She held up the teapot, and when he declined a refill, began to gather the tea things briskly together. Pausing with the pot in her hand, she traced a flower on its lid with her forefinger. 'Odd, isn't it, how much chance plays a part in one's life? I never thought I'd hear myself saying that, considering what I thought of Bibi's silliness – and I'm not saying she was right, mind, but –'

'Chance, Jane?'

'How one small thing can change the lives of dozens of people? There we were, last evening, nothing different from usual and then . . . well.'

'Perhaps Saturn squared Mars or something equally diabolical.' He'd only been attempting to cheer her up, but immediately regretted his facetiousness, surprising the look that flashed across her face.

'I thought we'd heard the last of all that!'

'Joke, Jane. Perhaps not in very good taste in the circumstances, but we're none of us at our sparkling best, are we?'

'What I meant was, if you'd been here on time, we

should all have been having supper and Bibi wouldn't have wandered outside and – and nothing of this would have happened.'

'Oh, that makes me feel really great!' He grinned this time to indicate the joke but it made no difference.

She said sharply, 'It had nothing to do with you, and it's ridiculous to pretend it had! If it hadn't been for an incompetent airline, is what I meant. But oh, if . . .' She laid a hand on Jonathan's arm and looked at him earnestly. 'Well, never mind. Life never lays burdens on us, my dear, that we're not strong enough to bear. Always remember that.' She picked up the tray. He held the door open for her and watched her erect little figure marching down the corridor towards the kitchen.

Now just what had all that been about? How much did she know?

Crouch, sitting at his desk in Felsborough, preparing an initial report on the case as it had gone so far for Bob Vincent, was of the opinion that the scant information Chip Calvert had offered had posed more questions than it answered. After that revealing outburst about the letters the victim had been receiving, he had more or less shut up like a clam, and Crouch was experienced enough to know when he'd pushed a witness far enough. Let it go for now, he'd decided, come back to it when he'd been left overnight to stew, and had meanwhile sent him down into Felsborough with DC Hanson to identify the body formally. After that salutary and chastening experience, Crouch thought he might be in a sufficiently altered frame of mind to be receptive to a little more questioning.

His alibi was cast iron. After letting him go, Crouch had had him checked up before anyone else. Routine procedure. The spouse – or the partner – was necessarily always the first in line as suspect, and the one who, quite often, turned out to be the culprit. But there was no possibility Chip could have been anywhere near Membery at the time

111

Bibi Morgan was murdered. A City dinner, a hundred unimpeachable witnesses could be invoked to prove he was innocent. Unless, of course, he'd arranged for someone else to do his dirty work. It had been known, and had to be borne in mind, but Crouch wasn't regarding this as likely, at the moment, or indeed at all. Not that he'd dismissed the man as being incapable of murder – anyone, in Crouch's opinion, could kill, given the right circumstances – but Chip, over and above other considerations, seemed the hands-on type, one who might lose his temper on the spur of the moment, but not one to brood and plan a murder. Crouch knew he'd come back to the idea of a surrogate killer only when all else had failed.

Jonathan Calvert and his girlfriend Jilly Norman also had unassailable alibis if, as they claimed, they had been marooned in the baggage reclaim at Heathrow, waiting for a suitcase that never turned up, though that too wouldn't be allowed to pass without some verification. Leaving, of those closest to Bibi, Francine Calvert and the two old ladies. Crouch was a man who was willing to believe most things of most people, but at the moment he wasn't yet down to regarding these last two old dears as suspects.

As for Francine Calvert, the first person on the spot, who had found the body in the pool at the foot of the waterfall, she'd apparently been genuinely upset at the death of her friend – not that he would allow himself to be fooled by that. There was something about her that gave pause for thought: determination and a strong will, something hidden behind those smoky blue eyes. Though slender, she was a fit young woman and could easily have tipped the even slighter body of Bibi Morgan into the stream after stabbing her, perhaps having met her on the stream-side path on her way up to Membery and later, when the body had tumbled down the stream and slid over the lip of the waterfall into the pool, raising the alarm. Murderers before now had found it expedient to be the first to 'discover' the body. She was near to her own home, with no one else around, she could easily have showered and changed her clothes if they'd been bloodstained. Light summer clothes, easily washed. Though of course, there might have been very little blood if, as Logie had stated, the massive haemorrhage had been mostly internal.

She would also have had to have the weapon with her, and that implied a prior knowledge that Bibi would have been there, which in turn made Bibi's impromptu stroll along the stream seem a little less impromptu. More like a pre-arranged meeting. And not having found the weapon yet was worrying Crouch – that slightly off-centre triangular blade which had made the single incision that had caused her death.

There were three kitchens where a knife might have come from: the original kitchen at Membery Place, one so old-fashioned it made him think of his old grandma's kitchen in Lewisham, though four times as big. It was not a room where trendy knives of that sort were likely to feature, however. A one-knife-does-all sort of kitchen, with the addition of a bread knife and a potato peeler, perhaps. The second was the pretty, remodelled kitchen in the converted wing of the house belonging to Chip Membery, replete with serious culinary equipment, where Bibi Morgan was said to have enjoyed cooking, and no doubt had used such knives. The third was at the The Watersplash, where there were undoubtedly knives for every imaginable task, but all neatly in their allotted spaces, looking as though they had never been disturbed. In none of the kitchens was there one which exactly filled the bill regarding shape and size, or one which appeared to have gone missing. Maybe they ought to be looking for that builder's pointing trowel, as suggested by Hanson.

But . . . where did the child's disappearance fit into all this? Crouch worried his chin with his hand. Nowhere, so far – unless, as Francine Calvert had been quick to suggest, he had been removed because he'd seen what had happened to his mother. But he had supposedly been put to bed before she'd gone out for that fatal stroll.

'It was a hot night,' Kate had pointed out. 'Children

don't always go straight off to sleep. He might have wandered downstairs, looking for a drink perhaps, seen his mother out of the window and gone after her.'

'Or his mother might have been got rid of in order to get at the child. Seems more feasible to me. Someone killed her and then went upstairs and snatched him from his bed. If he cried out, no one would have heard him, not from that wing of the house.'

'And stayed to make his bed, afterwards? Straightened the duvet, smoothed the pillow?'

Possible, but not very likely, Crouch had to admit. He'd simply been following up a theory put forward by the Super, not one of his own. Bob Vincent was convinced that this was a simple case of a child being snatched by his own father, whoever and wherever he was, in which case they might never hear from him. If he had murdered Jasie's mother, he was unlikely ever to apply for legal custody of his child. As soon as they found out his name, they would have all exit points from the country watched, though logic said this might already be too late. Crouch had put the computer gurus to work on it, and no doubt they would come up with results, but even with the marvels of modern technology, these sort of enquiries took time, and after thinking about it, Crouch didn't see why Chip himself shouldn't speed things up and make life easier all round by being made to tell the truth. Which Crouch thought he knew already.

He had told Kate caustically that he didn't need a lie to jump up and hit him in the face before recognizing it: it seemed obvious to him that it was Chip, despite his denials, who was Jasie's natural father. But what about those separate bedrooms? That still bothered Crouch.

The evasiveness of the answers Chip had given about how he and Bianca Morgan had conducted whatever relationship they'd had was a puzzle. Had she been blackmailing Chip? Emotional blackmail, if nothing else? A home for herself and the boy in return for having his child to live with him?

Whatever, Crouch felt more than ever that the answer to this particular murder did not lie outside the family. Perhaps that was a dangerous assumption to make, but Crouch was never averse to making assumptions, dangerous or otherwise, and buttressing them with whatever facts he could find to fit, and he was convinced there was something funny going on – and the more he thought about Chip Calvert, the more he believed this.

All the same, instinct alone could be a dangerous thing. He couldn't afford to ignore the routine approaches to this crime. His men had been busy during the day, up and down the village here, asking questions. It hadn't taken long. Of all its two hundred-odd inhabitants, almost all, except the few who were away on family holidays, had now been seen. Results had been negative. No unrecognized cars had been spotted, no stranger or anyone peculiar (which was tantamount to the same thing) had been noticed hanging around, or Middleton Thorpe wouldn't have missed it.

Everyone who worked in the Membery Place Gardens had been rounded up and questioned: those who came in only on the garden's opening days – the women who worked in the tearooms, served in the garden shop, took the money at the gates and so on – plus those working behind the scenes, which included men for the heavier work and several women who packed up plants for delivery by post, more who were employed specifically to weed the extensive beds and rock gardens – and swore they enjoyed it! The notable exception to all these was Gary Brooker, who had mysteriously been busy elsewhere all day and couldn't be found whenever he'd been summoned for questioning. They'd pin him down eventually. He was an unpleasant little git, and as an outside chance, he might possibly have been moved to kill Bibi Morgan for some reason, but for the life of him Crouch couldn't see him abducting the child. And the two crimes had to be connected.

As with enquiries in the village, the results from all

these interviews had been negative – but then, Crouch hadn't expected otherwise. The country club where Bibi Morgan had worked was marked down for tomorrow, but he set little store by what his team would gather from there, either. An added complication was that the gardens had been open to the public yesterday. Nearly a hundred visitors had passed through the gates, but it would be virtually impossible to trace them all – and though access to the private grounds was easy enough, through a wicket gate from the nurseries, it was no easier than getting into the gardens by other routes – via The Watersplash and along the stream, for instance.

Meanwhile, there were other things to occupy Dave Crouch's mind until he and Chip encountered each other again – like considering how to deal with the press, who were already baying at the door. All we need, he thought, running a hand through his hair. But he knew they were a necessity, he needed their co-operation, to put out a plea for information, circulate the boy's description. He'd grant them an interview, give them just enough to be going on with, put a taste in their mouths. And if there was still no news by tomorrow, the Super had let it be known, they'd have to consider setting up a TV interview, with someone close to Jasie to put in an emotional appeal. The problem there was that there was no mother in this case to pull the nation's heartstrings. Though the added fact that she herself had been murdered – perhaps right in front of her child's eyes – might evoke an even better response.

Crouch had left his men to get on with the search for the boy under the able direction of an experienced, unflappable sergeant by the name of Osborne, who had collected a formidable team around him – local civilian volunteers as well as police, among whom were officers who were fathers themselves and had given up their days off, declared themselves willing to forgo overtime, willing to work around the clock if necessary. But faces were grim. With every hour that passed, the odds against finding the little boy alive lengthened.

Chapter Nine

How long could a day last? For ever, if you'd spent it waiting for news that never came, everlastingly making cups of tea for Alyssa – and for the police, whose capacity was almost as fathomless – and for anyone else hanging around waiting to be interviewed, come to that.

The glorious weather, in direct contrast to the dark forebodings, the evil that had overshadowed the sun-filled day, had become intolerable. Membery was a house that was in any case rarely comfortable when the temperature soared, and no one had been at their best. Tautened nerves, coupled with the oppressive heat and the lack of air inside the house, had stunned everyone and made them morose and unlike themselves. Tempers frayed. They'd become snappish and impatient. Then guilty, ashamed of such trivial behaviour in the circumstances, which had in turn made them over-compensate with too much unaccustomed consideration and politeness, as if they were strangers, and not family: how could they be acting like this when such a terrible thing had struck all their lives, when there was still no sign of Jasie?

The woods had been searched all day, until darkness made any further attempts counter-productive. They would start again at first light, they said, but though it hadn't been put into words, any hope of finding him in the locality had dwindled. Fran could see it in the faces of the police. By now Jasie would be long gone and – dead or alive – miles from Membery.

Perhaps it's the grief, and a kind of impotent rage at

whoever has committed both senseless acts, that's made her barely able to think through the situation clearly. The unbelievable fact of murder – raw, violent, disruptive, with no seeming reason for it – is bad enough, but the abduction of a child, and not any child, but Jasie, is so mind-boggling that so far it has blocked all her constructive thought processes. She suspects that the events have affected everyone else in the same way, at any rate none of them have seemed able to do anything but go round in circles. Alyssa has kept on asking, futilely, all day, why Mark doesn't ring, as if that's the only thing that matters.

'I expect he will, soon.' Fran has been in no mood to discuss possible reasons why he hasn't. Mark acting so out of character on top of all this is beginning to be more than she can take. But at least it has once more served as an excuse not to stay overnight at Membery, as Alyssa suggested, though there is, after all, no reason why she should: she doesn't share Alyssa's conviction that the murderer is still hanging around and that Fran, sleeping down at The Watersplash on her own, might be the next victim. She is dazed and light-headed with tiredness and can't wait to curl up in her own bed. Besides – the delightful thought had slipped into her mind and immediately become of paramount importance – her own house has beautiful, blessed air-conditioning. She revels now in the coolness of it against her skin, like a benison after the dim stuffiness of the rooms at Membery.

No one has felt inclined to eat much at all today, not even Jane Arrow, who can discipline herself to do anything if necessary. While waiting for news that never came, they'd nibbled throughout the day at bits of sandwiches and sausage rolls, biscuits, the kind of food that fills but doesn't satisfy, with the result that no one has been able to face the evening meal produced by Rene Brooker, who pulled herself together and stayed on, long beyond her normal hours. She isn't employed to cook, but over and above her usual cleaning duties, she'd made a chicken casserole as a gesture of sympathy. It gave her something

118

to take her mind off things, and she'd remarked philosophically that if it was left uneaten, which it had been, it could be put in the freezer when it had cooled.

Fran feels it would be sensible to try and eat something nourishing now, but she can't think what. Unable to conjure up anything more inspired than a plate of cheese and crackers, she puts some out and then impulsively measures out an unaccustomed whisky to go with it. She doesn't normally like whisky, but there has to be a reason why it's Mark's favourite tipple, and she reasons tonight might be a good time to find out why. Sloshed over a tumblerful of ice, she finds it just palatable, and after a while the results begin to live up to everything Mark claims for it.

She sits back, sipping, muscles relaxed, a little swimmy in the head, and looks at the answering machine, willing its red light to blink, but it doesn't obey. It seems impossible that Mark is blithely carrying on with his business across the Channel, unaware of the cataclysmic events happening here. Unaware and uncaring, too, she thinks self-pityingly, taking another swig of Glenfiddich, that she might be worried about not hearing from him. All right for some.

She pushes the glass away. The whisky is evidently a mistake, it's making her maudlin. And it tastes even nastier now that what's left of it is diluted by the ice into a watery non-drink.

It really is time to try and look at the whole muddled situation objectively and begin to take steps towards coming to terms with it. But that's a lot easier said than done. All right, begin, then, as Crouch had done, with that telephone call Bibi had made to her at the office during yesterday afternoon. Was it really only yesterday? It seems like a month ago. Crouch is a bloody-minded man but, honesty makes her admit, he's thorough, nor would it ever do to underestimate him, she's sure. She reminds herself of his obviously sincere concern about Jasie and is cheered. Perhaps he has children of his own.

He would keep harping on about that note which had been waiting for her when she got in, though. Was she sure, he'd asked yet again, that Bibi hadn't said why she wanted to see her? And why, he repeated, had Fran destroyed it?

Yes, she was absolutely certain that Bibi had given no hint of why she needed to see her, Fran had answered – but then, she didn't need to give reasons for dropping in, even without any previous warning. They were friends, weren't they? And the letter – she had destroyed that because she was learning to be a tidy person, she had felt like saying crossly, only she hadn't. Pushing it down the waste disposal unit had been the sort of gesture that was by now becoming automatic. He asked why she hadn't put it out with all the other junk mail, ready for the council binmen to pick up. Or why she hadn't put it with the confidential mail, to shred. Because Bibi's message had only been a note, not worth the bother of taking it up to Mark's study to where the shredder was, not worth thinking about, after she'd read it. She'd begun to see how suspects felt, when asked to explain every trivial action – for which there were often no explanations. Why did you peel the potatoes with that knife, instead of this, what made you take road A rather than road B? Why didn't you tell anyone where you were going that night, so that you could have produced a cast iron alibi? It could drive you nuts. And yes, she was positive the signature on the note had been Bibi's. Impatiently, she'd picked up a pen and demonstrated how unmistakable that signature was, in the round, girlish handwriting complete with the encircling curlicue of the final 'a' – which had immediately disproved her point: it would have been child's play for anyone to have copied it.

But why should they?

'Does nobody keep any correspondence in this family?' Crouch had sighed exaggeratedly. 'Not even the letters from the so-called stalker?'

Fran had looked at him, unable to conceal her dislike.

'Perhaps Bibi would have kept them for you if she'd known she was going to be murdered!'

He was too thick-skinned to wilt under irony. He'd met her sort before, his look said, posh house, posh accent, didn't bother him. 'No need to get uppity. Were they obscene, made her throw them away? Did they contain threats?'

'I've told you,' she'd said through clenched teeth, 'I didn't even know she'd *had* any letters.'

She'd escaped at last, and found Chip, the only one who had known about their existence. He doubted very much if Bibi would even have mentioned them to him, he said, if he hadn't picked up the post once or twice and recognized the same, environmentally friendly envelope, made from rough, recycled paper, the tree design on it scarcely leaving room for the address. Bibi had never let him read them, she said they weren't worth bothering about, they were from some sad weirdo who had nothing else in his life and wasn't responsible for his actions. She'd refused to report it to the police or to let Chip do so, either, swearing him to secrecy.

'Thinking about it, though, I'm surprised she didn't mention them to you, Fran. If she told anybody, it would be you.'

'If, Chip. But she didn't, did she, ever? Confide in anyone?'

He wasn't to be drawn on that. His eyes slid away. He didn't seem to find it strange that Bibi had kept the contents of the letters secret from him and Fran wondered just what he'd told the police about his relationship with her, the astonishing circumstances of her precipitate arrival at Membery, an unknown woman with a child, whom he had never previously given an inkling of being involved with. He was revealing aspects of his personality Fran hadn't even suspected before – a propensity for secrecy that she would never have dreamt he possessed.

'What's the matter, why are you looking like that, Fran?'

He said slowly, 'You *do* know who might have sent them, don't you?'

'No, not really – I haven't a clue, but we-ell . . . you know, it could have been Gary.'

'Oh, come on!'

'He was always mooning about after her, everybody knows that. And that might have been the reason she kept quiet, even if she'd suspected – or knew – it was him. You know what Bibi was like – she wouldn't have wanted to get him into trouble, even though he was such a pain in the neck. Blushing and falling over his feet to do things for her. On the other hand, she may have spoken to him about it – you did say the letters had stopped recently, didn't you?'

'Oh no, that's too much of a stretch! It'd be a surprise to me if Gary Brooker can write at all – over and above his name, that is.'

'There's more to Gary than meets the eye, Chip.'

'Just as well! What does meet it doesn't give one much hope for the human race. Anyway, if it was him, the police'll be on to him like a ton of bricks.'

Gary was Rene Brooker's grandson. Tall and thin, etiolated and spotty, sporting a Number One haircut and never to be seen without the requisite amount of ironmongery distributed about his person to establish his street cred. He was nearly eighteen and he'd lived with Rene practically all his life, ever since her unmarried daughter had taken off for God knows where and left her baby behind. But six months ago, after all those years of skimping and scraping on her widow's pension, trying to do her best and worrying over him, Rene had reached a stage where she couldn't cope with him getting into any more hot water and had taken her troubles to Alyssa. 'He's not a bad boy,' she'd vowed, as mothers (and grandmothers) of bad boys the world over have been wont to do since time immemorial. No doubt Genghis Khan's mum had said the same thing. 'It's them as he goes around with, but if he had a regular job to keep him out of mischief . . .' Her eyes had pleaded, and Alyssa, smothering her doubts, had agreed to employ him as an odd-job man in the garden, with the result that Gary now had more money to swagger around with among his mates, and consequently his capacity for getting into trouble had increased. Despite Alyssa's misgivings, however, he'd turned out to be useful in the garden – contrary to what his appearance might indicate, he was as strong as a horse and, as long as he thought no one was watching him, he appeared to enjoy the work.

The odd thing was that this hard-case character had been reduced to a jelly whenever Bibi had been around. She could smile that dazzling, totally impersonal smile she bestowed on everyone, regardless, and Gary would take it as being entirely for him, hold it to his heart and blush to the roots of what hair the barber had left him. She'd only to ask him for a bunch of the flowers that were grown for cutting and he met himself coming back in his hurry to carry out the task. Delivering a letter to The Watersplash would have been the equivalent of a knight errant being sent off to the Crusades at his lady's behest.

But – supposing she had confronted him with writing those letters to her, would his adoration have continued, or turned to fury? Gary, Fran had no doubt, could be a very nasty customer if the occasion warranted it.

Well, Crouch had him in his sights. And no doubt Fran wouldn't be the only one to have made the connection, including those who worked with him in the garden. Most of the staff had been questioned throughout the day, much to Alyssa's distress. She was sure they would all give in their notice and leave in a body.

'How do you think they must feel, under suspicion like that?'

'Like the rest of us, I suppose. I know how I feel, and it's terrible,' Jonathan had said, exchanging a smouldering look with Jilly, and after that escaping back into the music room for yet more practising. How could he? Fran wondered. How could he shut himself away from all the activity? Even *begin* to concentrate? But that was Jonathan, whose passionate belief in his work completely overrode everything else. Ruthless, in a way. Anything, but anything, that got in his way was put into a separate compartment, labelled later.

Does he mean they suspect one of us? Fran asks herself. Surely not. But she's seen enough television, read enough crime novels, seen enough statistics in newspapers, to know that people who kill are usually known to their victims. It's not a happy thought.

Undressing before her shower, preparing for bed, she scrunches up the cotton shirt of Mark's she's been wearing all day, ready to toss into the linen basket, and hears a papery crackle. She puts her hand into the breast pocket. Smoothing open the piece of paper, relief hits her like an adrenalin shot when she sees a telephone number written on a scrap torn from the kitchen pad – thick, black, italic, very stylish, the sort of writing you'd expect from Mark. Perhaps he'd been wearing this shirt before he left, she couldn't remember – and stuffed the paper into the pocket and forgotten to give it to her, folding the shirt in his neat way over the chair back. But the realization brings a return of her exasperation with him, though she actually feels she ought to be more mad at him than she is, as she punches in the number. After all, the fact that she's not known how to get hold of him doesn't explain why *he* hasn't seen fit to contact her. He ought to have realized, when she didn't ring . . . On the other hand, there may be all sorts of explanations: he may not know he'd forgotten to give her the number where she can reach him and could be expecting her to ring him . . . possibly he's tried to ring while she's been up at Membery . . . the answerphone might not be functioning properly . . . the client he's visiting is known to be very demanding and he may not have had the chance . . . or what if there's been an accident and he's languishing in some Belgian hospital with loss of memory . . .?

Pull yourself together, Fran, get real! Stop acting the fluttery, anxious little wife who can't let her husband out of her sight for five minutes without fussing! Hold on to your stated belief that day-long proximity with someone you love isn't a necessary component of loving. When Mark is absent, he's still with her, part of her, inside her, for twenty-four hours a day. She believes he would be if he were dead, and she knows Mark feels the same. Space between them has nothing to do with it. She's never before expected him to have to worry about reassuring her as to just where he is and what he's doing every minute, when he's away conducting important business. But the more she tells herself these reassuring truths, the more the huge bubble of fear grows inside her chest, rising into her throat, making it difficult to breathe, so that she feels something near to a panic attack. The annoyance and the slight unease at his thoughtlessness is beginning to coalesce into a tight, unbearable knot of certainty that something must surely be wrong. Whatever she tells herself, never before has he left her in quite such a limbo as this.

She dials the code for Brussels, then the sequence of numbers. She lets it ring twenty-five times – she isn't going to give up easily, now that she's found the blessed number at last – before she has to admit defeat. It isn't a hotel she's ringing, that much at least she does know, it's a house owned by what'shisname, the client, so it must have been ringing into empty rooms.

This is absolutely not on: there has to be some way of speaking to him!

She tries desperately to remember the client's name, a Belgian reputed to be a zillionaire, but whatever name it is has been erased from her memory like computer data in a power cut. Think, think! It must be lurking somewhere in the retrieval system. He is someone, she knows, who is rich enough to have his every whim acceded to, and his latest one is to have built for him a house to his own fancy ideas, but with Art Nouveau overtones. There have been mutterings under the breath about this at The Watersplash over the last few weeks. Mark was damned if he was going to design some outlandish Disneyland fantasy, but at the same time, he knew he'd be damned financially if he didn't pander to this potential client, who had seen in Brussels the elegant Stocklet house that Joseph Hoffmann designed, and the wonderful exuberances of Victor Horta, and had decided a combination of both, plus some of his own bizarre ideas, was what he wanted, to show off his wife's fabulous Tiffany collection. But Fran has argued with Mark that whatever his personal opinion of these extraordinary notions, he can't afford to turn down the possibility of a commission. They're thin enough on the ground as it is. It's pretentious to be so precious.

'OK, OK, no need for sarcasm – I get the point.' And he'd agreed to do it.

Fran puts the phone down and sits thinking. The situation is too silly for words, yet oddly enough, this failed attempt to reach Mark has made her see things in better perspective – it can't be beyond the wit of woman to find out where he is. Perhaps it's desperation, or the spur of the whisky, but she suddenly knows just what she's going to do.

First, however, she has her shower, blessedly cool and refreshing, then wraps herself in a cotton kimono before going into Mark's beautifully equipped studio on the mezzanine. She throws the switch that operates only the angled reading lamp, making the big desk on which it stands spring into an eerie, isolated life among the drawing boards and plan cabinets looming in the background. It's now quite dark outside and her own reflection in the black glass of the windows reminds her with a shiver of the owl imprint on the mirror, the sounds she's heard outside at night. Feeling suddenly quite dithery, she quickly presses the switch that lowers the blinds electronically, sealing herself within a silky cream box, as if in the interior of a Japanese house. That's better. Whatever might be there, real or imagined, is outside.

The room looks alien without Mark. It's very much his own room, full of his presence, his working paraphernalia, old black and white architectural drawings framed and

126

hung on the pale walls alongside some of his own artist's impressions for earlier projects. It's oddly disconcerting not to see Mark himself there, in shirt-sleeves or casual sweater, in front of one of his drawing boards, either perched on a stool with his legs twisted into some impossible contortions around the support, or simply leaning back, his behind perched on the seat, arms folded, considering the work he's engaged on. She has an absurd longing to feel her fingers running through his thick, dark hair, smoothing it back from his forehead where it falls into a dark comma. Shaking herself free of such thoughts, she walks over to the desk. It's large, ebonized and antique, a single, intentional anachronism amongst all the other modern, functional items of furniture. And all the drawers are locked.

He's taken the keys with him. And why has he done that? It isn't as if she ever goes into his desk. As if he fears she might pry while he's away. Which, of course, is just what she is doing.

She takes a deep breath and while she thinks what to do next, she dials the Brussels number again, and though, as she'd expected, there's still no reply, it has become evident by the time she puts the phone down that there's only one way to get into the bottom left-hand drawer, where she knows Mark keeps his client files. All the other drawers lock automatically when the top centre one above the knee-hole is locked, so that there's only one keyhole. She only has to open that drawer and there'll be immediate access to the rest. The desk isn't, after all, intended to be burglar-proof so much as private. Except that Mark has never previously locked the desk that she knows of – or perhaps he has. She has never, after all, tried it before. At any rate, she doesn't have a clue how to start breaking open the drawer without using brute force and vandalizing the unique, expensive, two hundred and fifty-year-old black Egyptian-style desk, solid as one of the pyramids. Nail files, the stock fall-back of female private eyes in similar situations, do not immediately spring to

127

mind as the ideal solution. She has never had much faith in plastic credit cards either, after once having forgotten her Yale key and getting her card chewed up in the process of trying to open the lock with it.

In the end the solution is much less dramatic, in the shape of the collection of junk Mark laughed at, the stuff she'd picked up at last week's church jumble sale. Inside the rusty old tin box which had once held Karamel Kreeme toffees, among the buttons and buckles, the odd ear-rings and the pinless brooches, the hairgrips, safety pins and old suspenders, are dozens of keys, ranging from a mammoth specimen capable of unlocking the Bastille, to tiny ones for long-abandoned suitcases. The seventeenth of all the keys of approximate size that she tries fits, and the top drawer slides open.

She riffles through the file-drawers with no success. He has obviously taken his client's dossier with him, along with his laptop, which she might have realized he would have done if she'd thought about it. She opens the others, just in case. Nothing, until she comes to the bottom right-hand drawer.

A current like electricity suddenly shoots up her spine and almost lifts the hair on her head as she looks at what Mark has left in there, hidden away in a locked drawer.

Chapter Ten

A mobile incident room was now parked in a farmer's field adjacent to the Membery Place Gardens, from which the search operation was being mounted. It was the usual thing when crime scenes were in out of the way places, it made sense, being more accessible than the headquarters in Felsborough, but even as a temporary centre of operations it was less than perfect. It wasn't a good place to work and conduct interviews in for one thing, and for another, its limitations of size posed problems, especially for one of Crouch's dimensions.

In the end, Alyssa had been persuaded to allocate a room in the house where Crouch himself could spread out and work in greater freedom, formerly the library but now a room of unspecified function, though it was still so called, justified by the tall, glass-fronted, solid oak bookcases lining one wall. It smelled damp and unused, with the nose-twitching, musty odour emitting from the long unopened law tomes and books of jurisprudence ranged on the shelves. It could never have been anything other than cheerless, being situated on the same side of the house as Bibi's room: like hers, it could rarely have seen the sun except for a short period in the late afternoon or early evening. No doubt that hadn't mattered when a roaring fire was kept constantly lit in a fireplace big enough to roast an ox – as it was, the room's one virtue now was that it was the coolest spot in the house.

'You'll leave everything as you found it, I trust, when you've finished?' Miss Arrow had asked, nay threatened, finally allowing herself to abandon her supervisory activities and eyeing with disfavour the various pieces of up-to-date technology already littering the floor.

Bloody sight better than before we came, Crouch had muttered under his breath. And so it was, after Kate had gone round the lampshades with a duster in an attempt to gain more light, and had persuaded the technicians to fit light bulbs of somewhat higher wattage than forty to the ancient electrical fittings. Rolling their eyes, muttering at the dodgy state of the wiring, they'd all the same finally managed to set up all the necessary electronic equipment, and without, moreover, blowing the fuses for the whole house. It still felt as though they were working under the sea. Even this time in the morning, Crouch had to suffer the indignity of wearing his reading glasses in order to see his notes. Sure, there was the privacy he needed here for interviews, but he wasn't making much headway in controlling his irritability.

Chip Calvert was not at his happiest to have been summoned there either, at barely 8 a.m., hardly having finished his breakfast. 'Look here,' he began, 'I need to get down to my office in London for a while. I do have business to sort out there, you know, and I've already told you all I know.'

Crouch eyed him over his spectacles. 'All in good time. But let's make it clear from the start, Mr Calvert, I'm not here for my own amusement, either. I'm here to sort out this case. And it doesn't improve my temper when witnesses hamper me by not giving me the full facts.'

'I don't suppose it does, but how does that concern me?'

Crouch toyed with his pen. He sat at the foot of a mighty oak table, ten feet long, with Chip to one side of him and an empty chair waiting for Kate at the other, his papers spread over the green baize with which Miss Arrow had ostentatiously covered the polished wood. His back was to the glassed bookcase wall of great, leather-bound volumes, never opened for nearly a century and maybe not much

130

before then at a guess, judging by their size and weight and the off-putting titles on their well-preserved spines. He'd chosen this place to sit so that he would have the advantage of seeing the people he was talking to with what light there was on their faces, but he wasn't sure he'd picked the right spot: on the edge of his vision, he was aware of yet another portrait of Judge Calvert, hanging broodingly over the fireplace. It was the fifth of those Crouch had already counted, variously disposed around the house. That guy had really loved himself.

Chip threw down a packet. 'You said you wanted photographs. These are better than the snap I gave you.'

Crouch made no move to open it. Indeed, he seemed in no hurry to get on with the interview at all, and sat with his elbow on the baize, one hand supporting his chin, flicking through his notes with the other. Chip shifted uneasily in his seat, looking warily at him but not inclined, after that first barbed remark, to precipitate the situation by asking him what he'd meant. Eventually, Crouch opened the packet and fanned the photos out on the table in front of him, studying each one carefully. He took his time about that, too, as if he were waiting for something.

When at last Kate came in, it was obvious she'd been hurrying. Fanning her heated face, she handed Crouch a sheet of paper, giving him an almost imperceptible nod as she settled herself, and he immediately lost interest in the photos, leaving them where they were for her to gather up, while he read what she had given him.

She took the opportunity to select a very much clearer picture of the little boy than the previous one they'd been given. She saw that he was very like his mother, but with darkish brown hair, rather than blonde, that flopped in a curve over his brow. He had the promise of a firm chin, which would no doubt save him from looking in any way girlish, or like a copy of Bibi, as he grew older. By then, when his childish features had matured, with those sort of looks, he'd be all set to break a few hearts. Now he was

131

just a sturdily built little boy with a beaming smile that betokened a sunny nature.

It was a long time since Kate had prayed, but she found herself doing so now. Not using words – she couldn't have found any that were adequate – but just absorbing this happy, beautiful child into her own being and willing everything she had that no harm would come to him.

The last photo she picked up was another of Bibi herself, and again as she looked at it came the thought that the future could be read in that face. Inescapable as it seemed to be, however, Kate was a practical policewoman and felt she ought to regard this rather fanciful idea with some scepticism: how could you really tell what a person was like from any photograph, however good? Wasn't she looking at it with hindsight? There hadn't been time yet for any in-depth interviews, no opportunity to find out, by talking to people and drawing conclusions from what they said, what this woman had really been like, to have formed some idea as to what had made someone hate her enough to take her life and deprive her child of his mother. She made a note to find time to talk to Francine Calvert, who seemed a sensible person and the one, apart from – or even including – Chip, who she thought had been closer to her, in age and in other respects, than anyone else.

Dave Crouch was at last talking to Chip, starting from where he'd left off. 'It would have made life a lot easier, Mr Calvert, if you'd been straight with us from the beginning.' He glanced briefly at the paper Kate had given him and tapped it. 'As it is, I think we'd better start again, hadn't we? And this time from the beginning, with the truth.'

Chip blustered. 'What the hell's that supposed to mean?'

'I think you understand me well enough. Why didn't you tell us the real reason you brought Bibi Morgan to live here?'

'Does it need saying? Why do people usually decide to live together?'

This sort of arrogance was not calculated to gladden

Crouch's heart. 'Please don't answer one question with another.'

'What's happened now has nothing to do with what happened then.'

Crouch leaned forward and fixed him with a look. 'Let me get this straight. You're saying you *knew* there'd been threats against her life before this, when she lived in Yorkshire – and which had very nearly succeeded – and you're expecting me to believe you thought there was no connection?'

Chip went suddenly pale under his tan, with anger, Crouch thought, gratified to see it. Anger was a channel to get through to people. It left them exposed, vulnerable, without control over themselves. 'The reason I thought there was no connection is because the man who made them is bloody well in prison!'

'Was, Mr Calvert. Graham Armstrong *was* in prison.'

There was a measurable silence. 'Still is. He was sent down for seven years – and that was just over two, two and a half years ago!'

'Haven't you ever heard of remission?'

'They don't give remission to somebody as mad as he is, when he hasn't served half his sentence!'

'Oh yes, they sometimes do. Our caring society is very sympathetic to people like Armstrong,' Crouch said drily. 'At the time he was sent down, he was a very disturbed personality, but he's apparently responded well to the treatment he's had in prison, and after psychiatric assessment and showing remorse for what he did, he's been judged fit for release – under licence, of course. He's been out for nearly three months.'

Chip's face was a study. The scar stood out lividly. He looked round a little desperately, but this time there was no bottle of Dutch courage, such as he kept in his study, to help him out.

'Why don't you begin by telling us exactly what happened, right from when you first met Bianca Morgan, and this time not just an approximation of the truth?'

133

Chip ignored the suggestion. 'I can't believe what I'm hearing! You're saying they let that maniac loose, after he tried to kill her, her and Jasie? Don't you realize what he did? He only set fire to the bloody house, deliberately, when they were both in bed and asleep – Christ, he's a mad beast, he ought to have been locked up and the key thrown away!'

'You weren't with her, the night this happened?'

'If I had been, none of us would be alive to tell the tale. But I saw the smoke coming from the house, the flames behind the windows. If I hadn't come along then, it would have been all up with them.'

Crouch tapped the papers in front of him. 'You were something of a hero that night, it seems, Mr Calvert.'

'A hero? That's one way of putting it.'

His fingers went instinctively to the healed scar-tissue on his face. He hadn't felt like a hero, then or afterwards. A crass fool, more like, for not realizing what was happening and preventing what might well have been a tragedy. If he hadn't happened to go out for a walk round the village before going to bed, to cool a head that had felt like a bucket after throwing several drinks too many down his neck in order to try and make some sense out of the situation, it would have been too late. But that had been the end of it, not the beginning.

He said, his anger rising, 'If you know all this, why are you badgering *me*?'

Crouch was still looking at him as if he were some other species, arrived from some distant planet, perhaps. 'Didn't it even occur to you,' he asked slowly, 'to think it *might* have been Armstrong who killed her?'

There was a long pause. 'Possibly.' Chip studied the tip of his polished loafer. 'Briefly. Well, yes, maybe it did,' he admitted after a while. 'Then I thought no, it can't be. People don't escape from prison, just like that. They'd have let her know if he had. Never in this life did I imagine they'd just open the door and let the bastard go free – it's beyond belief.' He glared at Crouch. 'Why the hell haven't

134

you arrested him? He should be the one you're giving the third degree, not me!'

'That's all being taken care of. It would help even more if I wasn't working with one hand tied behind my back.'

'Meaning?'

'Meaning we now have the basic facts here,' Crouch said, tapping the papers on the table in front of him, 'but I need to know the background, everything that's led up to this, and only you can tell me that.'

The clock above the old coach house struck nine. The strokes sounded tinnily across the quiet morning stable yard.

'I don't see why, but all right,' Chip said eventually. 'It's a long story.'

'We're not going anywhere. Take your time.'

For a while, Chip sat with his big frame hunched in the chair, his elbows on his knees, breathing deeply, not knowing how to tell it. He began haltingly, but then, as he spoke, it became easier, as if a boil had been lanced, and all the pain was draining away.

The start of it all had been years ago, when he'd first walked into the Ascomb Arms with a gang of his racing chums, and seen her there, behind the desk, with her silver-gilt hair gleaming against the dark panelling of the reception area, her smile of welcome lighting up her face so that you thought she was smiling for you alone. He'd fallen for her like a lovesick teenager – hook, line and sinker. So much so that he'd stayed on for several days, after the rest of the crowd had gone home. He'd taken her out, wined and dined her, charmed her, softened her up – if nothing else, that was the one thing he did know how to do. She was a very young twenty-year-old and he could see she was more than a bit dazzled by his attentions, which was flattering, and perhaps if she'd given into him as girls usually did easily enough, his infatuation would have worked itself out naturally, as that usually did, too. But she didn't. That ought to have warned him, but strangely enough, he hadn't minded; for once in his life he was prepared to wait, to woo her, because he'd been confident that he'd win her in the end. This, he'd already decided, was the girl he was going to marry . . .

She had a divorced mother who owned and ran the hotel where she worked – another beautiful woman, from whom Bibi had inherited her looks but not her reserved nature. Carys Morgan was an expansively dramatic woman, who had once worked as a small-time actress and had been married for a short time to a moderately wealthy businessman. Using the money from her divorce settlement, she had worked her socks off to make a good life for herself and her child. Twelve years later, the determination to get where she was had begun to show in the hard lines around her mouth and the calculation in her eyes. It had cost her a good deal to turn the Ascomb Arms from a village pub into a small, decidedly upmarket place, furnished in country house style and with a growing reputation for comfort, care and excellent food. She employed a superb French chef and organized gourmet weekends, which were booked up months ahead, where she swanned around among her guests, made up and dressed to the nines, a gin and tonic in one hand, cigarette in an amber holder in the other, keeping an eagle eye on everyone and everything.

She had not approved of Chip, whom she saw as an obstacle to her plans for Bibi's future. Bibi, she'd long ago decided, would continue to run the profitable business built up so arduously over the years when she, Carys, retired. Of course, that wouldn't be for years yet, Carys had no intention of throwing in the towel in the foreseeable future. But it would take some time, anyway, for Bibi to learn enough to assume her mantle. She wasn't cast in the same mould as her mother and was still a little naïve, unprepared. And perhaps Carys hadn't met Chip in a good light, seeing him among his rakish cronies, who didn't impress her with their money and their noisy cars and their Hooray Henry lifestyles.

But more than that, she saw he had every intention of

taking Bibi away and installing her in his family home. Carys wasn't unaware of the advantages to Bibi of marrying into what she thought of as the county set, but she'd made it her business to look into Chip's affairs and what she'd found there hadn't reassured her. There was no money behind him, and Chip himself didn't impress her as being the sort who would suddenly turn into a solid proposition. She thought it very likely, taking it from the perspective of her own ambitions and inclinations, that he was out for what he could get, namely the ownership of the Ascomb Arms at some future date.

So she'd put her foot down. Her daughter was of age, her decisions were her own, but Carys had made it clear that if Bibi went ahead and married Chip, she could expect nothing from her, now or in the future. There hadn't been nearly as much opposition as she'd expected, confirming her opinion of Chip as a man of straw. In fact, Bibi had been no match for her strong-minded mother and, torn between the two, had given in and chosen to stay with Carys. Perhaps she had, after all, inherited a little of her mother's self-preservation.

'It's only for the time being,' she'd pleaded with Chip. 'She'll come round, I'll make her see . . .' But this wasn't what Chip, hurt and rejected, had wanted to hear. He'd shrugged, pretended not to care, and left. He'd never in his life had need to force his attentions on a girl who didn't reciprocate and he wouldn't start now. There were, after all, plenty more fish in the sea.

A couple of years later, again with a crowd, up for the racing, he'd gone back to stay at Ascomb, as an act of bravado, perhaps, or to reassure himself that he'd done the right thing in leaving Bibi, and was cured of her. He'd found her still there, still as beautiful as ever, and discovered himself still in the throes of his infatuation. Yet . . . he saw a remarkable change in her – the same lovely face, the remote delicacy that had so charmed him, but even more elusive. She'd gone vegetarian. She wore clothes of a vaguely ethnic nature and talked of alternative lifestyles.

She liked to think of herself as a free spirit, full of beautiful thoughts. Yet, behind it was a stubbornness he wouldn't have suspected. He might have said ruthlessness if he hadn't been so besotted. Before, she'd seemed young for her age, over-protected by that Welsh dragon of a mother; at times she'd seemed a child almost, but now she was a woman, with a mind of her own, and this only added to her attraction. All his old feelings came rushing back.

'Well, Bibi.'

'Well, Chip,' she'd replied coolly.

'So you're still here? And your mother?'

He learned with a shock that Carys was dead, that she'd been killed a couple of years before when her car collided with a tractor coming out of a farm-turning on the road from York, and Bibi was trying her best to run the hotel on her own. It was fairly obvious, however, that Carys had been proved right. Bibi might be older, she might have the willingness, but she was woefully lacking in her mother's business sense. The hotel, now, was not well run. Chip saw signs of neglect everywhere, the French chef had left and the food was not up to the old high standards, reflecting too much Bibi's own vegetarian inclinations. She had no chance of emulating her mother in the nicely judged way she mixed with her guests, either, cordial and welcoming, yet keep-your-distance. She couldn't even control the noisy excesses of the group of young men Chip was with – though she tried, as her mother had, by chatting with them, being friendly, accepting the odd drink. More than the odd one, if the truth were told. There'd been a riotous party on the last night which had resulted in vociferous complaints from the other guests in the hotel.

Chip paused in his narrative, passed his tongue round his dry lips. Kate reached out to the carafe of iced water she'd placed on the table earlier and poured him a glass.

'Thanks.' He took a deep draught and smiled gratefully, though the ice in it that she'd begged from the kitchen had long since melted.

Up to this point, Crouch had allowed him to carry on

without interruption. Now that Chip had at last begun to talk he didn't want anything to interrupt the flow. But there was something he needed to know and this pause gave him the chance to ask it. 'What about the child?'

Chip stared at him. 'Jasie wasn't born then. I still wanted to marry her and take her away from it all – things were in a hopeless mess, and there didn't seem to be a lot of hope of retrieving them. She wasn't Carys, she hadn't got her push.'

'And what did she say to that?'

'She said she realized that things were not going as well as they should, but everything was about to change. She had in fact already hired someone to come in and manage the place. He was arriving the following week and between them they'd soon have things back to what they had been. Anybody with half an eye could see it wasn't going to work, the place had gone too far downhill for someone as unfitted for the job as Bibi to pull it back. But she insisted she could, and this manager, she said, had come highly recommended . . . together, they'd get the hotel on its feet again. How naïve can you get?'

'It was Armstrong? Graham Armstrong was the new manager?'

'Yes,' he said bitterly. 'And he turned out to be a total disaster, though I'd no idea of this until later. There was nothing I could do to influence her. She still refused to marry me, so I left and that was that. As far as I was concerned, it was over. Done with. Finis.'

And yet, whatever he'd said and thought about other fish in the sea, he hadn't been able to get her out of his mind. She'd haunted his dreams, wouldn't be dismissed from his life. He didn't let it show, outwardly he went on being the same good old Chip, hail fellow well met, with women still featuring largely in his life, plenty of whom he fancied, but none of them enough to want to marry.

'Then, years later, out of the blue, I had a telephone call from her. She begged me to come and see her. She said she was desperate, but wouldn't say anything more until I got there. I drove up, didn't bother to book, and when I arrived I found the Ascomb Arms had been taken over by someone else. It was a comfortable enough place to stay, the food was OK but nothing special, they'd redecorated and made it spruce again, but – ordinary, somehow. I suppose they just lacked Carys's flair. They told me Bibi still worked in the hotel a few days each week, but she was married now, and she had a child, though she was separated from her husband. She still lived in the village, in a cottage down a narrow lane, just off the main street. There was something cagey about the way they spoke about her husband. I suppose I wasn't really surprised to hear that he was the bloke who'd come to manage the hotel. Armstrong.'

Chip drank some more of the tepid water. He hadn't been sure whether it was a good idea to see her or not, but he'd gone to the address the hotel had given him, all the same, and found her with this little boy, about six years old, Jasie – or James, he'd still been then. Chip had always thought the boy's insistence on being called by the new name his school friends in Middleton Thorpe had given him was one way of pretending that the life he'd left behind had never happened.

If Chip had been surprised to see the change in Bibi the first time he'd returned, this time he was astounded – and enraged – at what marriage to this man Armstrong had done to her. She'd never been an assertive person, but now she was cowed and seemed frightened of her own shadow. She'd clutched the child to her, he'd clung to her, and Chip wasn't sure who was protecting whom.

'When she saw me she burst into tears. "I knew you'd come," she said, and begged me to take them both away. I could see how desperate she was. I thought at first that Armstrong had been abusing either her or the child, but it wasn't that – not physical abuse, anyway. He was just simply paranoic, insanely jealous if she so much as looked at another man, which was unfortunate, the sort of work she did, meeting different people all the time. I wondered

140

why in God's name she'd ever married the man. Then I realized she'd never had the chance to find out what he was really like – they'd been married within a few weeks of his arriving in Ascomb. That staggered me. A bit quick off the mark, wasn't it? I said, but she just shrugged and said well, he could charm the birds off the tree when he wanted.'

A bitter pill that had been to swallow, after his own rejections, one he hadn't quite managed to down even yet.

'Even if she'd suspected he was out for the main chance, her mother had left a will that stopped anyone but Bibi getting their hands on the hotel. If she sold it, she'd only get half the proceeds, the rest would go to some charity or other. And anyway, he was a great ideas man, she said, and she believed him when he told her she was sitting on a little gold mine, that he could help her put the place back on the map, if she'd give him his head.'

Chip looked down at his shoes. 'Later, I came to think she'd actually been under no illusions, she understood he was offering his services in return for marriage. I suppose she thought she could do worse, it was a fair enough exchange. But she couldn't have had any idea what her life would be from then on. She became pregnant straight away which gave him the excuse to take complete charge of everything to do with the hotel, and maybe it would have worked out OK, except that gradually, her personal life became hell. She swore she'd tried to make the marriage work – Jasie needed a father – but it was no use and in the end, she found courage enough to sell the hotel over his head, sue for a divorce and walk away from the situation. It didn't stop him from pestering her, though. He followed her everywhere she went, besieged her with telephone calls and threats. He tried to get possession of Jasie, but he was refused, and ordered to stop persecuting her, which of course he didn't. She applied for a court order, a whatyoumaycallit -'

'Restraining order.'

'Whatever. Fat lot of notice he took of it. Well, anyway, she got desperate, and that was when she rang me for help, when I went up there. I went to the cottage several times, walked her home after she'd finished work at the hotel . . . and he must have seen us, or found out. That last night, the bastard set fire to her house – with her and Jasie in it. It was sheer bloody good luck I happened to be there and saw the smoke . . . it was off the beaten track, along a lane that led to nowhere, not a place anyone actually had reason to pass. Minutes after they got out, it went up like a torch.'

It was some time before he was able to resume. 'Two lives nearly sacrificed – and what did he get for it? Pleaded diminished responsibility and was sent down for a mere seven years – one of those bleeding heart judges who believed him when he said he hadn't known they were in the house at the time, that he'd been provoked by being denied access to his child. Despite the fact that he'd said at the trial that he'd intended if he couldn't have Jasie, nobody would.'

There was a long silence.

'He's admitted the offence, addressed his problems and showed contrition. A psychiatric assessment has judged him no longer a danger. If he really *wants* the child,' Kate said, 'he won't harm him.'

'Psychiatric my backside . . . I've no time for that sort of claptrap! She'd tried to take her own life, you know, and afterwards . . . well, that was why she asked me for help, she was just so all out desperate, I'd no illusions about that. It was a long shot, God knows, after all those years. But she'd nobody else to turn to and I'd always sworn . . . Anyway, I took her away, brought her down here. The whole thing had knocked her absolutely sideways, ruined her life – and not just hers . . .' He shifted on his seat, reddened. 'You know how it is, this sort of thing has a knock-on effect, it's not only the victim that suffers.'

'Yes,' said Kate, 'that's true, it damages a woman's self-esteem and –'

'If that means she wanted nothing more to do with men, that's it!' He looked sorry he'd said that, and stopped abruptly. 'Where is he now? If I get my hands on the bugger . . .'

'That's the trouble,' said Crouch, 'we don't rightly know. Not yet. He hasn't reported to his probation office for two weeks and he seems to have disappeared.'

Chapter Eleven

At some point, just about when Chip began sweating his way through his story to Crouch, the shrilling of the telephone drags Fran from the submerged depths of the violently disturbed dreams and half-waking terrors which have passed for sleep. Her hand gropes for the phone as she struggles out from under the damp tangled sheet. She forces her eyelids open, feeling as though she's been drugged, not knowing where she is, totally disorientated. And then, in the space of a heartbeat, she's awake. Jasie! They've found Jasie!

Filled with a mixture of hope and dread, her hand hovers over the receiver, unwilling to pick it up, petrified by the thought of what she might hear. At last she forces herself to move, and speak, her throat dry, her heart still pounding.

'Fran?'

'*Mark!*' For a panicky moment she's back in the dark shadows of her dreams, chasing a man she knows to be her husband – who, every time she catches him, turns a featureless face towards her, and then slips like water from her grasp again. But then her mind clears and everything comes back, the awful day yesterday, the worst day of her life, and the discovery in which it culminated. 'Oh, *Mark!*'

'Something tells me you haven't surfaced properly yet, love. Hope I haven't woken you up, but I thought you might have decided to go out, seeing I've abandoned you for the weekend, and I wanted to catch you before you did.'

'Mark, I've been trying to get you for two days! You forgot to leave me a contact number.' Her voice isn't her own. Like a mother who's been out of her mind with worry over a child who's run off and been lost for half an hour, she wants to shake him, shout at him, hug him and cry over him, all at once. She pulls herself together, indulging in such emotions is just pathetic, in the circumstances – though she doesn't draw the line at adding, sharply, 'You might have rung.'

'Sorry about that,' he says, briefly apologetic. 'You just wouldn't believe how hectic things have been here.'

'They haven't been exactly slow at this end, either.'

'What's happening? Everything's all right, isn't it? You sound upset.'

'No, Mark, everything's all wrong.'

'Everything? That sounds pretty ominous!' Teasing, prepared to humour her. Over-hearty, quite unlike his usual ironic self. Not really believing in anything disastrous, real or imagined.

'It's Bibi.'

'*Bibi*?' The change in tone is palpable. Sharp, peremptory almost. 'What's happened?'

'Prepare yourself for a shock, Mark. She's – dead. She's – I'm afraid she's been murdered.'

The long, fraught silence at the other end is worse, much worse, than anything he could have said. Oh my God, Fran tells herself, I was right, oh God. Then he says, quite calmly, 'Tell me about it.'

'She was stabbed and thrown into the stream, on Thursday evening. I – I was the one who found her, in the pool.'

'In the – *you* found her?'

'And there's m-more. Jasie's disappeared.' She rarely cries, but tears are very near the surface now. The phone is slippery in her grasp. She transfers it to her other hand and wipes her sweaty palm on the bed-sheet, then transfers it

145

back. 'The police are out looking for him but there's been no trace . . . Mark, I can't tell you how awful it's been!'

There was another, even longer silence. 'Hell's teeth, what a mess!'

She can see, in her mind's eye, his hands, typically, running through his hair as he concentrates his thinking. After a few moments, he says, 'Look, can you bear with me while I get things sorted this end? I'll be home by tonight, latest. This guy here, Duchêne . . . he's difficult, to put it mildly, but that said, he's given me every facility to work with here. He wants to see the plans as soon as possible at least in rough draft, and I've been working all hours to have something to show him. The thing is, it's actually turning out to be the most bloody marvellous commission, and I don't want to blow it. You know how it is.'

No, actually, she isn't at all sure she does know how it is, but having wanted nothing more than to fly into Mark's arms ever since the moment she'd first seen Bibi's body floating in the pool, now her only wish is for him to stay in Brussels and make a success of this commission. He sounds quick and excited about it. She knows Mark in that mood. When he's caught up with an idea, he's a glutton for work, overflowing with ideas. How can she ever live with herself if she encourages him to upset his new patron and he loses the biggest chance he's had for ages?

'No, Mark, listen, there's no need –'

She suddenly realizes she's talking into a dead telephone. She jiggles it about a bit but there's no response. She waits for him to re-establish the connection, but when he doesn't, she gives it time then dials the Brussels number, by now indelibly engraved on her memory. The ringing tone goes on in a way that has grown nastily familiar. What sixth sense tells you that a phone is ringing into a vacuum? Clearly, he's been calling her from somewhere else – perhaps this place he's been given to work in – and unless he rings again, she still has no idea what number that is. Oh, sod it!

Never mind, he'll ring back, Mark isn't the sort to leave

unresolved conversations hanging in the air. If nothing else, he likes to know just where he stands. It's just bad luck that they've been cut off like that . . . isn't it? All her doubts come rolling back, as she drags herself downstairs to make some coffee. She takes it outside and sits huddled on the bench that overlooks the clearing. The sun is hot on her face, though her fingers wrapped around the mug feel icy cold. She wants nothing more than to curl up and sleep under a tree, hide away from what's happening to her, invading her life, but she knows she'll have to face up to what she saw in that drawer last night in Mark's study, sooner or later. Face that, and what else?

The air is heavy, oppressive and humid. Unlike yesterday's cool, clear morning, even this early it's stifling hot, in the shade or out of it. A breathlessness that betokens a storm later hangs like a blanket. Not a thing stirs, but for the occasional tree leaf trembling in the thermals. She swipes the back of her hand across her damp forehead. After only a few minutes out here, she's sweating, she can feel it trickling down between her shoulder blades, under the cotton wrap.

From somewhere out in the forest comes a tremendous crash. She jumps a mile, the hot coffee splashing over her wrist, but then she knows what it is, only the limb of a tree falling to the ground. Sometimes, in this sort of heat, a big tree will inexplicably shed one of its heavy branches. At first, it used to frighten her, that this could occur so randomly, so dangerously, but Mark was used to it. 'It happens. There's a scientific explanation for it which I can't remember, offhand, something about transpiration.' He gave one of his lopsided grins. 'But I don't believe it. I think they've just had enough, poor devils, standing there with their arms everlastingly above their heads. Imagine it, year after year, centuries maybe. I've always felt sorry for them ever since I was cast as a tree in a kindergarten play.'

'You are a fool,' she'd said, laughing.

Oh, Mark, what fun we used to have, she thinks now,

when we first came to live here, in this magical place. It had been a kind of enchantment. But magic wears off. Not for her, but yes – perhaps – for Mark . . .

That bundle of letters, last night, in the desk. Well, three, to be precise. But enough to shatter a dream. Or to feed your fantasies, whatever. If you let it. She pulls herself up sharply. There's probably some quite rational explanation why Bibi gave those letters to *Mark*, of all people, though at the moment what that might be is totally beyond the scope of her imagination. They'd never been particularly close – in fact, Fran has always been aware that Mark didn't particularly like Bibi. He'd tolerated her because of Chip, but made no secret of his scepticism of her weird New Age philosophies, he laughed at her credulity in believing the heavens could tell her how to live her life when sometimes she didn't know Tuesday from Sunday. He raised his eyebrows and made caustic remarks about the style of dress she favoured (except when on duty at the country club, Bibi always knew which side her bread was buttered), the layers of ethnic clothing, and the silver rings and chandelier ear-rings that dragged down the lobes of her ears like some African tribeswoman. And Fran had always suspected that what he disliked most of all was the way her own friendship with Bibi had developed. Why, then, had Bibi trusted him, and no one else, with the letters?

She doesn't like any of the explanations that come to her.

Last night, she'd sat for over an hour, just looking at them lying in the drawer, held together by a rubber band, unable at first to believe what she was seeing, though the top envelope left no room for doubt that here were the missing letters – rough, greyish, recycled paper with a shadowy pattern of trees printed on it, a Save the Trees logo, Bibi's name and address typed in what space was left. For an hour she'd been unable to touch them, telling herself there was no way she was going to take out the contents of those envelopes, this business was absolutely nothing to do with her. But in the end, as she'd known from the first she would, obeying some inner compulsion, she'd read all three.

They had made her feel physically sick. Not that the language was abusive, or indecent. It was the quiet venom with which the writer had reiterated the same message, though differently phrased, in each one: that one day he would get Bibi, unless she returned what belonged to him – presumably Jasie. No matter how she tried, was the repetitive warning, she couldn't hide from him for ever: he'd already found out where she was living, hadn't he? She would have done better than to use her maiden name, but then, she never had been particularly bright, had she? Every time she went out, she should be looking over her shoulder, because he'd be there, somewhere around, and would be until he finally finished her. The letters had begun without preamble, and were, of course, unsigned – unless you counted the tiny horse's head drawn at the end. No, not a horse, she'd seen as she looked closer, it was a unicorn's head, complete with twisted horn.

She understands now why Bibi had begun to look so hag-ridden lately. A sharp word and she had been ready to burst into tears, as if all the world was on her shoulders. Difficult to please sometimes, Bibi, she'd thought. Manipulative. Up one minute, down the next. But it's a source of amazement to Fran now, how she'd kept her sanity at all.

Common sense tells her she ought to take what she's discovered straight to Crouch, but she finds herself oddly reluctant to do that, off her own bat. There has to be a reason why neither Bibi nor Mark took them to the police, and numbly, she refuses to consider why this should be so. But surely the circumstances now warrant it – even compel it?

A car swishes through the watersplash, then makes the sharp-angled turn into the drive of the house, the bark chippings scrunching beneath the wheels.

*   *   *

149

'You're a right berk, Gary Brooker,' Becky Jameson said, preparing a big batch of *Hydrangea petiolaris* cuttings for the propagating frames. 'You know that?'

'Oh, I am, am I? Well, you don't do so bad yourself sometimes,' Gary retaliated. But he said it half-heartedly.

He'd known Becky all his life. They'd both lived in Middleton Thorpe for all of their eighteen years, after being born in the Felsborough Hospital maternity unit within a week of each other. They'd attended play school together and been in the same classes throughout their time in the village school. When they were eleven, they'd both begun to attend the comprehensive in Felsborough, at which point they had ceased to tread life's path together. This last wasn't a circumstance that worried Gary unduly. Becky, in the A stream, and he in the C, rarely had cause, and at no time the desire, to meet, and only ever did so on the bus home, when he never actually acknowledged her presence. Well . . . heck. Gary didn't want his mates to think he couldn't pull anything better than this dragbag, did he? His sort of girls misbehaved as badly as he did, and looked as though they did, whereas Becky had a plain, scrubbed face, ginger hair and a figure that owed much to her mother's home cooking. She did her homework on the bus.

Gary wasn't thick. His exasperated teachers repeatedly told him so, in an effort to instil some sense into his head after all other methods had failed. If he'd put as much effort into working at his school subjects as he had at avoiding them, they said, he would no doubt have been in the position Becky was now, working here at the Membery gardens in the interim period before she went on to horticultural college – or somewhere else with some equivalent goal ahead of him. Bollocks to that, thought Gary.

'Here, come on, get your finger out. We've got to get this lot finished before we can go home,' Becky admonished sharply, though not unkindly. The gardens, though closed to the public until further notice, couldn't be let go, and

150

Becky and Gary were working Saturday morning to make up for the disruption of yesterday.

Listlessly, Gary picked up a cutting and began pulling the lower leaves off.

'Not like that! Take them off with the knife. They're liable to get fungus infection, else.'

It was steamy and humid at the end of the greenhouse where they were working. The bench in front of them was grainy with compost from the bin behind it, and stacked with three-inch flower pots. Becky's face was beetroot red and damp, her ginger hair stuck to it. Her square, capable hands, ingrained with dirt, worked deftly and lightly, taking up handfuls of sweet-smelling compost from the bin and lovingly inserting the cuttings into the three-inch pots. They would all be sold for a profit in the garden shop next year. If there was a next year. Her mum, who worked in the entrance kiosk, taking the money and dishing out tickets as people came through the gates, was of the opinion that this murder would be the end of Membery Place Gardens. It had fair knocked the old girl sideways, she said, meaning Alyssa. You didn't get over shocks like that at her age and besides, Becky's mum had said, she'd thought for some time that Alyssa was losing interest.

Gary, seeing someone noseying around outside, suddenly remembered a more important job to do and decided to abandon the cuttings. 'You finish these. I'd better go find some stuff to get that shed winder fixed afore old Arrer comes round. Been on about it for days, she has.'

'And don't forget to clear the glass up outside, neither. If you hadn't put all them heavy pots on that shelf it wouldn't have collapsed and they wouldn't have gone through the window in the first place. *Miss Arrow*,' Becky enunciated pointedly, 'could've given you the sack over that.'

'Who cares? I'm sick of this lark, any road. I could pull in a lot more down Tesco's, like, shelf-stacking.'

151

'But you won't, will you?' Becky said shrewdly. "'Cos you like it here – even though *she's* gone.'

'Who said that?' Gary demanded, his ears reddening for more reasons than one.

'I said it. And you can't dodge the police for ever, you know. They have to see everybody, stands to reason. Best get it over and done with – if you haven't done anything wrong, you've nothing to worry about, have you?'

What did she know about it? She'd never even seen the inside of the Felsborough nick, much less done community service for twocking a car, when he'd been like, tanked up a bit. Never forgotten that, they hadn't, the fuzz. Nor the time he'd nicked a cheapo video from Curry's and later tried to sell it at the car-boot sale in Dawson's field. Not even the ruckuses of a Saturday night after a few bevvies. They were ticking names off a list now and sooner or later, he'd be the only one left and he'd have to answer their questions.

'What am I going to do, Beck?' he moaned. He wasn't above asking her advice, in an emergency. She was that sort who always knew the answers. She'd had her life planned out from when she was in Year Nine, and ever since he'd come to work here, she'd been on at him to do likewise. It had been a mistake to let her see he didn't mind a bit of gardening. Well, it was all right, seeing things grow, like. But she thought he ought to go and get himself some GCSEs, then an A or two, and then go to college. What a laugh! Gaz going to college! His mates would piss themselves laughing if he did – not that he'd ever have a hope of getting in, never mind what old Beck said.

'What are you feeling so sorry for yourself for?' she asked suddenly. 'You look like a dying duck in a thunderstorm. All you have to do is tell the police she asked you to deliver that note.'

Gary looked hunted. Becky followed his gaze and saw that the woman detective who'd been asking for Gary yesterday and had been looking purposefully around outside for the last ten minutes, had now come into the

152

greenhouse and, dodging the hosepipes snaking along the floor, was making her way down the centre aisle between the staging to where they were working at the very end. He slipped out of the back door but he knew he'd left it too late.

Kate had left the uncommunicative Gary Brooker behind without regret. He'd obviously been ill at ease, but that wasn't surprising. The likes of Gary and his mates were rarely at ease with the police, usually having something they wanted to hide. No doubt what it was would be revealed in the fullness of time: meanwhile, she had managed to get out of him the admission that he had indeed delivered the letter to The Watersplash, and had been asked to do so by Bibi herself. He'd blushed painfully at the admission – *Gary Brooker*, blushing? Thoughtfully, she drove on until she came to the house in the woods.

Fran looked up as the car stopped by the front door and out of it came Sergeant Colville without her suit jacket, wearing a white sleeveless blouse tucked into her grey skirt as a concession to the heat. 'Hot, isn't it?' she greeted Fran.

'It's cooler inside. Come in and I'll get you a drink. Cold, or would you prefer coffee?' Her own coffee had cooled and grown a disgusting grey skin. She'd been sitting there for over an hour and a half without noticing the time passing. 'Sorry I'm not dressed yet.' Nor showered, and her hair not even combed. Dark circles round her eyes, too, no doubt. Enough to frighten the horses. 'I'm afraid I had a bad night. I slept late.'

'Not surprising, after yesterday. It was a rotten day for everybody. Yes, a cold drink would be lovely, thank you.' Looking disgustingly bright-eyed and bushy-tailed, the sergeant followed Fran into the kitchen and gazed round at the granite working surfaces and the stainless steel equipment, noticing everything with miss-nothing, detective's eyes as Fran took ginger beer from the fridge, held it up and, receiving a nod, poured it into a tall glass. 'Nice kitchen. Wouldn't I just love one like it?' She laughed. 'In your dreams, Kate! Cheers.' She perched on a chair and raised the glass. 'I have some news for you, good and bad.'

Fran, sitting opposite with her elbows on the table, felt a roll of fear. 'Jasie?'

'Uh-huh. The good news first. We think there's every chance he may be alive and with his father.' And before the relief had time to flick in, she added, 'The bad news is that we don't know where his father is, and we can't be sure what his intentions are.'

Fran had known, of course, that the person who had written those letters must have been Jasie's father, though nowhere in them had this been openly stated. Now was the time to hand them over, yet somehow . . . well, they were Mark's property, she reasoned, not hers to do with as she saw fit, or at any rate had been left in his keeping. Giving them to the police now, without telling him – well, there was the question of loyalty. On the other hand, telling *him* how she had found them might conceivably be worse. And yet, when she remembered the threats in them . . . No, she told herself, she'd no right to withhold them from the police, even though they seemed to have worked it out, anyway. And yet –

The telephone rang again. 'Fran, it's me. We were cut off, I'm sorry.'

'Where are you ringing from, Mark? Tell me where I can ring you back, I can't talk just now, I've got someone from the police with me.'

She immediately wished she hadn't mentioned that when he said sharply, 'What are they doing there? OK, don't answer that, they'll be all ears . . . I wish you weren't having all this hassle.'

'Me too, but I can't do anything about it – and it's OK, really. I can cope.'

154

He hesitated, but then gave her a number readily enough, which she carefully wrote down. 'Sure you're all right, Fran?'

'Yes, sure. In about half an hour?' she said hurriedly. That would put a time limit on her deliberations, force her to make a decision about those letters, and what she should do.

'Bye till then. Love you, all the time.'

'Love you, too, Mark.'

Sergeant Colville didn't trouble to hide the fact that she'd been listening and understood the side of the conversation she'd heard. 'Your husband?' she asked as Fran turned from the telephone.

'Yes. He's in Brussels.'

'For long?'

'I don't think he'll be home just yet. He's an architect and he has this commission there, you see, it's important –'

'Well, I don't see anything would be gained by interfering with his work,' she said reasonably. 'Where were we?'

'Jasie?'

'Right, yes – well, we have to hope his father has no intention of harming him, and simply wants to gain custody. But there's no knowing what he might do if we try to take him away, people don't always act rationally in such situations, especially men like Graham Armstrong.'

Graham Armstrong. The name gave more substance, added another dimension to the dark shadow, the evil persona behind the spate of hatred poured out into those letters. 'He surely can't expect he'll be allowed to keep Jasie, a man like that – and after murdering his mother!'

'Hang on! We don't have any proof yet that he did.'

'But surely –'

'I'll admit it looks like that but – hear me out, Mrs Calvert – Fran, if I may?' Fran nodded. 'And I'm Kate. Let me put you in the picture.'

Fresh from the interview with Chip, Kate had it all at her fingertips, and gave Fran the gist of it crisply, stopping just short of the point where Armstrong had set fire to Bibi's house, watching Fran closely to see how the news was received. She'd a pretty shrewd idea, from the way Fran had reacted, that she'd been in the dark until then about Bibi's previous life, but she still hoped that the half-hour she'd allocated to spend here might not turn out to be a complete waste of time. She was, however, beginning to have her doubts about it. Fran seemed vague and disorientated this morning, no doubt due to having slept badly, as she said she had, last night. At the same time, Kate was convinced that hidden behind that veiled, smoky-blue regard was something that she was keeping to herself.

Fran decided she needed more coffee before hearing what else Kate Colville had to say, and this time Kate agreed to join her. When it was made, Fran sipped and listened in silence to the remainder of the sorry story, as related by Chip. Her eyes widened in horror as she heard about the sick attempt by Armstrong on Bibi's – and Jasie's – life. There was so much in it that explained Bibi – what she was and how she'd acted. But even so it left a lot still unexplained. Why, for instance, had she refused to confide in anyone when she began to be threatened once more? Miserably, Fran felt this as a personal failure on her part – she really ought not to have taken so literally Chip's request not to question Bibi about her life before she'd come to Membery. Surely, if she had approached it sensitively, Bibi might have felt she could help? Though in the end, perhaps she *had* begun to feel that she needed to unburden herself about those awful letters – yes, that was surely why she'd rung her at the office in such a state. But what had happened that day to force her to do that? If only she'd spoken sooner! The only explanation was that her fear of her ex-husband's reprisals must have been over-whelming enough to keep her worries from everyone, even Chip, though in a way Fran thought she could under-stand this last. Chip wasn't renowned for being the most sensitive of souls, and like most men, he would have taken an aggressive stance, which might only have made matters worse.

Yet she had confided in Mark.

'So that's it,' Kate said, 'that's what we know so far.'

'So this madman's got Jasie? But that's terrible!'

'It looks possible. We can only hope he won't do anything stupid. Everything will be done to make sure he doesn't.' Kate was cautious, mulling over in her careful way what they had learned, smothering her own doubts about this and other aspects of the case which she hadn't yet felt able to come to terms with, and Fran looked anything but reassured. 'We should know where he is pretty soon. He was released on licence, he's under probationary supervision, which means he has to report regularly to his probation officer. And notify him of any change of address.'

'And you believe he would do that? In the circumstances?' Fran couldn't hide her scepticism.

Kate drained her coffee but declined a refill. 'Let's cross bridges when we come to them. I'll keep you informed as and when we hear anything. For now, I'd better be getting on, or I'll have Dave Crouch on my tail.'

'Rather you than me.'

A quizzical look, followed by an odd little smile. 'He's not all he appears on the surface. He's a damn good detective, you know.'

'I'm sure he is.'

'Just not very good with people.'

The hard-nosed policeman with a heart of gold? Fran wasn't going to fall for that one. Policemen were no different from anyone else. Some, just like other men in other jobs, were simply bastards.

'How long have you been working with him?'

'About five years.' She smiled at Fran's expression. 'It's better than the Domestic Violence Unit, where I was before.'

'Five years? I'd be a nervous wreck in a tenth of that time.' There were different kinds of violence, Fran thought, and being put down all the time wasn't the least of them.

Kate didn't pretend not to understand what she meant. 'Don't take any notice of his manner. It's an essential requirement for some men in the force to react to women colleagues the way he does, they're simply throwbacks to the old days. It's not my problem, it's his.'

'Hmm.' She had a point – perhaps it was all in the way you received it.

'Anyway,' Kate added cheerfully, 'it's all academic. I'm lumbered with the bloke, I'm afraid. Seeing as how I happen to be married to him.'

'Oh, wow! Sorry, I've really put my foot in it, haven't I?'

'Don't worry, you're not the only one who looks on Dave like that, though if they had his problems . . . He was in the Met, see, doing a job he really liked and was good at and then – well, there was an incident, not his fault, but it was better he left. I could tell you the whole story, but I won't bore you. Just that it's made him a bit stroppy at times. It could have been one of those incidents with a commendation at the end of it, if it had turned out different. As it was, he got the mucky end of the stick. He doesn't complain. Whatever else, he has guts.'

'I'm sure he has.' Those unfeeling, brutish men often were brave. No imagination to hamper them about what the consequences might be, Fran thought unfairly. 'Isn't it unusual? Husband and wife working together?'

'Unusual, yes, but not unheard of. We're a good team, believe it or not, that's why we're kept together.'

With a smile she dismissed the subject, finished her coffee and delved into a big shoulder-bag for something rectangular wrapped in polythene that she slid across the table. 'Before I go, take a look at this.'

'Oh, a photo of Bibi. I thought for a moment it was her book of days.'

'You mean that one about myths and legends? Unicorns and virgins and all that?'

'Unicorns?' For a moment, Fran seemed fazed. She

blinked rapidly. 'No, no, I've never seen that. It was a sort of diary, I suppose, though not quite. She told me once she just wrote down anything she considered interesting, but she was paranoid about letting anyone see what she wrote. It was just like Bibi to give it such a name.'

Kate was alert. 'No, we haven't come across anything like that yet.'

'You'll know it when you do. It's really lovely. Sort of old, with a red watered silk cover and gilt edges to the pages, and a fancy clasp. She said it was too nice to be called a plain old diary, a book of days suited it better, and I suppose it did, really. Oh, this is lovely – one I haven't seen before.'

The framed photo had obviously been taken years ago – Bibi with a short, designer haircut, her soft, feathery curls blow dried and disciplined into a smooth cap that accentuated the fine modelling of her face.

'A good likeness?'

'Brilliant, but – she looks different, and I don't mean just because she's so much younger. Perhaps she just looks – *happier*, than I ever remember seeing her. Though that's probably hindsight, wouldn't you say, after what you've just told me?'

'Mmm. Maybe. Are you saying she wasn't happy, even before those letters started coming?'

Fran took a swig of her own coffee, looked down again at Bibi's face staring up from the table and knew it wasn't her own imagination that saw the shadow behind the transient impression of happiness. 'I don't think,' she said slowly, 'it was in her to be really happy.'

Chapter Twelve

In Chantry Street, not above a hundred yards away from where the historic old Saturday market was held in the Market Square in Felsborough, the aggressively modern brick police station sat like a complacent squatter, thumbing its nose at its ancient neighbours: the beautiful Abbey Church, a row of mellow stone cottages and the gracious buildings of the old chantry school, now the Edward the Sixth Grammar School, that had given the street its name. The nick was new, functional, and unlovely, standard design for the county, but inside it had certain definite advantages over the other buildings, especially today when it was refreshingly cool. The heating and the air-conditioning both worked like a dream, there was iced water available at the turn of a tap, coffee from a machine. Crouch couldn't understand the moans of the old guard who said they missed the solid old Victorian building on the corner, before his time, spacious and sound-deadened as it was remembered to be, but where apparently you alternately froze or sweltered, depending on the outside temperature.

He took a mammoth bite out of a rare beef on soft white bread sandwich from the canteen, spread as ordered with more mustard than butter. It made his eyes water, but it went down a treat with his half-pint of bitter. He wolfed it down with all the enjoyment of a man who hadn't eaten since a hurried breakfast at six that morning, after only a few hours' sleep, and then went out into the corridor for

160

coffee, brought it back and sat down to address the progress report he was compiling for Vincent.

He'd been chuffed at how much quicker the case was going down than he'd expected, how much simpler it was turning out. No blind alleys. No complications. From the moment when Armstrong's name had first been mentioned, the reason and motivation for the murder had become clear to Crouch, and his original opinion that it was bound to be a Calvert family matter had undergone a swift reversal, his doubts about motives receded: Armstrong wanted his son; he also wanted his revenge for his incarceration in prison, ergo, he had killed his ex-wife and abducted his son. Simple. All wrapped up. The main thrust of the operation could now be concentrated on collecting supporting evidence, a task that should be made much easier now that they knew who the perpetrator was. Whether Jasie had seen his mother killed or not, it was obvious that it was his father who had done the deed, and then taken the boy.

The only one who remained not totally convinced had been Kate. 'We don't actually *know* those letters she received were from Armstrong. She seems to have thought they were from some weirdo.'

'And what's Armstrong but a weirdo? It's the same method the bastard used before to frighten her – writing to her, ringing her up, following her everywhere.'

'I know the probabilities are stacked against them being from anyone else, but I'd feel happier if we'd seen them.'

'So would I, Kate, so would I. But it's the only lead we have, so far. And if he is innocent, I'd be more inclined to believe him so if he hadn't chosen this moment to do a runner.'

'That does seem funny.'

Yet she was basically right. Amidst all the euphoria following the discovery of Armstrong's existence, Crouch realized that he had brushed aside the difficulties of apprehending him and now, though he wouldn't have cared to

161

admit it, the good feeling that it was all over bar the shouting had evaporated like water in the Sahara after hearing that he had broken his parole and disappeared. Dammit, he might have known. Given his luck lately, things weren't likely to be that easy – though he was still convinced they were steering a straight course in the right direction. However . . .

If Armstrong had any sense, it went without saying that he and the child would be out of the country by now. And then, even supposing he were found, getting him, or the boy, back could be a long-drawn-out affair. These tug-of-love cases, as the press delighted in dubbing them, and which was essentially how this had started out, were a bugger.

The child's disappearance was already generating too much interest for his liking in the media, blast them. But these were sentiments he couldn't afford: their co-operation was needed.

Usually, by now, two days after the opening of an investigation, information would be trickling in, however slowly. But not on this one. The facts surrounding Bibi Morgan's stabbing remained stubbornly obscure. As for Jasie, there had been the usual false sightings by people who claimed to have seen him, from Edinburgh to Clacton on Sea, but none of it could be given credence.

Crouch had been pinning his hopes on the local police up in Yorkshire, feeling sure that they would have gone some way towards tracing Armstrong by now, but so far those guardians of the outposts of the Empire hadn't come up with anything – probably knocked off for the weekend, he thought irritably. Armstrong had been living in Morley, a suburb of Leeds, since his release, in the house his lately deceased father had left to him, but he'd failed to report to his probation officer two weeks ago and had simply vanished, without a word to anyone. The house was reported to be as locked up and silent as it had been during the interim between Armstrong senior's death and the release of his son from prison.

Crouch wasn't actually sanguine enough to believe that the man they were looking for was certain to be found at all, though he would never have admitted this to anyone. If he had disappeared into the maw of one or other of the big cities, that might be the end of it. He had, after all, lately been living in the company of those used to existing outside the law, and if he hadn't known all the tricks and dodges by which it was possible to disappear before he went inside, he would now. Outside, there was always someone ready to employ casual labour and no questions asked, if he was without means of support, which he might well be, since how much ready cash he had was debatable. Though he now owned the house, its contents and an old car left to him by his father, they were assets which would need to be realized and, with the possible exception of the car, that wasn't easy to do without discovery. He might soon be living hand to mouth, but even in this bureaucratic age, it was possible to exist without papers. Doing so with a small boy in tow might be more difficult.

'Let's try to work things out, how it happened,' Crouch had said to his assembled team that morning, the thirty or so men and women brought together on this assignment, 'working from what facts we have.' First, he'd outlined the case as he saw it, simple on the face of it: after his release, Graham Armstrong had started threatening Bianca Morgan with the letters and the threat to 'get' her. She had gone for a walk in the grounds of Membery, he had been waiting for her, had killed her and tipped her body into the water, then snatched his son and made off with him. Either by force or by persuasion.

This last would explain, argued Crouch, why the boy had made no fuss.

'With respect, sir, I don't think that'll wash,' Kate had objected. 'According to Chip Calvert, Armstrong had terrified the child by letting him see how he upset his mother. He wouldn't have gone willingly with him – certainly not without his mother's say-so.'

Crouch thought for a moment. 'All right, by force, then.'

There was a moment's silence, at the thought of this man who had lost his hold on reality having the boy in his grasp. Not one person who didn't remember reading in their briefing notes what he'd said at his trial – that if he couldn't have Jasie, no one else would.

And yet, a judge had freed this man on the understanding that he had shown remorse and was no longer a risk, basing his judgement on the reports of psychiatrists and psychologists, care workers and prison authorities and his own assessment of the prisoner at a Parole Board hearing.

'Forgive my cynicism,' Crouch had remarked on hearing that, an understandable reservation, given that within weeks of being released Armstrong had restarted his campaign of intimidation against his ex-wife and their son. Now, it seemed as though that might have been justified, that Armstrong had snatched the child. There had been no one to hear but the two old women. The big old house had thick walls, which would have deadened any sounds from outside. Even the shrill screams of a terrified small boy might not have penetrated as far as the small sitting room where the two old women had been watching the Channel 4 news, relaxing and sipping aperitifs, waiting for Jonathan Calvert and his girlfriend Jilly Norman to arrive for supper.

Crouch very soon closed the meeting and went to telephone Yorkshire yet again, to waken the dozy buggers up there in the sticks. He had never been very good at waiting.

After Kate left her, Fran had showered and dressed, washed her hair, and now feels more sense of being in control before ringing the number Mark has given her. The speed with which he answers tells her he's been waiting

164

for it to ring and that makes her feel good, but his short, sharp, 'Yes?' diminishes the feeling somewhat.

Fran has always hated the telephone for conversations like this, or for those requiring any degree of intimacy for that matter, when you can't see the face of the person you're speaking to, or their body language. All the same, as she and Mark talk, she does sense that during the time that has passed since their last conversation, he's absorbed the shock of what she'd had to tell him, has got himself together and thought it through. This time he comes over strong and supportive – the old Mark – and she feels a surge of relief. Everything's going to be all right. It had all been her imagination, thinking he was holding back.

'Right. Now, here's what we'll do,' he begins decisively. 'Just hang on there, I'm arranging to come home, just as soon as I can sort things out and get a flight.'

'But –'

'No buts.'

'No, listen, don't do that, Mark, there's really no need.' She puts a smile into her voice. 'Anyone would think I can't see a thing like this through without a man beside me.'

'You've been talking to Claire again.'

She laughs. 'We had a meal together, Wednesday evening.' Actually, Claire's bright decisiveness, her clear-sighted certainty when faced with any problem, is just what she needs now – only Claire's in Spain for the weekend, meeting her future parents-in-law for the first time, out of circulation until Monday. 'But this has nothing to do with Claire.'

'Makes no difference, you shouldn't be on your own.'

'You call being five minutes away from Membery on my own?'

'No, but if I know you, you won't be creeping up there into the bosom of the family for protection, and yes,' he adds positively, 'I am coming home, no arguing. You're far too vulnerable down there at The Watersplash with a homicidal maniac at large.'

165

Fran likes, and at the same time despises, the warm, protected feeling this gives her, but she says, 'What makes you think he'd be after me? Anyway, listen – the police think they know who killed Bibi now, and he's not a homicidal maniac – at least not that sort. They think it was Jasie's father, a man called Graham Armstrong. And that Jasie's with him now.'

She rather belatedly realizes that Mark, with his quick intuition, and in view of those letters in his desk, must have made that connection already, but he gives no indication of it. 'Do they? Well, let's hope they're right,' he says non-committally. 'They're on the track of this guy, you say – this Armstrong?'

'Yes.' She proceeds to tell him all that she's learned from Kate Colville, though it really hurts, knowing that most of what she now knows about Bibi, if not more, can't be news to him. She can't imagine what sort of game he and Bibi were playing, but she can't see she has any alternative at the moment but to carry on as though she isn't aware there was anything between them. A quarrel about something as important as this at long distance isn't something she's prepared to initiate. She takes a deep breath and says, 'So you see, there's no need for you to mess everything up over there. Don't let it interfere with what you're doing. Armstrong isn't interested in anyone else.'

She hopes she sounds convincing, because she isn't convincing herself. Truly, she doesn't feel she's in the least danger from Armstrong, or anyone else, but she can't rid herself of that spooky sense of impending disaster that's been with her ever since she saw Bibi floating in the pool. Actually, it had started even before that. Looking back, she can date everything from the moment when she had that telephone call from Bibi, and then came home and saw the impression of the white owl on the mirror. Or even before that, with that creepy sensation that she and Mark were being watched. Tell herself as much as she will that it's all rubbish, she can't rid herself of the nagging feeling that

166

something else is flowing along there, like a subterranean current beneath the surface of the murder.

'How can the police be so cocksure?' Mark is saying. 'Seems to me like an unwarranted leaping to conclusions.'

'Mark, he's got Jasie, and that's all he wants. We have to leave it to the police, it's in their hands. There's nothing we can do,' she adds mournfully, 'but watch the clock and wait for something to happen.'

'God, yes, that's what it amounts to, doesn't it,' he says soberly after a moment, adding, as he had before, 'What a bloody mess it all is.' Then, 'How's Ma taking this? And Chip, of course?' he asks, with a sort of delayed reaction.

'You should ring them, your mother would love to talk to you.'

'I already have, but the line's forever engaged.'

'I expect that's Chip on to his office in London. He's frantic about some unfinished business he has on the go. The police have a direct line they've set up – Mark, they have an incident room in the library!'

'The holy of holies? Did they get Jane's permission?'

'With difficulty.' She laughs shakily. How liberating only a little laughter is. How it unravels the knots of tension inside. A minute before, she'd felt Mark was beginning to waver and now she seizes the advantage, pressing home all the arguments she can muster. She can be pretty persuasive, when she wants to be. In the end, he says, 'Tell you what – we'll leave it until tomorrow and see what gives, OK? Surely they'll have found Armstrong by then.'

'I'd feel much more comfortable if we did that, rather than you come charging over here to no purpose.'

'Well, I still don't feel good about it at all, but as things are here . . .'

With a sigh, she replaces the receiver when they've finished talking. She hadn't, in the end, said anything to him about finding the letters and it has left her with a guilty feeling that perhaps she had in fact never had any intention of doing so.

*   *   *

Her stomach rumbles. Perhaps this downbeat feeling might be due, at least in part, to the fact that she's had no breakfast, nothing much at all, in fact, over the last two days. Shopping is clearly indicated when she examines the distinctly unappetizing contents of the fridge, consisting mostly of the leftovers from the meal she and Jonathan had eaten together. They look more depressed than she is, and are in any case more than a little suspect by now. Some bendy-looking celery and lettuce so wilted it's going slimy, smoked salmon that has dried and curled up, all ready to die, and several slices of avocado that are evidently in the final stages of the Black Death. The last morsel of the Brie that had been just ripe when Jonathan brought it has run and spread all over the plate on which it's been standing. It's still edible, however, and she scrapes it off and eats it, but she makes a clean sweep of the rest of the once-tempting offerings, which leaves only some scaly-looking Cheddar, a couple of rashers of bacon, half a pint of milk and two cartons of tomato juice. Oh, and the oranges, filling up half the crisper drawer. She takes two of them out, frowning. Again, that uneasy moment as she remembers coming into the house and seeing them on the table in the black dish. Determinedly, she shakes off the shivers the thought inexplicably induces and juices the oranges to drink while she makes herself a bacon sandwich and be blowed to the fat content.

She feels ready to face the Saturday shopping in Felsborough after she's eaten. Finding somewhere to park there will be a pain, but still, there are things she needs apart from food and it's a pleasant place to shop, a small country town with pretty buildings and some interesting shops off the High Street. Everything she wants can be found there, dispensing with the hassle of a safari to the big Tesco's on the edge of the town. Things like cheese from the specialist shop, fruit and salad from the Saturday market that lines the High Street. An hour should see it finished.

Chapter Thirteen

Papers, papers, papers! Chip, sorting, putting aside for the shredder. Being suddenly decisive, ruthless in clearing out the debris, the questionable, being very efficient about it, too. Making sure there could be no comeback, nothing that would connect, if ever it came to the crunch . . . not that it would, he'd hadn't actually done anything strictly illegal, yet. Not committed himself, thank God, either here or at his London office. He'd spent hours on the telephone and his affairs there were now as much in order as they ever would be, as were these here. Not a whiff of anything unsavoury left. He was clean as the day he was born.

'What are you doing?' asked his mother, from the doorway.

'Sorting out my life,' said Chip. Her face told him there was still no news.

'Chip.' She came into the room. 'My darling boy.' She sat down on one of the big, shabby chairs and waited, while her handsome son sat at his desk, amid the chaos of papers. She turned her head so as not to be caught watching him, and gazed out of the open windows. Not a cloud in the sky, a burning bright blue. Where, under that sky, was Jasie?

Chip swiped the drops of sweat from his forehead with the back of his hand, looked at the bottle on the sideboard, then at his mother, and decided not. At any rate, not before he'd told her what he'd told the police. He was sick of explanations, he absolutely didn't want to go through the whole bloody rigmarole again, but he couldn't dodge it.

She'd hear the story from Crouch, anyway, if not from him, and he owed her that much. She'd accepted Bibi, and Jasie, no questions asked. Which, for Alyssa, was a great deal, and now she had a right to know why she'd been asked to do it.

'All right, Ma,' he said. 'There's something you should know.'

He began to tell her the bits of the story she hadn't already heard – which was most of it, he realized, and at the same moment, wondered for the first time why there had been the need for all this secrecy. Bibi had been paranoic, that was why, unsure of herself. Even using the bloody stars to counteract her insecurity.

Alyssa knew, she always had known, when it was time to listen, when any of her boys had something to confess. Even before he began to speak, she felt instinctively that this wasn't going to be a small graze that could be made to feel immediately better by the application of an important-looking bandage. But when he'd finished, she wondered, with a flash of insight, how deep the hurt was – and how far Chip's commitment to Bibi's son would go. Even Alyssa could not envisage her son, on good terms as he was with Jasie, taking on the permanent responsibility of another man's child – always supposing the monster who called himself the father could be persuaded to release him.

Although Crouch believed it was all sewn up, now that Graham Armstrong was in the frame, and though Kate for the most part agreed, she thought there was an element of wishful thinking involved in his certainty. To her mind, there were still gaps to be filled and inconsistencies which were not going to clear themselves up as easily as Crouch imagined. She knew she would have to go on doggedly, as her police training had taught her and her nature compelled, with the business of talking to people, again and again if necessary, for as long as it took to get a clear picture of what had happened on the day Bibi Morgan met her death.

The decision as to who should come first on her list was made when she saw Humphrey Oliver working in the small front garden of his house as she made her way through Middleton Thorpe, driving yet once more between Felsborough and Membery. She drew her car up on the road outside and went towards the gate.

There was nothing to distinguish Humphrey's house from its neighbours in the row, except that it was the end one, and a privet hedge limited its outer garden boundary. They were a row of three charming little houses with Gothic front porches and pointed windows in fretted frames. Gingerbread houses. Dolls' houses. You could amost believe the fronts would swing away to reveal all the rooms inside. The gardens of the other two houses were untidier, but prettier, than Humphrey's, with Dorothy Perkins clambering round the porches, and sweet peas, marigolds, rigidly staked dahlias, gladioli, rows of beans and tomatoes in clay pots growing happily together in old-fashioned confusion, with nothing so finicky as a plot of grass in the centre. Humphrey, on the other hand, didn't appear to go in much for flowers, but his square lawn was a tribute to mathematical precision and although the hedge was already barbered with military severity, he was trimming its stray hairs with garden shears to make it even neater. He looked up as her car door slammed and when he saw who it was he immediately put down the shears on the tiny lawn and came down the path to greet her, raising a panama that had seen better days. 'There's news of the little fella?' he asked immediately, his face creased with anxiety.

His straight shoulders seemed to sag a little when she shook her head. 'I'd like to have a few words with you, Mr Oliver.'

'By all means. Come in.' He led her in through the oak-panelled front door with its old-fashioned iron knocker and into a tiny hall. He had to duck to avoid hitting his head on a beam that crossed it. 'Like a cup of tea? I was just about to put the kettle on.'

'In that case, yes, I'd love one, thank you.'

He waved his hand to an open door. 'Make yourself at home. Take a pew. Won't be a jiff.'

With a glance into a tiny, and what she guessed was a largely unused room, furnished with an unimaginative three-piece suite, a prickly cactus placed dead centre on a polished table, and smelling strongly of meadow-fresh furniture polish, she said, 'I don't mind the kitchen, if you don't.'

'Rather not. Where I live most of the time, anyway.'

She could see why when she followed him in through the door. Light came from a big window over the sink in the side wall. There were old-fashioned kitchen appliances, and the old coal range, comforting in winter, had been left in situ, but the far wall had been entirely removed to accommodate an extension that stretched half-way out into the back garden to form a big, light living-room, glazed by long windows, Gothic-arched like the ones at the front of the house. The other walls of the extension were almost entirely covered with shelves which held books, tidily stacked magazines, miscellaneous objects, some plants and a music system. A shipshape, masculine room, unpretentious and comfortable, with nothing extraneous in it. He waved her to a big chair, deep from back to front, with a remote control and the *Daily Telegraph* on the arm, directly facing a TV set, and while she hesitated between occupying the chair which was plainly his, or turfing off the enormous Persian cat that immovably occupied the other armchair, he busied himself with mugs and the kettle at the kitchen end. 'Indian, or I think I have Earl Grey somewhere? Can't offer you any of that herb muck everybody seems to have taken to drinking nowadays, sorry.'

'I actually prefer Indian, thanks.'

He nodded approvingly. 'Sugar?'

'No sugar, just a little milk.' She stroked the cat. It didn't even open an eye or twitch a whisker. Perhaps it was dead.

Not wishing to put it to the test, she perched on the edge of Humphrey's chair. He approached with two mugs, one in each hand, handed her one, then with a single economical movement he lifted the still-sleeping cat expertly with his free hand and sank into the chair it had occupied with it on his knee. It still didn't open its eyes.

'So it's Jasie's father who took him away, and killed Bibi, eh?' He explained when she raised her eyebrows, 'Alyssa rang me. Told me Chip had spilled the beans. Damn fool, first thing he should've thought of when she started getting those letters. All this might never have happened then. Wonder sometimes about Chip. Drinking too much, y'know, like his father, and *his* father too, I hear. Always been a curse in that family, drink, they haven't the head for it, but they can't leave it alone. Pity he isn't more like his mother – one glass after a hard day in the garden and she can hardly keep her eyes open!' He grinned engagingly. 'Don't tell her I said that. And don't get me wrong – wouldn't go so far as to say Chip was a tippler, but he's bending his elbow more than's good for him. Understandable, in a way . . .' He broke off, then added, almost as an afterthought, 'Bibi too, on occasions, she could knock the gin back . . . Ah well. Jasie's father, eh?'

'That's what we're working on at the moment.'

He regarded her shrewdly. 'Not certain, though?' She inclined her head non-committally. 'You'd hardly be questioning me, if you were,' he said.

'We're simply trying to get a clearer picture. We might think we know, but nothing's certain until we've got him in our sights, and even then we shall still need witnesses, hard evidence. Meanwhile, we're anxious to eliminate as many as possible from the enquiry.'

'And that includes me, does it? Am I a suspect?'

She smiled and drank some of her tea. 'Not unless you've been fiddling the evidence – which doesn't seem likely.'

He'd been in Cornwall to attend his daughter's Silver Wedding. The day before returning home he'd visited the

Eden Project with a nephew who was a keen gardener. Their tickets were timed and docketed. On his journey home, he'd filled up with petrol twice, and kept the receipts, both of which were dated and timed. One filling station was near Taunton, another nearer home. 'Noticed the petrol was two pee a litre down, so I thought I might as well fill up,' he'd said, producing the receipts. There was no possibility that Humphrey could have been near Membery when Bibi Morgan was killed and Jasie taken away.

'Then if it's not me, you're here to talk about the others,' he answered her shrewdly.

'Well, I suspect you know more about the Calvert family than anyone else.'

He gave a short bark of laughter. 'If that's what you're after, it's Jane Arrow you should ask. Not much she doesn't know about the family, one way or another.'

Of course. All those photos crowded in her sitting room when she and Crouch had called on her the morning after the murder, before they knew Jasie was missing. The Calvert boys at every age, on every occasion. Dozens of them.

'No family of her own,' Humphrey went on, 'Alyssa and the boys mean everything to her. Surrogate sons, isn't that what they say?'

She was beginning to like Humphrey. She'd suspected before that his bumbling stereotype was all a bit of an act and that his initial remarks when he'd arrived at Membery to be told of the murder hadn't been simple gaffes – he might not have said them intentionally, but they were what he had been thinking. He was a shrewd observer, seeing, and interpreting, far more than he saw fit to let everyone think. He might turn out to be a very good witness indeed, she thought, as she met a direct glance from very blue eyes.

She said, 'What did you make of Bibi's arrival at Membery? Didn't you think it odd that there was this conspiracy of silence about her past?'

'Yes, I did, but that was her business – and Chip's. Nothing to do with anyone else. Let them get on with their lives, that's what I told Alyssa. Didn't affect anyone else, anyway.' He paused as if to consider his next words. 'Let me just say – don't believe all you hear. All that about everyone loving her. Largely a myth. Created by her, if you ask me. Bit of a troublemaker on the quiet, even allowing it wasn't always intentional.'

'Give me an example.'

After a moment, he said, 'For one thing, she was trying to persuade Alyssa it was time to get rid of the garden, and move out.'

'Move out of Membery?'

He reached out a hand to one of the shelves behind him and picked up a pipe. He stared at it hard for a moment or two then put it back. 'Gave it up three months ago, mustn't start again now.' Hunching himself forward, he folded his long stork's legs up into a more comfortable lap for the cat, which he began to stroke compulsively instead.

She continued to wait patiently for an answer. As a reformed smoker herself, she understood the temptation, but she wondered why he'd needed the prop at that particular moment. It had been to cover his embarrassment, she decided, as he finally said, 'Fact is, Membery isn't Alyssa's. Left in trust for the three boys. She can live there as long as she wants to, but it doesn't belong to her. There's no reason for her to stay there, she could move in with me. Get married,' he finished gruffly.

She had guessed at something of the sort between them.

'It'd make sense. She could sell the garden, or better still, get a manager in, still make herself a tidy little profit. Can't understand why she won't. She had a hell of a life with that husband of hers, and I've been a widower over fifty years. M'wife died in childbirth, the child too. Sort of thing doesn't happen much, nowadays.'

'I'm sorry.'

'It was a long time ago. Water under the bridge.'

175

'So, in fact, Bibi was actually on your side, persuading her to move out?'

He snorted. 'Bibi was never on anybody's side but her own, whatever they tell you! No, she hated Membery, found it dark and depressing. Reason she was manipulating Alyssa into leaving was so that Chip and the boys could sell up.'

'Would they do that?'

He shrugged. 'Hard to say. Bound to have caused dissension. Though maybe Mark wouldn't have been averse. And Jonathan, too, perhaps. I'm not sure about him. He's not there enough for it to matter, but he's very attached to the place. She'd have had a hard job with Chip, but she had a lever there . . .'

'Is that what you meant by saying Chip's drinking is understandable? She was holding her favours out as a carrot on the end of a stick, so to speak?'

'Something like that,' he muttered, making her think she'd gone a little too far beyond what he'd be prepared to answer. She should have remembered that men of his age – men of his type, anyway – didn't think such topics suitable for women to discuss, but after a moment he growled, 'Bibi . . . supposed to be his "partner" but – well, egging the poor devil on to think . . . let's say it wouldn't have done for me when I was his age! Used to have a word for her sort when I was younger.' He looked down into the empty bowl of his pipe. 'Forget I said that. Rotten bad taste. How about another cuppa tea, eh?'

Reaching the flower-filled roundabout at the bottom of the hill, Fran turned in the direction of the station, where she could take advantage of its car park and walk up into the town. Free of commuters' cars today, it was relatively empty, since most people would rather jostle for a space in the town centre than walk the half mile or so from the station.

The question of whether to go in to work on Monday

176

morning resolved itself as she walked across the river bridge and then up into the town. There were certain tasks on her agenda that she needed to deal with personally, she told herself, knowing it was a specious argument, more to do with the fact that she was experiencing a guilty longing to remove herself from what was happening here. The lurch of the heart whenever she remembered Jasie. The silence of the forest she loved that was beginning to feel threatening. Maybe this was partly what Mark had meant, when he'd talked about her vulnerability, living in this house without any gates that could be locked to keep out intruders. She suddenly had a yen for the big city, people, even one of those mad shopping sprees with Claire – like buying expensive shoes she didn't really need. For people who hadn't been overtaken by a tragedy happening in their midst. Gossip. A little fun. O.S.O.T., in fact. Yes, she'd definitely go in on Monday, she'd be contributing nothing by staying at home.

She hurried through her errands as quickly as possible, ending up at the market. No one wanted to eat heavy meals in this sultry, oppressive heat, and she queued impatiently at a greengrocer's stall, in search of salad like every other shopper today, smothering thoughts of what Alyssa would say if she knew she was actually buying things she could have had for free from the kitchen garden at Membery. But Alyssa had enough on her plate at the moment, without being bothered with requests for tomatoes and stuff.

When it came to her turn, Fran bought tiny, locally grown new potatoes, some misshapen, non-supermarket-graded tomatoes, guaranteed delicious. She asked for a pound of juicy purple plums, a couple of ripe Comice pears, and looked at the big pile of oranges at the front of the stall. She picked one up, feeling its gravid weight in her hand. Oranges? What did she need with more oranges? There were still five big Jaffas in the fridge. The remaining ones from those she'd removed from the glass-topped table on Thursday evening, when she'd arrived home from work . . .

'You gonna buy that orange, love?' asked the stallholder.

'What? Oh no, sorry, I was miles away.' She put the orange back on top of its pile. 'I'll have one of those cos lettuces, please.'

'Wish I was. Miles away,' said the stallholder, wiping his forehead with the back of his wrist. 'Iceland for preference, eh? Good downpour and we'd all feel better, clear the air. That all? Four pound twenty pee to you then, my lover.'

She drove unchallenged through the gates at Membery and left her car by the front door, the idea being to make her way on foot down to The Watersplash. That way she'd avoid coming across any of the inquisitive reporters Alyssa had rung and warned her to beware of. It seemed her fears in that direction might have been unwarranted. She'd approached the house cautiously, half expecting to be stopped, but everywhere was quiet, with no sign of the press – or, for that matter, police. The number of their vehicles had diminished to only two, parked to one side, under the shade thrown by the big Cedar of Lebanon in the front lawn. Perhaps the reporters had got tired of waiting for any activity.

Her ideas of the place being guarded suffered a distinct jolt when she found that even the front door was unlocked, so that anyone could have walked straight in, as she did herself. Inside, apart from the ever present, distant sound of Jonathan on his cello, silence reigned. She peered into several rooms, and for a moment stood in the centre of the big hall, undecided. Jane had most likely bullied Alyssa into going over into the garden to do some work, and quite rightly too. Nothing ever perked her up quite as much as poking about among her plants when she was worried, or upset.

She was about to wander across there when the distant

cello notes caught her attention again. Any time that Jonathan was known to be practising, it was an unwritten rule that he should not be interrupted, but the difference in this particular music indicated he wasn't alone. Intrigued, she went outside and round the side of the house, to where she could see the french windows of the music room wide open.

They were so preoccupied, even the sounds of her footsteps scrunching on the gravel went unnoticed. She stood outside, reluctant to interrupt the scene within. Rehearsals for Jonathan's concert in London were to start tomorrow, but this wasn't the Schubert Quintet he was practising.

The room was in semi-darkness, with the dark green rep curtains on the opposite window fully drawn, and those on the french doors pulled half-way across. Through the gap in the open doors, Fran could see the sun streaming in a shaft and lying along the polished wood floorboards, dust motes dancing in the air. At the piano was Jilly, looking amazingly different without her glasses, presumably wearing contact lenses, tanned and smiling in an ankle-length dark blue sundress, patterned in turquoise. Jonathan in white T-shirt and jeans, one finger plucking a sophisticated, syncopated rhythm that Fran half recognized. She stood, rooted to the spot, as Jilly sang softly to the music, not in the sparrow's chirp that might have been expected from her but in a sweet, husky, seductive voice.

'Tell me the truth about . . .' she sang in a minor key, her eyes all the time on Jonathan. 'Tell me the truth about . . . love.' The last notes hung on the air as the song came to an end on a dying fall. In the silence, the smile they gave each other was one whose meaning would not be mistaken by anyone in the world. And then, quite suddenly, Jilly burst into tears. Jonathan put his cello aside and in one stride was by her side. 'Oh, Jonathan, what are we going to do?'

'We can't do anything, my love, except go on as we have done.' He was kneeling on the floor, her hands in his. 'If

179

we keep on sitting tight, no one's going to have any reason
to suspect.'

'It's all going to come out now, anyway.'

'Not now it isn't,' he said sharply. 'Seeing she was the
only one who knew.'

'Oh, how can you be sure of that?'

'Because I was the bloody fool who told her, wasn't I?
And I've never said a word to anyone else.'

There was a silence.

'You know you can't go on like this, Jon. Make an end
of it.'

The silence lengthened. At length he said, in a quietly
desperate voice, totally unlike his normally controlled
tones, almost pleading, 'Let me have the concert, Jilly, and
then I promise. I can at least ask that much.'

Fran fled, regardless of the sound of her footsteps on the
gravel.

She wouldn't have cared now whether she met a dozen
reporters, if she'd given it a thought. She grabbed from the
car the tote bag into which she'd packed her shopping, her
fruit and vegetables, now grown unaccountably heavy,
slung it over her shoulder, and hardly noticing its weight,
slithered and scrambled her way back down to The Watersplash, ignoring the grazes on the palms of her hands she
received when she slipped on the rough path and tried to
save herself.

Chapter Fourteen

Crouch would much have preferred to go haring off up the motorway to Leeds in person, looking for Armstrong, he could scarcely restrain himself from doing so, but Vincent had said no, leave it to the locals until there was something concrete, until they'd gone further along the road towards locating him, so it was Sergeant Nick Hingley up in Yorkshire who responded to the call from Mrs Mavis Brayshaw on Sunday morning. She was Graham Armstrong's maternal aunt, and attempts had been made to contact her previously, but she and her husband, veterans in the international army of globe-trotting pensioners, had been abroad for the last fortnight. They arrived home late on Saturday evening and she rang the police station at ten o'clock on Sunday morning.

Hingley, who was a large, placid young man who rarely hurried but had all his chairs at home, arranged to meet her at the house which had previously belonged to Armstrong's father, and where he had been living, prior to his disappearance. She was waiting for him when he got there, her car parked on the drive of a neat, brick-built semi just off the Leeds-Halifax road, in a street of similarly neat houses. It was a small, well-kept house, and unlike the one next door, which was dirty and neglected, with a number of grubby children playing about and a lopsided For Sale sign stuck in the weeds that comprised the front garden, the garden of number twelve showed signs of recent attention. The grass had been cut and the edges trimmed, though the tubs of busy-lizzies either side of the front door appeared to be dying from lack of water. The path was swept, the windows were polished, the net curtains clean. There was a quick response to Hingley's ring on the doorbell.

'Come in, sit you down.' Mrs Brayshaw was knocking seventy but going strong. Short, well-cut grey hair, dark eyes and a rather dried-up tan from over-exposure to the sun on her recent holiday. Neatly dressed in white trousers and a blue overshirt. No flies on her, no airs and graces, a sensible Yorkshire grandmother.

'This is Eric, my husband.' She introduced a stocky, truculent-looking man with a crest of white hair and a mighty case of sunburn, clearly reluctant to dispense with his holiday garb of shorts and open-necked shirt. He responded with an unsmiling nod and a curt how-do.

'We've just been on a lovely Saga holiday to Greece,' Mrs Brayshaw told Hingley over the cup of coffee that had been ready and waiting. 'We only got home yesterday, but as soon as I opened the papers this morning, I knew, didn't I, Eric? "That'll be our Graham," I said. "In trouble again." I knew it were too good to be true, he'd been that quiet, ever since he came out. It weren't like him.'

'Talkative sort, is he?'

Eric Brayshaw snorted.

'No, that's not what I mean, love, he doesn't go in for chatting much, never did. I meant he never said a word about *her*, or the little lad neither, so I knew he were brooding about it. He won't give up, you know, once he's set his mind on something, never. Stubborn? We've seen mules this holiday less obstinate than him! Our Marion spoiled him, and that's the truth. My own sister, but it has to be said. Mind you, it were something in his nature, in the first place. Born like that, our Graham.'

'Imagines everybody's agin him, that's his trouble,' Eric interposed bluntly. 'That flamin' sensitive, you've to mind every damn word you say in case you hurt his feelings.'

His wife nodded agreement. 'We used to try and tease him out of it when he were a kiddie, but it only made him

182

worse. You couldn't get mad at him, it were like scolding a wounded puppy . . . but I don't want to give you the wrong impression, he were a grand little lad most of the time. It's just that he couldn't ever forgive anybody if he thought they'd slighted him. I bet all that time he spent in *there* – in prison – he were just biding his time until he could get his own back.' She sighed gustily. 'It's a thousand pities it's all happened, I thought it had all come out right for him when he married her and took that hotel over – just up his street! He did right well on that hotel management course . . . I'm sorry, I'm talking too much, that's always been my problem.'

'No, no,' Hingley said, thanking God for a garrulous witness, steering her back on course. 'So you think it's likely him that took the boy away?'

'It'd be a miracle if it was anybody else!' said Eric. 'That one never forgets, never forgives.'

'Oh come on, Eric, I'm not saying it's right, what he did that time, but she led him a right dance, by all accounts, that Bibi.'

'Aye, according to him!'

'When was the last time you saw him?' asked Hingley.

'Just before we went on holiday. I brought him two or three meals I'd cooked, for his freezer, and a few buns. He liked sweet stuff. I think he waited till we were away, like, before he pushed off.'

'Maybe I'd better take a look around,' suggested Hingley, having finished his coffee.

Mrs Brayshaw seemed to feel it necessary to apologize in advance for what he might find. 'Me and my husband's looked after the place as best we could. Kept it decent like, while he's been in there, but it wants decorating top to bottom, it's never been touched since our Marion died – I tried to get him to do it, thought it'd give him something to occupy him till he got another job, but he'd no interest. He just sat there, in front of the telly, didn't matter what were on, he'd watch it.'

'*Teletubbies*, *Neighbours*, Open University, game shows,

you name it,' said Eric disgustedly. 'All he did, watch telly.'

'Well, what could you expect, being in that place all this time? It's like you've always said, Eric, they get institutionalized, don't they? Wouldn't even cook for himself,' she told Hingley, 'though he always used to love his food. I brought him some decent meals in every now and then, I couldn't stand to see him living off all them pizzas and curries.'

'And Joe Soap here went on, daft as a brush, cutting the grass for him like I'd done all the time he was inside, and what's more, he bloody let me – never raised a finger! Never even stirred hisself to water the tubs, idle sod! You wouldn't catch me doing that, I tell you, for nobody but Mavis.'

'Well, you couldn't let the place get into a slum like next door,' his wife said placatingly – 'what would folks have thought?'

'What they already think – that we'll be letting the bloody Pakis in next!'

'*Eric*!!'

'Bad enough having a jailbird here. I've heard that said, an' all, down at the Red Lion.'

'He'd paid his debt, Eric.'

Brayshaw's face had turned from sunburnt to puce, and Hingley hastily stood up, sensing signs of marital dissent, and not anxious to ignite any more of Mr Brayshaw's smouldering prejudices, but his wife hadn't finished with Hingley. 'If it turns out he *has* killed her – well, we'll just have to accept it. But I'll just say this. Taking James like that's just the sort of thing he would do, but he fair worships that little lad. He wouldn't harm a hair of his head.' Suddenly she burst into tears. 'It's all my fault – I told him, when I was visiting him once, she'd gone to live down south with that chap that was a witness at the trial.'

'Now then, Mavis. He'd have found out where she was, choose how.'

184

'That's right, Mrs Brayshaw. He knew his name, it wouldn't be hard to find out where he lived.' She looked relieved and Hingley said, 'Well, the first priority is finding 'em both, your nephew and the little lad. Let me have a mosey round.'

The search didn't take long. The house was shabby, the carpets threadbare, the kitchen units were an old DIY job, circa 1950, that needed replacing, but everywhere was spotless, due, no doubt, to Mrs Brayshaw's ministrations. He soon returned to the front room.

'I can't find anything to suggest a child's been in the house.'

'Oh aye? So that's what you've been looking for, Sherlock, eh? Flamin' hell,' said Brayshaw, 'even I can see he wouldn't hardly've brought him here – he's not that daft!'

'Maybe you can suggest somewhere else he's likely to have taken him, then?' Hingley asked sharply, nettled.

Husband and wife looked at one another. Some sort of agreement seemed to have taken place in Hingley's absence. 'As a matter of fact, there is one place he might likely be,' Mavis Brayshaw said.

The congregation at the family service in the church of St Michael and All Angels in Middleton Thorpe on Sunday morning was very nearly as big as even the vicar, whose three-weekly turn it was to preach there, could wish for. Regular churchgoers or not, an unusually satisfactory number of people from the village filled the pews this morning.

Dr Paul Anderson, who lived in Middleton but whose practice was in Felsborough and who, it just so happened, was the police medical examiner who first saw Bibi's body, led the choir with his fine baritone, struggling against the organist, old Roger Capstick, who invariably pitched the hymn tunes too high and too slow. There was just one other man in the choir, a newcomer to the village who

185

worked in computers and had been persuaded to make up the numbers. His voice wasn't up to much, he was the first to admit, but he was enthusiastic. The rest of the choir were women, mostly middle-aged or elderly. None of the youngsters of the village, boys or girls, could be persuaded into joining, although a fair sprinkling of children had been lugged along to church this morning by their parents, since prayers were to be said for their schoolmate. A television camera crew was hanging about outside, hoping to catch some of the children weeping for Jasie.

Humphrey stands next to Alyssa, barking out the words of the hymn in the tuneless manner he invariably falls back on, since he can't hope to reach the high notes and has never been able to carry a tune, anyway. 'On!-ward! Chris!-tian! So!-oldiers! . . .' What was good enough for Rex Harrison as Professor Higgins is good enough for him. When it comes to the responses, he gives the familiar ones he's learned as a child from the Book of Common Prayer and has continued to use, regardless of whether anyone else is using Rite A or Rite B or any other new-fangled rite. He refuses to shake hands at the Peace. No one around him is unduly surprised by this eccentricity. They're used to Humphrey.

Alyssa is amused at his stiff stubbornness, but all the same, she herself can't help sighing for the loss of the beautiful prose of the old Prayer Book, such a comfort. She can never comprehend why those who are said not to understand it cannot be taught to do so. Despite the loss of the old familiar words, however, she feels comforted by the service, and immensely supported by all the family being here today, though none of her sons are regular attenders any longer. She hasn't slept properly for two nights, being very troubled in herself by having remembered something which she hasn't told the police. Is it important enough for them to need to know? Even if it is, she's not sure whether she'll tell them. It probably has no significance, she thinks, willing herself to believe it. The hymn creaks to its end and she watches Jane Arrow, in the choir, lead the 'Amen' in a high, reedy soprano.

Jane settles herself back while the vicar mounts the pulpit to begin his sermon. She hopes the Reverend Treece, who is a terrible old windbag, will restrict himself to the prayers said for Jasie and not make mawkish appeals in his sermon. As it is, it's going to be enough of an ordeal for Alyssa, who looks ready to weep. She notices that Humphrey has closed his eyes, as he usually does during the sermon, and purses her lips, waiting for his head to jerk up to the amusement of all. She's pleased to see that Chip has turned up, looking resolute. And Jonathan, too – even though she knows this so-called music is hard for him to endure.

She's quite right about that. The choir is abysmal, Jonathan is thinking, and no boys in it, but what's new? He'd been dragooned into swelling the numbers before he went away to school and occasionally after that, when he was home, but even then it had been a painful experience, quite unlike the occasional near-ecstasy of being part of the choir at school, which happened to have a music master who was passionate about boys' voices and church music generally: his mentor, who had eventually persuaded him to consider seriously the idea of music as a career. He exchanges a wry smile with Jilly. It's not realistic to expect much more than that from a tiny village choir. But he did wish they had a better organist.

As the vicar begins to speak, he looks at his watch. He has half an hour exactly before he must set off in his mother's car for London, and his first rehearsal. The vicar has been asking their prayers for Jasie's safety, and though prayers haven't featured much in Jonathan's life lately, he prayed then. For Jasie, and for himself. Perhaps he should have done that long ago. He shuts off the vicar's words.

Kate heard the sound of hymn singing coming from the church as she drove past on her way to Membery. A

187

nostalgic sound, inescapably associated with Miss Marple films, where church bells rang for Matins, you could almost smell the roasting beef, and little girls wore their Sunday shoes and straw hats. Alas, this was Middleton Thorpe, similar sort of name but a different story. In St Mary Mead they'd never heard of men in vests washing cars on Sunday mornings to the accompaniment of head-banging music. Large, uncontrolled mongrel dogs didn't run out into the road and bark at traffic. Neither did godless little boys on roller blades flirt with death almost under the wheels of cars. She narrowly avoided hitting one of them and momentarily regretted she hadn't when he gave her the old one two.

By contrast, the gardens at Membery Place were manna to the soul. They were still closed to the public, but she had a key to get in, and was alone to wander quietly along the herbaceous borders and the sunken garden, to smell the roses and climb down among the cascades of rock plants on the escarpment overlooking the valley . . . Come on, Kate, you're not here to enjoy yourself!

Sometimes, she wondered why she'd joined the police, and when she had to work on Sundays was one of those times. Though to be truthful, she didn't have to be here. She'd been yo-yoing between here and Felsborough ever since Thursday evening and ought to have been glad of a respite.

She sat on the top one of three sun-warmed stone steps leading down into the rose garden and sipped from the bottle of mineral water she had in her bag. As the cool water gurgled down her throat, she flicked back through her notebook. She was convinced that she'd registered something at the beginning of the enquiry which had lodged in her mind, something that would help to build up a picture of Bibi Morgan's last hours, but she couldn't catch it. She was a meticulous note-taker and she quickly found the place where she'd underlined the time of that telephone call Bibi had made to Francine Calvert at her office – around half-past two, as far as Fran could remem-

188

ber – which seemed like a starting point for the sequence of events leading up to Bibi's death.

No one else who had been questioned had reported anything unusual about that day. Apparently, Bibi had spent most of the afternoon in the garden in a deck chair under the cedar on the front lawn, reading and resting her weak ankle. Jasie had been playing that afternoon at the home of a friend, where the main attraction was a junior trampoline the other boy had been given for his birthday. He'd been given his tea and then brought home by his friend's mother. Kate turned to what she'd written down when she'd interviewed this woman.

'I told her Jasie would need to go straight into the bath,' Mel Barrington had recalled, laughing. But she'd added that if the noise they'd been making was any indication, they'd tired themselves out – he shouldn't need any rocking to sleep that night.

'It was brill, Tom and me kept jumping from the tramp into the paddling pool and we got *soaked*!' Jasie had said. 'But I had my trunks on, so it was OK. Thank you for having me, Mrs Barrington.'

'I told her he could have stayed longer, you know. But he'd told me his mother had said he had to be home by five, and she said that was right, that was what she'd told him.'

'I don't suppose she said why?'

'No, and I didn't ask. Whenever he came to play with my kids, she always made clear the exact time he had to be home – she either picked him up herself or I brought him back. She was very protective of Jasie, you know. But that's no bad thing, these days, is it?'

'Absolutely not, Mrs Barrington. You can't be too careful.'

So that was five o'clock, when they'd last been seen together. An apparently uneventful afternoon. Yet Fran reported that she'd sounded frantic when they'd spoken. Had something happened – apart from the onset of a headache – between then and the time she'd asked Gary

Brooker to deliver the note – which was half-past five, according to Kate's notes?

Kate had gone after Gary when he'd scarpered so fast out of the greenhouse on seeing her yesterday and, following the girl Becky's instructions, found him outside a potting shed, just starting to sweep up glass from one of its broken windows and shovelling it into a wheelbarrow. He'd looked shifty, and avoided her eyes, but even he had been able to see there was no longer any way he could avoid her.

He towered above her, and she didn't want to give him that advantage. She looked around for somewhere to sit, but could only see the brick edge of a cold frame with its lid up. She perched on it and indicated the space next to her. He ignored the invitation but chose a similar perch on the frame opposite, leaving the brick path between them.

Kate riffled through her notes to remind herself of what she'd written down then.

It had been like pulling teeth, but at last she got Gary to admit that at half-past five, Bibi had come through the gate from the private garden, caught him just as he was about to go home, and asked him if he wouldn't mind doing something for her and delivering a note she'd written to young Mrs Calvert at The Watersplash.

'So you took the note down to The Watersplash as a favour for Ms Morgan. What did you think of her, Gary?'

He'd flushed a dull, unattractive red. 'She warn't bad,' he mumbled, not raising his eyes from the path. He had his elbows on his knees, his head supported in his hands, which still wore the thick, protective gloves he'd been using while he prised out the last pieces of glass from the window. 'She was OK, I suppose. Didn't have all that much to do with her, though.'

'OK, so that was half-past five. How long did it take you to ride down there?'

'I didn't like, ride down, exactly.'

'Come on, Gary – what do mean, you didn't *exactly* ride down?'

'I walked, then. Cut down the side of the stream. We're not supposed to go there, into the private bit of the gardens, we aren't. But like, I reckoned I was doing it for her, warn't I, so I was entitled. And it took me fifteen minutes of me own time, there and back, maybe a bit longer, so I didn't think she'd have no grumbles.'

'Fair enough. But why didn't you ride down and deliver it on your way home?'

''Cos it ain't *on* my way home, is it? Ten minutes in it, that way round, and I knew I just had enough juice to get me down into Felsborough later on, didn't I? Like I had a date, that night. No way I wanted to run out half-way there!'

'No, that's reasonable. So – fifteen minutes there and back. Means you got back here about ten to six to pick up your bike?'

'That's right,' he said, looking again at his feet. The dark fuzz on top of his head was starting to grow out furry.

'What else aren't you telling me, Gary?'

'Not that I met her on the path and done her in, if that's what you think! I liked her, she was real nice to me, which is more'n you can say for some folks round here.'

'Which folks in particular?'

But for the moment Gary had said all he was saying. He had the mulish look which told her she'd get nothing more out of him for the moment. He was obviously in a panic at being spoken to by police and given his past record that wasn't surprising – but what was it he was hiding?

'Did you see anyone else while you were walking down there?'

'No.'

'Are you positive about that?'

'I bloody said so, didn't I?'

'All right, Gary. All right for now,' she'd said, and let him go.

She closed her notebook now, stood up and, taking the

191

same way he'd taken, went through the gate into the grounds around the house, noting that it was marked 'No Entry, Private' but that it wasn't locked. Perhaps it was deemed unnecessary, now that the public gardens were temporarily closed.

She bypassed the house, and walked straight down to the stream. The still unanswered question was, what was it that had happened between half-past two, when Bibi had rung Fran in a panic, and half-past five, when she'd written the note to Gary to deliver? Something that had removed those earlier fears?

If so, her relief had been misplaced. At the end of that hot and sultry day, at about half-past six, Bibi had popped her head round the door at Membery and told the two old ladies she was going outside for a breath of air. At seven twenty, Fran had set out for Membery Place and found her dead in the waterfall pool.

When Kate reached the place along the stream where the bank had been broken down and the murder had been assumed to have taken place, she sat down on the grassy edge, still trying to see some sort of pattern in the ideas that were forming in her mind, and though she didn't know that she was a great deal further forward, she knew it was important that she should try.

It had little to do with her own ambitions – she wasn't ambitious in that way – but it had everything to do with her and Dave Crouch. Whether to offer him her ideas on a plate, or claim her rightful share of the kudos. He'd understand if she was right and give in, if not gracefully, in his own way. 'One up to you,' he'd say, as if they were on opposite sides, each needing to score, not seeing that it wasn't like that. He was her partner in life, as well as at work, but she needed to step out of his shadow sometimes – for his sake, as well as hers. And yet . . . the sooner he notched up a few Brownie points and got back to his old job, the happier everyone would be – including Kate. OK, then, tread softly. Don't poke the tiger with a stick.

The water in the stream was cool and crystal clear, fast

192

running, with purple loosestrife and red-stemmed balsam growing at the edge, and on the bed sharp flints and some of the larger rocks that she'd learned were called pudding stones – flinty pebbles embedded in a matrix, rather like fruit in a lump of plum pudding. The sun cast glittering reflections on the small, polished pebbles and gravel lying on the bottom. They looked like semi-precious stones, one in particular looked just like a tiger's eye. She dipped her hand idly in the water and tried to pick it up but it wasn't where she thought it lay. The water was very much deeper than it looked. Nothing was as it seemed, she thought, it was all an illusion. Those glittering diamond chips in the sand were only mica. The richly coloured stones would just be flat and dull if they were taken out of the water and dried.

She gazed down, her thoughts wandering. The water eddied and swirled around the pebbles in a miniature whirlpool. She caught her breath. Suddenly alert, she got on to her hands and knees, and then lay flat on her stomach, the better to peer into the water. She stared, mesmerized. After a while, she scrambled to her feet and sat back on the bank, hugging her knees. There were grass stains on her new, light cotton trousers.

Glory be, Dave Crouch, I think I've found your murder weapon.

Chapter Fifteen

When the service was over, Fran, with Jilly and Jonathan, came out of the church by the side door so as to dodge the TV cameras. Jonathan rushed off to his rehearsal in London and the other two walked in the direction of Membery, although the usual mandatory Sunday lunch of Alyssa's overcooked roast beef and two veg, where everybody met, had been abandoned today by tacit consent.

Jilly touched Fran's arm. 'How about walking over to the pub at Endbury for a drink and a snack, maybe? Anything's better than this awful waiting.' She sounded on edge, and waited nervously for Fran's reply. 'What do you think?'

Fran hesitated. The erstwhile White Horse, now facetiously renamed the Rat and Radish, and suffering under equally dire assaults on its decor, was a place Fran would normally have avoided like the plague, the in place at the moment, popular with Felsborough's G & T brigade, many of whom she met daily on the station platform, most of whom were scarcely able to wait to board the train before pulling out their laptops and checking in with the office on their mobile phones – and none of whom she wished to meet in the present circumstances. It was a tiny, stone-floored inn with low beams and small-paned windows, and today it would be packed, smoky and noisy. Still, with luck, they might find a seat in the garden and getting there would mean a walk through the forest where it was cool and quiet, an opportunity to talk on neutral ground, which she felt might be Jilly's reason for suggesting it.

She smiled and said, 'Yes, OK. I'm on if you are.'

But they were nearly there before Jilly came to the point. 'Let's sit down here for a minute, Fran. I expect you've guessed why I asked you to come.'

'Not really.' It wasn't altogether a lie. She wasn't absolutely sure. They sat on the fallen trunk of a beech which had been uprooted in the storms of the previous winter, its exposed roots sticking up nakedly in the air, its bark already gathering moss and lichens.

'Yesterday, in the music room . . . you heard, didn't you?'

Fran saw that she couldn't evade what was coming, but wished she could. 'When you were singing that song?' she prevaricated. '"Tell me the truth about love"? Where have I heard it before? It's been haunting me ever since.'

'It's one of Britten's cabaret songs. But that's not important – I want to explain.'

'You don't have to explain anything. I was eavesdropping, though I didn't mean to. It's really none of my business.' Never mind that she'd spent most of the evening speculating on just what it was she'd overheard.

'I'd like you to know – please. I want to tell you everything.' Fran saw that Jilly was determined to go ahead with her explanations, so she made no further protests. Breathing deeply in an effort to control a voice that had grown dangerously shaky, Jilly sat with her hands either side, pressed into the trunk of the tree, as if she needed its support. 'I know it's not fair to put this on your shoulders but oh! I just have to tell somebody or I'll go mad. Jonathan and I – we've gone round this in circles and we just get nowhere. And I know you can be trusted.'

'It's something to do with Bibi?'

'Well, yes, though it wasn't, not until she came here.' She flushed angrily. 'Jonathan – well, he let something slip . . . you know what Bibi was like when she was being all feminine and sympathetic . . . when really, she was just so manipulative.'

'Yes, she was.' Fran saw how true this was now, though

195

she'd taken some time to realize and admit it. She'd been blind to a lot of things about Bibi.

Jilly began to pleat the material of her dress with nervous fingers, the same one she'd worn yesterday, its kingfisher colours a bright splash under the dark canopy of the trees. But she wasn't wearing her contact lenses today and looked solemn as an owl behind her large specs. She had quite lost that glow which had lit her up when she and Jonathan had been singing and playing together.

'Go on,' Fran prompted, wondering what she was going to hear, not wanting to, and very much afraid that she wasn't going to like it.

Jilly swallowed hard, licked her lips. 'It was something that happened when Jonathan was a student in Cambridge, just after he'd taken his music degree, in fact, and they were all ready for leaving. On the last night, a group of them went out to celebrate and well – it all got rather out of hand . . . you know he never drinks much. He really can't take it.'

'But he did get drunk that night?'

'Not really *drunk*, but enough to make him realize he was well over his limit. The party was breaking up, anyway, so he said goodnight and went to walk home. It was a long way but he thought it might sober him up.'

Well, yes, it was possible to imagine Jonathan, even then, having the self-control to walk out of a student celebration. Not many young people you could say that about, but Jonathan, yes. He was born taking himself seriously, Fran thought wryly.

'When he got outside it was pouring with rain – a really wild night. There was someone else out there in the car park that he hardly knew, in fact they'd met for the first time that night, a medical student. He was opening his car door and shouted to Jonathan, offering him a lift. When Jon got to the car, he realized the other guy – his name was Malcolm Farrant – was plastered – so he suggested he should drive. Farrant said OK and they set off. It wasn't long before Jonathan realized he was in no condition to drive, either, not in that weather, the car was all over the place and he could scarcely see through the windscreen. Luckily, the roads were deserted on such a wild night. Well, you can guess what happened . . .'

'An accident?'

'Yes, the car slewed off the road into a ditch. Farrant came off worse. He hadn't fastened his seat belt and he'd banged his head on the windscreen and was out cold. There was a lot of blood and Jonathan panicked. He was a bit groggy himself, though more shaken than anything. His seat belt had saved him. He got himself out of the car and ran to find a telephone box – but first he pulled Farrant across into the driving seat.'

'What?'

'Don't you see, if it was discovered he'd been the driver he could be prosecuted for dangerous driving. Even manslaughter, if Farrant was dead, which he thought he might be. The beginning and end of a promising career.'

Blighted before it had begun, the one thing that mattered to Jonathan above all else, and always had done. My God. 'And then?'

'He found a telephone and got the ambulance to come.'

'And I suppose he faded from the scene afterwards.'

Jilly looked up quickly. 'Well, yes, but he'd done all he could, hadn't he?'

'And the other guy – Farrant? Did he die?'

'No, his head injury was fairly superficial, after all. He was fined three or four hundred pounds, that was all. But the police weren't satisfied, they suspected there'd been another person in the car, one who'd been driving – the one who'd called 999. Farrant's injuries, you see, weren't consistent with his having been in the driving seat when the car crashed. But they never found it was Jonathan – no reason why they should, after all – he and Farrant were strangers, no one had seen him get into Farrant's car, and he left Cambridge for ever the next day.'

'Didn't Farrant tell the police there was someone else with him?'

'Apparently he was so out of his skull he didn't even remember the accident, never mind giving anyone a lift. It wasn't just booze he'd taken that night.'

'Lucky for Jonathan.'

'Fran, he was young, he was shocked, he just did the first thing that came to him! He got the ambulance, after all, he didn't just leave him, as he might have done! It wouldn't have made any difference if he'd stayed.'

'Except he'd have been the one who took the blame, especially if Farrant had died.'

She didn't know what else to say. Jonathan, the responsible, dependable one. The one with integrity. He'd always been more law-abiding, more respectful of authority, than anyone else she knew. She just couldn't believe that he, of all people, had simply walked away like that, until she thought of the reasons why he had, and then she could. Oh yes, if it had looked like interfering with his career, he would have done anything. But whichever way you looked at it, it wasn't a very elevating story.

'How did Bibi come into this?'

'Oh, it was shortly after she came to live here. Everyone else had gone to bed, and she persuaded Jonathan to let her read the tarot cards for him, just for a laugh. But after a while, it became serious, she swore she could read all the signs that there was something hanging over him that had happened to him in his past. She told him he'd never be free until he unburdened himself of what it was that was troubling him – or words to that effect, you know how she talked. I really don't know how she managed to persuade him to tell, but in the end – well, the upshot was, he confessed the whole thing to her. One of those confidences you make on the spur of the moment and regret ever after. But she had an uncanny knack of being around when people were ready to talk, didn't she? All that wide-eyed sympathy and understanding. But rather than sort of exorcizing it, as she'd suggested, it made things worse – not

198

that she knew, though there was that, but the fact that after all these years of saying nothing, he'd let the cat out of the bag.'

'Was she blackmailing him?'

'It was more subtle than that. She just found ways, every time they met, of letting him know she hadn't forgotten. He swears she didn't want anything from him – she just wanted him to know that she knew. Which meant that he'd never be allowed to forget. It was a kind of power, I suppose. Didn't you ever feel it, Fran, that dark streak in her?'

'Oh yes, I think I did, from time to time, without really recognizing what it was. It probably hurt her more than anyone else.'

They sat for a while, saying nothing. Insects whirled and danced in the shafts of sunlight coming through the trees. The silence was complete. Fran picked a piece of bark off the tree trunk and began to shred it. 'Supposing it were to come to light now – what would happen?'

'He thinks he could be charged with conspiring to avert the course of justice, or however they put it, and I expect he'd be fined. That wouldn't matter, he'd welcome it, in a funny sort of way, the chance to clear the slate. But think of what it would do to his reputation! That's something he'd never get over.'

'No one expects anyone to be perfect, nowadays. I've often wondered if there's anything at all that would put someone in the public eye totally beyond the pale. They can get away with anything. Most people would think what he did wasn't so very terrible anyway. He'd survive, people would forget.'

Jilly looked at her. 'But Jonathan wouldn't.'

'No.' Fran privately thought he might rather be enjoying wearing his hair shirt. 'But I can't see any good would come of resurrecting it now, except to relieve his conscience – and he's managed to live with that all these years,' she added drily.

'That's not fair! You don't know how it's preyed on his

mind. Not to mention how his work's been suffering, ever since Bibi got hold of the story.'

'Well, he won't have to put up with her any more now, will he?'

'Fran!'

Fran sighed. 'Don't take any notice of what I said, we're all on edge, aren't we? Look, I don't much feel like going on to Endbury. Come back home with me and I'll find us something to eat there.'

In a caravan on the cliffs on the edge of the North York moors, a man sat drinking coffee from a mug, staring out over the North Sea. A mongrel dog resembling a dusty black hearthrug sat expectantly at his feet, waiting to be let out, but the caravan was too close to the edge of the cliffs for comfort and he never let the dog out alone. The coastline around here was subject to dangerous rock falls. In fact, not too far from where the caravan was parked, a mere few miles away, whole sections of the cliff face had not long ago broken away without warning and slid with a great roar down to the beach below, taking everything that had been on the cliff top with them. Not long ago, a hotel in Scarborough had been swallowed by the sea. This van, now decrepit and unused, was the only one still left on a site that had once accommodated twenty or more, but no one would contemplate coming to stay here now.

The dog whined again, but he couldn't bestir himself out of the appalling apathy that seemed to characterize his days since he had come out of prison. Inside, the shrinks had encouraged him to put his past behind him and look forward to the future, not to bear a grudge or dwell on the circumstances that had brought him there. But Graham Armstrong had never been one to forget, much less forgive, a wrong done to him. He had brooded ever since the start of his marriage on what he regarded as the injustices he'd suffered – more than that, he was congenitally incapable of relinquishing thoughts of his child, or of accepting the fact that he was now permanently lost to him. The only thing that had stirred him and kept him going was the thought of the day when he'd have little James back with him. He was prepared to watch and wait for as long as it took. He would never run out of patience. He'd made one bad mistake and he didn't intend being defeated a second time.

Once, he'd had fresh-faced good looks, but he'd lost his hair and grown fat and pale and moon-faced, due to prison stodge and lack of exercise. He'd remedy that when he got out, he'd always told himself, trying to do as he'd been encouraged, and to look forwards, not to dwell on that one failure which had been the cause of all his later troubles. It had never worked. He was too deeply depressed for that. But he was also monumentally good at hiding his feelings, and a whole lot more intelligent than people gave him credit for. He had let them talk to him, made them think the rehabilitation programme they were putting him through was working, while inwardly he forbade himself to forget the wrong done to him by his ex-wife.

He cursed the day he had ever applied for managership of the Ascomb Arms, not because of his subsequent failure to make it once more a viable business proposition, but mainly because if he hadn't he wouldn't have met Bibi Morgan and then his life would never have revealed itself in all its inadequacies and hang-ups.

When he first saw the hotel, he'd admired what Carys Morgan had done to it and had been filled with enthusiasm for the idea of expanding on what she'd already achieved, knowing that he and her daughter, working together, complementing each other, could make an outstanding success of it. He had the necessary management skills: he appreciated the good things in life and liked to surround himself with them, in his working environment as well as in his home life. He knew how to look after money, none better. And she was beautiful enough to add that finishing touch, the grace note that would have the customers coming back, again and again. He imagined them, an urbane and charismatic partnership, she playing the same role as her mother had done, he with his epicurean good taste, as the top recommended hoteliers in Egon Ronay and *The Good Food Guide*.

It had only been a small step from that to imagining them as a married pair. At first, he'd hardly dared to believe that she – so far above him! – would look in his direction, but when he saw she wasn't at all averse to his attentions, in fact rather the opposite, he had looked at himself in a different light and reassessed his chances. Apart from the professional qualifications he possessed, he wasn't bad-looking: he had a good height and physique, with a round, fresh face and – his best feature – the big, soft dark eyes his mother had always loved, that girls had found melting and attractive. He had never before, however, had any relationship with the opposite sex that amounted to more than a passing attraction, though he recognized within himself an infinite capacity for tenderness, love and faithfulness. He loved children and family life and felt with a beating heart that he could ask no more in this world than a life of domestic bliss with Bibi . . . the sort of woman who had hitherto intimidated him, but whom he'd always admired from afar.

And, wonder of wonders, this paragon, Bibi, had accepted him.

For the first months of their marriage, life was idyllic. She was warm and responsive beyond his wildest dreams; within a few weeks she became pregnant, and though she gradually lost interest in having sex, this was only to be expected. After the baby was born, it would be different, he knew. Only it wasn't. She submitted to his needs, but under sufferance. What was wrong with him? he asked her, but she only shrugged. He began to look around, and see how she smiled at other men, how they responded. He could scarcely contain the great, boiling jealousy that seethed up inside him.

As a child, he'd been fascinated by the myths, fables and

legends he'd found in an old, beautifully illustrated book given to him by an old lady his father had worked for. In the same way that kids nowadays were obsessed by dinosaurs, he'd become obsessed by mythical beasts: dragons and mermaids, phoenix and salamander – and in particular, the unicorn, a wild animal elusive of capture by anyone except a spotless virgin. A beast so pure that drinking its blood would give you eternal life. Yet the paradox was that if you killed a unicorn your life was cursed – to eternity. He read until he knew by heart the legend of the Lady and the Unicorn, how her innocence and virginity tamed and protected the beast. He read until the two images were inextricably wound together in his mind and he could no longer distinguish one from the other. He had in fact never completely grown out of his childish obsession, the Lady had imprinted him with the image of his ideal woman.

He had searched for her for a long time. Virginity and innocence were thin on the ground, these days, but at last he believed he had found her. Only to discover that she was not the woman he'd imagined her to be. Her innocence was a façade. And he'd seen it too late.

They'd stuffed him with so many drugs in that place that even when they stopped them, he was like the walking dead. The thought of James had been the one thing that had kept him going, fired him, stirred him out of what had seemed to be a terminal apathy, made him feel alive, fuelled his sense of injustice and his desire to do something and be revenged against that two-faced bitch and have his son run back into his open arms. He had chosen to bury the knowledge of how James had shrunk from his father in terror because of the way he had frightened his mother.

'Why did you set fire to the house if you thought so much of the boy?' they'd asked him, time and again, and time and again he gave the same answer, that he'd believed she'd taken advantage that night of the arrangement she had for herself and James to stay in the hotel on the nights she worked late, in a former servant's room, so inconvenient it wasn't considered worth converting to a guest room. He swore he'd never meant to kill Bibi by setting fire to her house, despite his threats, but only to frighten her into letting him have James – and the precious Unicorn book he'd unwisely given her, in an access of love.

The sea had a rolling swell on it, it was a metallic grey except for the whitecaps further out, and despite the heat of the day it looked cold. An offshore breeze stirred the rough marram grass that grew at the cliff's edge, studded with cushions of sea pinks, yellow vetch and white yarrow. His paternal grandmother, who'd lived fifty miles up the coast, had gathered yarrow and made a herbal tea from it. It would have been better than what he was drinking now. He pushed the coffee away, only half drunk. The milk had gone sour and flecks of curdled white floated on the surface. He should remember to buy coffee creamer instead of milk in future.

Inside the caravan it was stuffy with used air and the smell of dog and last night's fish and chips that he'd brought in. It was a measure of his indifference that he'd left the greasy papers screwed up by the cooker all night, where they still were, now stinking, over and above the smell of cheap instant coffee and burnt toast. He hadn't yet got the hang of the tiddly grill on the even tiddlier cooker, but it didn't matter, they wouldn't be here long. His mother had always been the one to use the cooker, or one like it, when he and his parents had come on holiday to this caravan site when he was a child. He'd hardly been able to believe his luck when he'd driven past and seen the one caravan that hadn't yet been taken away. He'd parked his car where it couldn't be seen from the road, shielded by the van, and broken in. No one would ever suspect he was here.

The dog suddenly leaped to its feet and began barking. It had a permanently hoarse bark, due to having been chained up for most of its life in the untended back garden of the house next door to his father's, where the feckless

204

family had become new neighbours while Graham had been in prison. He had untied it one night when he couldn't stand the noise any longer, and the dog had joyfully followed him and been with him ever since. Armstrong let it stay. It was company. It went on barking now and he told it to shut up, but it carried on and when he looked out of the window on the other side of the van, he saw cars coming along the bumpy road that had once formed the backbone of the site. Three cars. A Ford Mondeo, followed by two others. Two men got out of the first. Police. Once, Armstrong might not have recognized them so easily, but now he knew them instantly for what they were, and why they were here. All up, then.

He was unsurprised. Maybe he'd been expecting it, right from the start. Maybe the foreknowledge of failure was so strong in him he didn't care now. His most urgent thought was what was going to happen to the dog.

They knocked on the door, making it rattle, and the whole caravan shook in sympathy. The dog's noise increased to a frenzy. He shouted to it and raised his hand and was immediately sorry when it cowered down, belly to the floor. He didn't like to see that. He'd never been a violent man, he thought, not seeing the irony of it. He reached out and patted the dog's head to quieten it and then went to open the door.

The telephone rang just after Fran and Jilly had finished their snack lunch. It was Kate Colville, true to her word, ringing to let them know what was happening. Fran listened without interrupting until Kate had rung off.

'What is it?' Jilly asked.

'Crouch is up in North Yorkshire. The police up there think they've located Jasie's father.'

205

Chapter Sixteen

Jesus, thought Crouch as the man came to the door of the caravan and the stench with him. The squalor some people could live in never ceased to disgust him – and this was clean, compared to some places he'd been obliged to enter, he saw as they followed Armstrong inside.

He wasn't what Crouch had expected. A heavyish, balding man with a round, melancholy face, he was pale, not with the prison pallor that should have left him by now, but possibly with fright: it was accentuated by unshaven jowls and big, heavy-lidded dark eyes, of a strange colour somewhat resembling peat, that swam with misery and self-pity. A feral smell of sweat and fear emanated from him. He blinked a lot and drew back his lips, and it was hard not to think of a hunted animal. Crouch trod warily. He might be armed. And unstable men like this could go for the jugular if cornered.

Yet the hardest thing of all for Crouch to imagine was how in the world this specimen had ever been able to persuade a beautiful creature like Bibi Morgan to marry him, not simply because he was, at the moment at any rate, physically unlovely, or that two more opposites it would be difficult to conceive, but because there was something inherently repulsive and abject about the man.

'All right, Armstrong, where's the boy?'

'What boy?'

Crouch sighed. 'We're talking about your son, Jasie Morgan.'

'My son's called James. James *Armstrong*.'

'No, his mother had his surname changed by deed poll. As you must know. You've been following her, up to your old tricks, sending letters to her. Not to mention breaking your parole – and you haven't done that and forfeited your remission for nothing. Where is he?'

'I've no idea. But I haven't got him. I don't know what you're talking about.' Not the slightest flicker in the strange, non-colour eyes. But this man would give nothing away. He was a well of secrecy, deep as Hades. For the first time, Crouch felt a plunge of uncertainty.

'That's a load of bull. Come on, where've you hidden him?'

'I've told you, I haven't got him. I haven't seen him for over two years. Why don't you ask his mother?'

'You'll be telling us next you didn't know he was missing?'

Something flickered in the peaty depths of his eyes. 'No, I didn't know that.'

'Haven't you seen the newspapers, heard the radio?'

Armstrong shook his head, slumped against the stained and split red vinyl of the banquette seat. It was hard to tell how the news had affected him. His doughy face was impassive. He wouldn't break easily under questioning.

'All right, let's get out of here,' Crouch said, suddenly sickened by the foetid atmosphere, unable to support it a minute longer, the smell that emanated from the man himself, that thick, nauseating compound of sweat and fear.

'Where are you taking me?'

'You're nicked, Armstrong. I'm taking you in for questioning about the murder of Bianca Morgan and the abduction of her son, James Morgan.'

At last there was a reaction in the mud-coloured eyes. 'Murder?'

Monday morning found Fran staring out of her office window, overlooking the canyon of a narrow road not far

207

from Oxford Circus. Below, cars slid through, cautiously approaching the bollards at the end that fanned off the road into a narrow alley. Two very elderly ladies, immaculately coiffed, hatted, handbagged and gloved, trotted off to lunch with never a notion that fifty years had brought about a sartorial revolution. From the corner of her eye she could see the traffic grinding laboriously towards Marble Arch.

She'd fondly imagined that the workplace was what she needed: people, bustle, routine, something to take the place of the churning anxiety which had possessed her for the last three or four days – and now that she had it, she couldn't reconcile it with an entirely contrary desire to be alone. She could settle to nothing. She might as well have stayed at home, where they were at least all in the same boat. Here, she felt apart, as though marked by stigmata: one of those persons, only previously encountered in newspapers or on television, who had been personally involved in the horror of a murder, and which might rub off with contact, though she suspected it was Kath, with the best of intentions, who had shunted people off. Good old Kath in her old brown mohair cardigan, out at elbows, which she donned on arrival every day against the air-conditioning, and wore over her shapeless skirts and jumpers or blouses. Specs permanently at half-mast on the end of her nose. Bullying Fran into thinking herself back into the partly finished design she'd been working at on Thursday, even if it did mean she was working with half a heart.

She went back to the screen and sat looking at it, unseeing. She thought about ringing Claire again. She'd previously been engaged elsewhere, and of course, she *would* be very busy after her long weekend in Spain, and that would explain why she hadn't yet returned the call when she'd be dying to tell Fran everything about the first time she'd met Mitch's mother. It was conceivable, by having gone straight to the office after flying in this morning, as Fran knew she'd planned to do, that she wouldn't have seen any newspapers and would know nothing yet of what had happened to Bibi, and Jasie. Actually, she thought that was more or less a certainty, otherwise Claire would surely have contacted her.

No, the call would have to wait now. She'd rather rashly promised to take her lunch hour at a time when she could slip in to Jonathan's final rehearsal at the Wigmore Hall. The tickets for the actual performance were all sold out anyway, since the string quartet he was playing with was world famous and the Schubert Quintet one of the most renowned pieces in their repertoire. Talking to Claire would have to wait a little longer.

She left the office, already late, knowing she was going to the rehearsal more out of a sense of duty than inclination, showing solidarity, if you like, but now rather regretting the impulse that had made her say yes to Jilly when asked. Music was a pleasure to her, but not a necessity of life, though on occasions it could move her deeply. Which was why she wished she hadn't promised to attend the rehearsal . . . this particular piece might be just too heart-rending to be endurable today.

The heat was like a blanket as she waited to cross Oxford Street, she was nearly suffocated by hot diesel fumes from the almost stationary traffic and the heat rising from the tarmac. 'Come on, come on!' she muttered. In the end, losing patience, she dodged between two buses, giving a conductor who was leaning out over the step with his arms wrapped around the pole the opportunity to blow her a cheeky kiss. Obscurely cheered by this, she grinned back, carried on and reached the other side without incident. Then as she cut across to Wigmore Street, a bookshop display caught her eye and quite suddenly she was rocked almost to a standstill with a sense of Jasie's warm little body in her arms, while she read Harry Potter's latest adventure to him, doing all the voices, one he could perfectly well read himself but still loved to have read to him.

She wished she could weep, but she was beyond that. Would it always be like this, catching one unawares?

Half-way into Monday, back in Felsborough, and they still hadn't been able to break Armstrong. He had no alibi for the time of the murder. He swore he'd been living in the caravan for a fortnight, and there was no one to say he had, but on the other hand, no one to say he hadn't. Crouch tried to wear him down, but he'd met his match. Armstrong simply went on insisting that he hadn't killed Bibi. He had no knowledge of where Jasie might be now, either, he repeated, his face white, his big eyes like muddy puddles.

'Then what about the letters you sent to her?'

In the same stolid, deadpan way, he also denied ever sending any letters, threatening or otherwise. This in the teeth of evidence to the contrary which Crouch had found stashed away in the caravan, in the shape of a pack of recycled paper envelopes in a cardboard box, alongside a battered, old-fashioned portable typewriter. Crouch had appropriated the lot – though it wasn't the sort of evidence he could be happy with, when the envelopes themselves, and the letters therein, had disappeared. Armed with the knowledge that Armstrong didn't know this, he tried to feel confident that sooner or later he'd be forced into an admission.

Several hours in close proximity with him on the journey from Yorkshire hadn't lessened Crouch's disgust for the man. Hadn't he washed at all since he left home? Grinding his teeth, he was being forced to admit that he wouldn't be able to keep him much longer. Unless he confessed to the murder, he'd have to be handed over to a lesser justice, to await punishment for breaking his parole, which would mean forfeiting the remission he'd earned and serving the rest of his sentence, but was nothing like the sentence he'd get if he could be proved to have killed Bibi and kid-napped Jasie. The worry was – if he *had* taken the child,

210

had Jasie now been left abandoned and alone? Crouch broke out into a sweat at the very thought, but he would have liked to think even Armstrong wouldn't be that much of a sadist.

Taking her seat next to Jilly in the womb-like interior of the Wigmore Hall – the holy ground on top of the mountain to chamber musicians and enthusiasts alike – sinking into the deep, crimson plush seats, Fran felt the hush of anticipation already upon the few people who, for one reason and another, had been privileged to be allowed to attend the rehearsal. One of the polished wooden doors at the back of the stage opened and the five musicians came on stage – the two violins, viola and two cellos – to a smattering of encouraging applause.

She'd thought Jonathan had looked tired, thinner than usual on her first sight of him the other night when he'd come down to The Watersplash. Now, he looked gaunt and exhausted, anything but ready to play a technically difficult and emotionally demanding piece. It could be just her imagination, or even the effect of the stage lighting, or the tension he must be feeling, though she doubted any of this, after what Jilly had told her yesterday.

The slow opening notes of the quintet began to flow around her, and determinedly she fixed her attention on the musicians as they bowed away at the lyrical opening bars of the first movement. The quartet had their own natural ease and fluency that came from playing together every day; and Jonathan's rehearsal with them yesterday would hopefully have established some of the same rapport. The lights were dimmed; the richly textured notes rose to the gilded decorative apse above the platform, and filled the hall with a slow, lyrical, inspired melody, as the different strings began to interpret Schubert's ravishing music.

Closing her eyes, Fran let the music wash over her, made herself let go, and sure enough the tight feeling that was screwing her up inside eased, a calmness and rationality she hadn't felt for days took its place. Things suddenly began to make sense.

Two large fresh flower arrangements had already been placed on the faux marble columns either side of the stage. Lilies. She could smell them, faintly, from here. She sat very still, breathing in their scent, hardly daring to move, lest by doing so the small embryo ideas that were beginning to grow and take shape would shrivel up obstinately and die. But she found that her hands, resting on the bag on her knee, were trembling. Trembling with suppressed energy, as it gradually became clear to her in that darkened concert hall, with the wondrous music filling her ears, that she'd suddenly and miraculously come to herself again, recovered her wits, seen what she should have seen right from the first.

The case would seem to be all but sewn up. Yet Kate Colville, she remembered, had from the first shown reservations about Armstrong, perhaps trying to warn her not to feel too euphoric – to remind her that even the police weren't quite as sanguine about the outcome as it might appear.

Her insides did a double roll. Yes, there had to be something else, other than her former husband's hatred, at the heart of Bibi's murder. Something darker and deeper than Fran had ever wanted to imagine. She couldn't refuse any longer to acknowledge the undercurrents which she had always known, if she were being honest, were there, running swiftly and dangerously under the surface. Because of those letters, in Mark's desk. *Had* Bibi given them to him? Or had he – maybe got hold of them some other way? With that monstrous thought, all mixed up with her other fears about him, Fran knew that whatever the outcome, she had to know the truth.

The music finished, those who had gathered to listen applauded enthusiastically, and though admittedly none of them were truly disinterested, being mostly friends, family, agents, the odd critic, it was enough to tell Fran that

Jonathan needn't have worried. If today was any indication, he would give the performance of his life tomorrow. Jilly turned a bemused and shining face to her, unable to speak. They hugged each other. There were tears in Jilly's eyes. Fran didn't want to break the spell for her, but she hadn't any time to waste. 'That was absolutely fantastic, but I'm sorry, Jilly, I have to go now. Listen.' She put her hand on Jilly's arm and spoke urgently. 'I have to go away – maybe for a couple of days, but I'll keep in touch.'

'What?' Jilly wasn't yet quite back in the land of the living.

'I'll ring Membery tonight,' Fran promised.

'Well, OK – but why?' she asked, still looking dazed.

'I can't explain. But trust me. Look, I have to go. Tell Jonathan I loved it.'

She gave her a quick kiss and hurried along the row, leaving a bewildered Jilly staring after her.

Out into the baking London streets again with wings on her feet, back to the office, no way of avoiding Oxford Street. Pushing her way ruthlessly through the shuffling masses, the souvenir stalls selling policemen's helmets and *I love London* T-shirts, the street food vendors. Gagging at the smell of fried onions, boiling caramel and chocolate. Her shirt stuck to her back. God, it was just awful! Did no one realize there were better places in London to shop? The need for therapeutic shopping of her own – even for shoes – had disappeared for ever, she must have been mad even to have entertained the idea, in these crowds, in this heat, she would never shop again. Then she remembered she would have to slip out later for a few necessities.

Back in the blessedly air-conditioned office, she punched in Claire's number and prayed. Her prayer was answered. 'Where have you been?' Claire exclaimed. 'I couldn't return your call straight away, it's been hectic here since I got back, but I've been trying to get you for ages . . . oh God, Fran, I've just heard! I can't tell you how sorry I am.'

Fran thanked her briefly, and as succinctly as she could,

she went through all that had happened. 'Oh God,' Claire said again. 'If there's anything I can do –'

'There is, angel.' For once, the universal, well-meant offer of sympathy in a crisis was one she could take up. Thank heaven for Claire's French mother and a friend who was therefore bilingual. 'Pin your ears back and listen, Claire. You know how abysmal my French is. I can get by in ordinary circumstances, but not on the phone. The thought of tracing an address through a telephone number blows my mind. I know how busy you are, but –'

'Bugger that,' said Claire elegantly. 'Ask away.'

They spoke for several more minutes. 'I'll see to everything, seat reservation and the lot, while you do what you have to,' Claire said at last. 'But listen, are you sure all this is necessary? Why don't you just ring him?'

'Don't ask. Just accept I have to see him face to face.'

'All right, then. I hope you know what you're doing.'

'Trust me.'

After that, she spent time clearing up essentials with Kath. 'Can you hold the fort a while longer? I'll be back in as soon as I can make it.'

'Just you carry on, if you feel it's necessary. We didn't expect you in so soon, anyway.'

'How long have I got?' She looked at her watch. 'Oh, Kath, my watch. My good watch – not this thing, it never keeps the right time – you don't happen to have seen it lying around anywhere? I thought I'd left it in my drawer on Thursday, but it's not there.'

'You were wearing that one on Thursday. You kept checking the time with me.'

'In that case, I must have left it at home.' But where?

'If somebody bought me a Gucci watch, I'd take more care of it,' Kath said.

'A Gucci watch didn't ought to have a dodgy clasp.'

But she hoped to God it was somewhere at home, that she hadn't lost it, just because she'd been too clueless to have the clasp fixed. It was Mark's last birthday present to her.

214

Another mad hour back amongst the crowds – Boots for a toothbrush and deodorant, John Lewis for a nightie and knickers, a few more necessities to tide her overnight – and she was back on the phone to Claire, stuffing her purchases into her big tote bag with her other hand.

'All done,' Claire said. 'Got a pencil and paper?'

The address was in a suburb of Brussels called Overijse. The name of a road that sounded like Oomklomp or something else that echoed with the thud of big boots, with the house number at the end. It hadn't occurred to Fran that it might be in a part of Brussels where the predominant language was Flemish.

'Everything taken care of. Seat reserved on Eurostar. Currency. See you at Waterloo to hand over your ticket.'

And there good, reliable Claire was on the platform with seat reservation, chocolate, magazines. 'Can I get you anything else?'

'Claire, love, I'm only going to be on the train for four hours max, but if it makes you feel any better, yes, I have my compass, thermal underwear, survival kit. The crossword, your magazines. And if all else fails, I have a Jeffrey Archer. Don't *worry*.'

'Seriously, Fran, be careful.'

Careful? Fran thought. Careful, when it's my own husband I'm going to see?

Chapter Seventeen

It's been a long journey. Not in terms of hours, but Fran
has discovered that time can stretch to infinity when cata-
strophe might well be the end of it. It's hot when she
emerges from Brussels Midi railway station for a taxi to
her final destination, but it isn't the heatwave weather
she's left behind in London. The air feels cleaner, less used-
up, there seem to be fewer people occupying more
space.

This comforting illusion is quickly dispelled, however,
as they're caught up in the maelstrom of the Brussels rush
hour traffic, as bad here as in any other major city, but after
a time, the taxi reaches Overijse, which turns out to be a
well-groomed, residential area. She's deposited outside a
pleasant, unremarkable house, surrounded by a fair-sized
garden, and the driver departs after being paid what
seems to be an inordinate number of francs.

She walks up the short path and rings the doorbell.

And there he is, familiar in working garb, jeans and a
soft, dark blue cotton shirt, sleeves rolled up, neat and self-
contained. He always looks right, whatever he wears. The
hair he's run his hands through falls in the usual cowlick
over his forehead.

'Fran!'

'You look surprised to see me, Mark.'

Shocked might have been a better description. After that
first astonished moment he answers not a word, just looks
at her, drinking her in, then opens his arms. For the space

216

of a dozen heartbeats, there's nothing else in the world. It's she who steps back.

It's just an ordinary house from outside, nothing special. But inside it's beautiful, unusual. He ushers her up two shallow steps into a wide, high hall, floored with black and white chequered tiles. Expensive-looking paintings hang on the walls. In one corner stands an old, decorated sedan chair with its door open, a lavish arrangement of leaves and berries which have been placed on its floor spilling artfully out of it. Mark's doing? More than probable. In the opposite corner is an antique rocking chair in which reposes a fox, so lissom and relaxed as it lolls over the chair arm that she recoils, thinking for a moment it's alive, grinning and watching her with its bright, shining eyes.

'Gives everyone a shock at first, meant for a laugh, I guess. Come through to the studio.'

He leads her by the hand into a room, fully equipped as a drawing office, which extends right out into a large area of rough grass, into which shrubs have been thrust, here and there, like afterthoughts. There's a square pool bang in the middle, surrounded by spindly metal chairs and a table. Inside the office, a stool drawn up to a drawing board shows where Mark has evidently been working. The room is up-to-the-minute modern, sparkling clean and the temperature is cool and air-conditioned.

'Nice place you've got yourself, here, Mark.' She hears the edge in her voice, but if he notices, he pretends not to.

'The house used to belong to an architect, and when Henri Duchêne bought it, he insisted the set-up in here was included in the deal, since he was interested in designing a house for himself.' He laughs. 'You should meet him, Duchêne, I mean. He's incapable of buying just a box of chocolates, it has to be the whole bloody factory as well. This house was bought for an old retainer, since departed this life.' He spins her round, holding her hands, looking into her eyes. It's as if he can't let go of her. 'Now tell me what you're doing here.'

She disengages herself. 'Where is he, Mark? Where's Jasie?'

For a long time he says nothing. 'How did you know?'

'Later. Where *is* he? Is he all right?'

'Hey, what's all this? Of course he's all right! He's staying with a very nice Belgian lady called Madame Bayard, who looks after her grandchildren during the day, and he's having the time of his life.'

'I'm not sure I can eat all this.' Fran faced the biggest dish of steaming *moules marinière* she'd ever seen in her life, from which arose a delicate odour of garlic and wine. A bottle of Chablis stood on the table, and a large basket of bread.

'Go on,' said Mark, tucking his napkin under his chin like the other diners, 'it's a feast for a king, I can vouch for it. On Duchêne's recommendation, so what could be better?' He began to eat his own *moules* and, having tasted the first, raised his glass to the proprietor, cooking behind his counter, who beamed and raised his own in response. 'Well?' he asked, turning back to Fran. 'They are good, aren't they?'

'Delicious.'

The fish restaurant was in an uninspired suburb of Brussels, the decor verging on the Spartan: a stone-flagged floor and white, rough plastered walls, wooden tables, but the food was cooked to order and every table in the small space was filled with apparently satisfied customers. Mark watched Fran as she began to eat and, once started, went through the shellfish as though she hadn't eaten for a week – which probably wasn't so far from the truth: her normally healthy appetite invariably deserted her when she was worried about anything, or upset. He signalled for more bread and another bottle of wine, he talked about this new assignment, his eyes brilliant – but it wasn't until the last drop of sauce had been mopped up that he allowed the real talk to begin. He held her hand again across the table, and she smiled at him. The smile didn't seem to take as much effort as before, and a weight lifted from his shoulders as he knew the magic between them was still there.

He took a deep breath and gradually began to tell her everything.

Over nine years ago . . . the York races . . .

Racing had never been Mark's thing, on the contrary it rather bored him, since he wasn't a betting man and couldn't see any other excuse for getting so worked up at watching one horse try to beat another. But Chip, looking forward to a convivial few days with a crowd of like-minded men, had prevailed upon Mark to join them. Great place, the Ascomb Arms, and besides, it had a pretty receptionist that he remembered from a previous stay, a real knockout.

Mark said all right, then cursed himself for being drawn into agreeing. He'd long outgrown his brother's ideas of amusement. He was past the age when a rowdy weekend with the lads could shift the blues.

But Chip had caught him in a savage mood. He'd just resigned from a partnership that was bringing him no satisfaction. Safe, but boring. Beginning to be contentious. His older partners, fearful of taking risks, had recently refused to back him in what he'd been sure was a winning design. He'd wanted a change, some space. Is this all the future holds? He hadn't reached a mid-life crisis at thirty, had he? Perhaps he could learn something from Chip, after all.

Nevertheless, he'd felt distinctly juvenile, roaring up the M1 in Chip's MG as if they were still eighteen.

They drove north and reached unfamiliar landscapes, with the Ferrybridge power station cooling towers rearing like primeval monsters out of the flat, coal-mining land-scape, belching out fumes, which did nothing to alleviate

219

his mood. Then later, sighting the square towers of the Minster rising from the gentle, rich, agricultural plain of York, where the sun lay like melted butter on the burgeoning corn, he began to feel better . . .

Sod it, he'd thought, putting his shirt on a dead cert at the races next day. What the hell? His inhibitions dropped away, he began to enjoy himself, though he lost more than he won, and drank more than he had since he was in college. Like Jonathan, he was normally a moderate drinker. Unlike Chip, neither of them had ever felt the need to demonstrate their masculinity by propping a bar up and drinking to excess. They couldn't forget their father.

But that weekend he'd felt reckless. Chip had been right, the hotel was good, the receptionist stunning . . . he'd joined the others in chatting her up a bit, persuading her to join in the party they had that night. He'd woken in her bed the next morning, alone and with no very clear idea of how he'd got there, or what had happened. He had a suspicion it might have been because somebody had spiked his drink, in all probability Jack Cavenham, whose idea of a joke that sort of thing was. He was desperately ashamed of himself, not least where the girl herself was concerned, and because he'd also been all too aware that Chip had been really smitten with her. Pulling a bird was one thing – though casual sex wasn't the sort of activity he went in for – poaching on his brother's territory something else.

The girl herself, however, already busy downstairs, had refused to enlighten him. Presumably, despite her virginal, untouched appearance, despite the vigilant mama Chip said used to preside over the hotel, this wasn't the first time something like this had occurred. *What* sort of thing? Mark asked himself. It was inconceivable that he wouldn't have known if he'd had sex with her; inconceivable, on the other hand, that he'd gone to bed with a beautiful woman without having sex. 'Did I – did we?' he'd begun, and she'd put her finger to his lips, smiling enigmatically,

220

whether to save him or her from embarrassment, he never knew.

The only saving grace was that Chip had been equally pissed and had remembered nothing of the previous evening. So, as far as Mark was concerned, it was a discreditable episode, best left where it belonged, in the past. Until Bibi had turned up at Membery with Chip, and a seven-year-old child in tow.

Fran knew she'd been right, the moment she saw them, standing together in the doorway, when Mark had fetched Jasie in from the garden where he was playing with the other children at Madame Bayard's. Perhaps she'd always known, subconsciously. Mark and his son. Her heart had turned over.

And now Mark is announcing proudly, in a way that leaves no room for doubt, that yes, he is Jasie's father. 'It suited Bibi to let everyone think it was Armstrong, including Armstrong himself, but that's a load of old cobblers. You've only to look at Jasie to know.'

The same lock of dark hair falling over the brow, the same turn of the head. Not enough to call it a startling resemblance, but enough, when you know. It explains a lot, but not everything. Chiefly why it was only then, when Bibi had turned up with Jasie, two years ago, that Mark had suddenly started avoiding the subject of children of their own.

'I suppose she was putting pressure on you?'

Mark laughs shortly. 'I don't easily succumb to that sort of thing. But it was a bloody impossible situation . . . For one thing, knowing how you felt about having children . . . I couldn't stand the idea of you looking at him, thinking, he's Mark's son – she has his child, but what about me? But children of our own, knowing that . . .' She swallows and bends her head. A strand of hair comes loose and strokes her cheek. Distressed at the pain he's causing her, he lifts it gently and pushes it back behind her ear, then takes both her hands. 'I thought, if we moved away, it might be different, but I had to find a good reason for asking you to do that. And then, there was Jasie himself . . .'

The restaurant is noisy round them, but they're in a quiet corner of their own. 'I know how much I've hurt you – it's crucified me, come to that, but . . . no, absolutely no excuses. I thought, I can take care of this, but I couldn't. Didn't want to believe it at first, even told myself it wasn't certain he was mine. The dates were right – but he could have been Chip's. In the end I asked her outright and she said of course I was his father, did I think she slept with every man she came across? She was really upset that I could think that.'

That was so like Bibi. The Bibi Fran's learned to know only since she died.

'She said if I needed convincing,' Mark goes on, 'just to ask Chip. They'd never actually slept together, then or since. Believe that, I thought, and you'll believe anything! But when I got to know her better, it didn't seem so crazy.' Fran remembers Jonathan saying pretty much the same thing. 'The situation was impossible. There he was, poor sod, hoping against hope, and there was I, wanting more than anything to acknowledge Jasie as mine. I hated him bringing up my child, supporting him, deciding on his life . . .'

'Don't you think it's possible that Chip might have known? He's quite capable of putting two and two together.'

'Sure it occurred to me. In fact I think that's probably what he has done.'

They fall silent while the waiter collects their plates and Mark orders coffee.

'Why ever did she marry Armstrong? When there was Chip?' (*And what about you?* she thinks, but doesn't say.)

'She wanted to keep the hotel at all costs – and Armstrong was there, wild about her, the obvious solution.

Only she bit off more than she could chew when she picked on him.'

She frees a hand to sip the last of her wine. She takes a deep breath. 'Mark, I've seen the letters Armstrong wrote. I'm sorry, I broke into your desk and found them in the bottom drawer.'

'You did what?' His grasp tightens around the other hand he still holds and he stares at her. That's done it. Will he ever trust her again?

But what she sees in his face isn't condemnation, only that he knows exactly what's been going through her mind – the suspicions, the fear, the terror – and she sees no blame on her for that. 'She gave them to me, Fran,' he says quietly. 'She knew, of course, that I was going to Belgium for a while, and she rang me on Thursday morning and asked me to take Jasie along, too. It was school holidays, she reminded me, and finding something to occupy him was a pain. Knowing how protective of him she was, I couldn't take that on board – I'm afraid I was a bit short with her and I told her it was out of the question – and then it all came out. She'd been getting these threatening letters from her ex, and she'd just had another which had really frightened her. I thought she was overreacting, but within half an hour she'd hobbled down to The Watersplash with them, apart from the one she'd received that morning – that one had really got to her, and she'd immediately destroyed it. "Read them," she said, "and then see whether you believe me." Well, you've read them yourself, you must know what I felt. Yes, Fran, I did advise her to go to the police, but there was no way she'd do that – look what had happened last time, she said. I hadn't much time before I had to leave, so in the end I agreed to do what she wanted and let Jasie come with me, on the understanding that when I got back she must go to the police.'

'You say she rang on *Thursday*? But you left before me on Wednesday morning.'

'I did, but on my way to London I had a call on my mobile postponing my meeting until the following day, so

I came home and rearranged my schedule to leave for Brussels on Thursday evening. It was sheer chance that I hadn't gone when I was supposed to.'

'So that was it. I knew the oranges must have been you.'

He blinks. 'Oranges? What oranges?'

She explains about seeing the fruit in the black bowl, her growing certainty that she hadn't, herself, subliminally arranged them. He smiles wryly. 'Right, I remember. Seeing the bowl empty, remembering the oranges in the fridge, putting them together . . . time I stopped having such predictable reflexes.'

'It started me thinking – that and the owl.' Barely repressing a shudder, she described the shock the image on the mirror had given her. 'It was weird. *Somebody* must have left the front door open, and I knew I hadn't. After a while I realized it could only have been you.'

'The front door? Sorry, not me this time. Why should I change the habits of a lifetime and not use the back door?'

Why indeed? They both tend to use the more convenient back door, all the time.

'In any case, on Wednesday evening, I shut myself up in the studio and got down to some work. I went straight to bed afterwards without going downstairs.' And no doubt, following his usual custom when he worked, had turned the stereo full on, deaf to any sounds below. 'Well, since I can't believe in the supernatural, the owl must have got in by more normal means – an open door,' he says.

That's something to think hard about. Gooseflesh rises on her arms, the back of her neck.

'There's a key to the front door up at Membery, Fran, for emergencies. Anyone could have let themselves in – Chip, Alyssa, Jane – even Bibi herself.'

'Why?'

'All right then, maybe I should have taken more notice of those noises you've been hearing in the night.'

'Don't, that's not funny.'

224

'Fran, I've never been more serious. As soon as we get back, I mean to get to the bottom of that.'

She said slowly, 'Anyway, surely – you couldn't have missed seeing the imprint on the mirror when you came down next morning?'

'Couldn't I?' he asks, smiling wryly.

She has to accede that he might. Mornings are never Mark's best time, he surfaces slowly, not really awake until after the third cup of coffee – especially if, as he says, he was wakened suddenly by that panicky phone call from Bibi, asking him to take Jasie away. If he hadn't done as she asked, would Jasie have been Armstrong's second victim? Thinking about that, she almost forgives him the last few days – almost . . .

'You might have saved us a lot of grief if you'd told us all this at the beginning.'

'Bibi intended telling you that evening – but she never got the chance, did she?'

'No.' There was a silence. 'But afterwards, when I told you she was dead? We were frantic about him.'

'Believe me, that really bugged me,' he said steadily. 'But it was a toss up between causing anxiety and keeping Jasie safe – which he wasn't anywhere until that bastard was caught.'

She's not sure she goes along with his reasoning – men, even the best of them, can be so obtuse. But they've crossed a barrier here tonight, so she just says, 'Well, whatever, you're going to have to face the music when we get back. Wasting police time and all that. Not to mention facing your mother.'

Crouch was taking a break from questioning Armstrong, back in his own office, with approximately the fifteenth cup of black coffee of the day in front of him, when Kate came in. Summing up the situation at a glance, she raised questioning eyebrows.

'He's admitted it – to sending the letters.'

225

'At last!'

He shrugged. 'It was only a matter of time, but he's still sticking out that he'd nothing to do with killing Bibi, or taking Jasie.'

He looked gutted. He was due for his second shave of the day and hadn't noticed. She resisted the impulse, even though no one else was there, to give him a wifely, comforting hug. But Crouch wasn't easy to comfort. And it was an unwritten law between them that home and office remained two separate worlds. He pushed his chair back and went to look out over the darkening town, his hands stuck in his pockets.

'You believe he's telling the truth about the rest, don't you, Dave?'

'Dammit, he can't be!' He slammed his fist against the window frame and swung round to face her. 'Who else is responsible, if not him?'

She took a deep breath and counted to ten. She was about to be shot down in flames and didn't want to think about it too much first. Then she said what she had to say, and waited.

'*Glass*, Kate?' In two words, he made her feel approximately the same size as Alice when she'd drunk the magic potion that enabled her to get down the rabbit hole. 'You're suggesting the murder weapon's a piece of *glass*?'

She stuck to her guns. 'That was my first reaction. How could a glass shard have been thrown into the stream without being broken? But you know, it didn't need to have been thrown in with any force, just slipped in, and it didn't have to break, either. Well, it *didn't* break, did it? It just lay there, flat on the gravel at the side.'

'And Forensics missed it when they were searching for the weapon? Hey, come on, that lot don't miss a grain of sugar in a pile of sand!'

'They missed this,' she insisted stubbornly. 'You could easily, you know. They were looking for a knife or something similar and I don't suppose they actually sifted through every pebble in the stream. Glass is transparent, and I only happened to see it by a trick of the light. Try looking at a piece of glass under water and you'll see what I mean. Anyway, Dave – the size and shape fit, they've looked at it and it seems to be the exact profile.'

He rubbed his chin, still highly sceptical but wanting to be convinced. 'How the hell would you manage to push it in with enough force, without cutting yourself?'

'Gary Brooker was picking out the shards of glass from the frame of a broken window – the same one this glass came from, is my guess. He was wearing really tough, heavy-duty gardening gloves.'

'*Brooker*?' He groaned. '*Brooker*? Oh, for God's sake, Kate!'

'No, I'm not saying he's the one. She was still alive at half-past six, and he says he left Membery after delivering the note at about ten to. We've only his word for that, mind, but his gran would know what time he got home – and it's unlikely the neighbours would miss the sound of his motorbike arriving, either.'

He was still gunning for Graham Armstrong, still hoping to be convinced he was lying. 'I suppose it's just possible that sad bastard could've been hanging around, noticed the glass and seized the opportunity to use it when he met her –' He broke off, knowing he was grasping at straws, though she could see he hadn't entirely thrown out the idea, knowing that scientific comparison of the glass shard with the wound would confirm whether she was right or wrong.

Kate was damn sure she was right, and there was more she had to say. She had at last pinned down that elusive idea she'd been chasing and, going back yet once more through her notes, there it all was, the possibility at any rate, a possibility so bizarre that she'd needed more time to work on it and let it mature in her own mind before amazing Crouch with her powers of deduction. She felt she'd come up with quite enough weird ideas for the moment, and her theory offered no explanation for the boy's disappearance, but since they appeared to have come to the end of the line with Armstrong, it could do no harm. She said slowly, 'Dave, I think you might have got it right. Right at first, when you were so adamant it was a family matter . . .'

He turned his gaze on her. Under the unforgiving fluorescent lights, she looked tired and anxious. She was wasted as a sergeant, bloody wasted on *him*, come to that, though she thought he didn't appreciate that. He felt remorseful. He would do better. And this time he meant it.

He grinned at her. 'Amaze me further.'

But before she could do so, the telephone rang. Since she was the nearer, she reached out a hand and answered it. A few minutes later, she replaced the receiver. 'That was Fran Calvert. She's in Belgium –'

'*Belgium*?'

'She's with her husband – and they've got the boy there with them.'

There was a short, sharp silence. 'So that's one thing Armstrong didn't do.'

'I don't think he killed Bibi Morgan, either. As we were saying . . . There are only two possibilities, really, aren't there?'

So, he thought when she'd finished, they now knew who, and they knew how. What they didn't know yet was why. But Crouch didn't feel that was important just now. People who killed had their own agenda, their own motives, quite often inexplicable to other people. It would all come out in the end.

He smiled at Kate and said, as she'd known he would, 'One up to you, darlin'. Now get me a line to Membery Place.'

It wasn't gracious, but it was enough.

Chapter Eighteen

The small gold watch on the black strap was expensive, way out of his league. Try to flog that and they'd have him banged up to rights in no time. Gary had meant to give it to Charleen Smith, but it wasn't her style, not flash enough. And smitten as he was at the moment, he knew she was dumb enough to try selling it if he did give it her. Keeping it here, on the other hand, was equally a nonstarter. His grandmother had eyes like lasers and a nose like a bloodhound that she poked into everything.

He couldn't think now why he'd bothered nicking it, except that, unlike everything else his covetous eyes had lit on, the watch had been a doddle, lying on the floor by that leather chair thing that he'd tried out and found so comfortable he could've nodded off, only at that moment there'd been the sound of a door opening and a blast of music from upstairs. And the frigging house was supposed to be empty!

He'd leaped up like a scalded cat, pocketing a couple of CDs on his way out, just for luck, and then just as he was getting the hell out the same way as he'd come, there was a big soft thud and then a scuffling sort of sound. Something big and grey rushed past his ears. He'd nearly pissed himself. Christ, that was one weird house! Never mind it was stuffed to the gills with all the most up-to-date gear, as he and his mates had reckoned. And nearly all of it built-in, as he'd seen, too late.

So, what about the watch?

He didn't hear the door open, but the next moment his

grandmother was standing there. 'What's that you've got there then, our Gary?'

Today Membery is a different place. The relief of knowing that Jasie is safe has made everyone light-headed, the telephone lines between Brussels and Membery have been alive. Jonathan and Jilly are preparing to depart for Philadelphia, with Berlin in between, Chip is returning from London. Mark and Fran, with Jasie, will be here any time.

After all the excitements, Alyssa and Jane walk slowly under the trees towards the head of the waterfall, bypassing the bank of the stream where Bibi died, drawn there by an invisible thread of tension. The sky is a lurid shade of yellow. Purple thunderheads are forming in the distance but nobody is giving much credence to their promise of rain. The weather's tried that trick once or twice too often in the last few days.

They reach the massed boulders above the fall and sit quietly for a while, the only sound the gurgle of the running stream and the splash as it hits the next rock below.

'I need to talk to you, Jane.'

Jane bends down and works a tiny cushion of moss off its rock, looking like smooth, Lincoln green velvet, but in reality a dense mat of tiny, individual stems and leaves. It resists with all its might but it has met its match in Jane. Triumphantly, she pulls it free.

'Look at me, Jane.' Alyssa puts a hand on Jane's brown forearm. The skin, like that on her own forearms, is dry and rough. Jane at last looks at her from under the brim of her fawn cotton sun-hat. 'I think you might have guessed what I'm going to say. I'm going to marry Humphrey, Jane.'

An aeroplane moves across the sky, leaving a vapour trail, heading towards North America, its passengers settling down after take-off, awaiting their first gin and tonic and the pleasure of a British Airways meal. One of the village rowdies, maybe Gary, roars distantly past the garden gates on a motorbike. A column of gnats rises in the air in front of them. Jane rubs the moss between her fingers until it goes to nothing. 'You can't do that,' she says.

'I've already told him I will.'

'You can't,' Jane repeats, suddenly shaking with anger. 'I won't let you!'

'Now, Jane, it can't come as any surprise to you. You know he's been asking me for years.'

'What's going to happen to – all this?' The wide sweep of Jane's arm encompasses the acres surrounding Membery Place, the garden, and the house itself. The family.

'I shall sell the garden – there won't be any shortage of buyers. It'll be up to the boys to decide what to do with the house.'

Jane's anger erupts. 'You must be mad! You'd never have entertained the idea if it hadn't been for her – that woman – that silly little bitch stuffing you with all that hocus pocus about the stars!'

Alyssa is shocked. In all the years she's known Jane, she's never heard her use strong language. But she knows now that she's never known Jane at all, something she's only realized in these last few days. Her heart is so heavy with foreboding and sadness she fears it might stop.

'Humphrey!' Jane says now, with scorn. 'He's all right, I suppose, but what use is he to you?'

'You're forgetting. He's a good man, and he's loved me for years, I know his little ways, and he knows mine. Such as,' she adds softly, 'knowing how to make my martini without overdoing the gin. I don't fall asleep when he makes it.'

Jane stiffens, her small, taut body braced like a spring. After a while, she says, 'You work hard enough. It's no sin to take a drink and a nap.'

'But you really overdid it on Thursday night – made it so strong that I couldn't drink it at all. I only took a few sips. No, Jane, stay where you are and listen to what I have

231

to say.' Alyssa lays a strong hand on Jane's arm and forces her to sit still.

'I'll admit I'd had a very hard day on Thursday, and I felt pleasantly relaxed over my drink. Perhaps I dozed for a few minutes – it's a habit you can fall into easily enough when you're our age, if you're not careful, without the benefit of gin! But I woke up after a few minutes and you weren't there. I took the opportunity to pour the rest of the drink away – far too strong, and I'd had quite enough. I watched the telly for a while but I was bored and closed my eyes. I heard you tiptoe in and thought how kind of you not to want to disturb me, so I kept them closed and pretended to be asleep. You were gone at least twenty minutes, Jane –'

Jane says nothing. Her mouth is turned down in the familiar disapproving curve, but there is wariness in her silence.

'– plenty of time to have followed Bibi down here – and done what there was to do.'

Alyssa was stunned by what she had been forced to believe was the truth. Jane had killed Bibi. Jane. Who loved Jasie, who loved them all. Jane, who had been her friend for over thirty years. No, it wasn't possible, she had thought at first.

But then she remembered how clever Jane was, how she had always succeeded in manipulating everyone in this, her adoptive family, even though they were always aware, at the backs of their minds, of being made to do things they didn't really want to do. Why had they submitted? Well, for one thing, it was often easier to knuckle under to someone like Jane, with her bright, birdlike fixations, than to fight her – and for another, she was almost always right in what she advised, or coerced, them to do. Alyssa recalled how she used to push them all, her children, especially Jonathan, remembered her absolute devotion to everything appertaining to the Calvert family. Paranoia? Maybe not, but certainly close. Look how devotedly she'd nursed Jonathan day and night through that bad bout of measles, insisting on doing it alone, until she almost collapsed herself from exhaustion. And how she'd given up any thought of holidays of her own and taken the children away to East Anglia every summer to give Alyssa a break when Conrad was at his worst. She had hated Conrad. For a fleeting, horrified moment, Alyssa had a vision of Conrad at the bottom of the stairs, his neck broken.

No! He had fallen. He was fuddled with drink. That was what Jane had said, and she had been the only one in the house at the time. No one had reason to disbelieve her. She had taken charge of all the arrangements, and Alyssa had let her, unconsciously setting the shape of all the years to come. From then on, Jane had lived a vicarious existence through them all, Alyssa and the boys. And to be fair, it would seem she had genuinely loved them, though she'd loved Jonathan the best of all.

Poor, twisted Jane. For all that, she hadn't been able to inspire a return love.

I only did it for love, Jane says.

She had laid her plans so carefully. The notion of getting rid of Bibi had been with her for a long time, ever since it became evident that she had every intention of pushing Alyssa into marrying Humphrey, with the consequence that Membery Place Gardens would cease to be open to the public, or be leased off to someone else, and the house itself sold to God knows who. What then would have been left for Jane? A lonely, pointless existence in her little house in Middleton Thorpe. But the idea had only crystallized when she'd read that book of Bibi's, the one she so fancifully called her book of days, and realized what was happening with Jonathan.

Almost everyone made excuses for Bibi, saw her as she liked to put herself forward, the victim of some unexplained past, the exception being Humphrey. How had he once put it to Jane, in a rare moment of communication between them? *Wants to see herself as virtuous, that one, and*

233

that's where the trouble lies. Interferes. Can't see that she has a core of selfishness. All I can say is, God save me from the attentions of a good woman. She and Humphrey, despite their differences, have always seen life as it is, unencumbered by romantic notions, like the Calverts. They both saw that Bibi was like two sides of a coin, pretending to herself that she was acting from the best of motives, while destroying everything around her . . . Alyssa's life here with me, thought Jane, Chip's . . . and especially Jonathan's.

Jane had had over two years for her hatred to grow.

It had come to a head when she'd read the entry in that book of Bibi's about what Jonathan had so uncharacteristically and foolishly confessed to her. If she hadn't read that book, Jane would never have known, but having noted how secretive Bibi was about it, she had watched until she found out where she kept it hidden: in her room, of course, but whenever had privacy stopped Jane?

There might have been other ways of getting rid of Bibi, but killing her was the surest. She'd been content to wait for the right opportunity, which had come with the arrival of those letters, that Bibi kept tucked inside the front of that same book, no doubt in case they were ever needed for evidence.

There were three of them. When Jane wrote the fourth, and last, she'd looked for the others to copy the same style and discovered that Bibi had removed them to some safer place – or perhaps destroyed them. So she'd had to rely on memory when she'd typed her own on the old Remington they'd used before Chip had urged them to computerize the office records. It was a pity she hadn't been able to find any of the same sort of paper, but she didn't think it would matter – and it hadn't. It worried her that she hadn't been able to copy the little unicorn signature on the bottom; it niggled her also as to what it meant, but Bibi had apparently never questioned that the letter had come from the same source as the others. Jane had watched her the morning it arrived through the post and had noted with satisfaction that she was entirely panic-stricken.

234

It was the wicked-looking pile of glass from the window Gary Brooker had broken that had suddenly given her the idea of how she could do it. She'd chosen a likely-looking piece and hidden it outside until the time arose when she would be ready for it.

Everything had gone her way. When Bibi had announced she was going out for some air, Jane had made Alyssa an extra-stiff drink, knowing she was certain to drop off over it, as had become her habit every evening. When she was sure she had, Jane had slipped out and picked up the heavy-duty gloves in the porch at the back door where she'd had them in readiness. No one would ever remark upon a pair of gardening gloves lying around anywhere in this house. She had followed Bibi down towards the stream, so absorbed in her own thoughts she never heard Jane creeping up behind her, didn't know what was happening until the cane was knocked away and she fell. A quick stab with the glass after that was all that was needed. Her nursing training during the war meant she knew exactly where to aim for. Bibi had scarcely moved before losing consciousness. Jane had felt for her pulse and when it stopped, had tipped her into the stream, and the glass shard after her and gone back to the house. It had all been so easy.

It was only when she reached the back porch that she found she had taken possession of the walking stick, that she was leaning on it, as a matter of fact, unable to walk without it because her breath was coming in great, painful gulps. But she had pulled herself together, stuck the cane into the stand amongst the other sticks and umbrellas, joined Alyssa and acted thereafter as though nothing had happened.

The following morning, before it was certain Bibi had been murdered, she'd burnt the book of days in the big garden incinerator, watching its red silk covers curl back like a monstrous, voluptuous flower, finally to disintegrate, along with the damaging secrets it contained. After it she had thrown the Judge's cane, waiting until the malacca

235

had burnt through, then retrieving the blackened silver knob and ferrule. She'd taken them home and buried them in her herb plot. Someone, sometime might recover them and wonder what they were.

She had been as confounded as anyone when she learned that Jasie had disappeared. It upset her. Almost as much as her own inexplicable lapse of failing to consider how his mother's death would affect him.

'The police are on their way, Jane.' Alyssa's voice was tremulous. She was more upset than Jane. 'They suspect, but they don't know.'

Jane Arrow said nothing. The sun glinted through the trees on to the windows of The Watersplash below, the pathway down to it was steep and rocky, the romantically ruined bridge spanned the stream as it ran swift, falling in a shining curl over the lip of the stepped fall, down into the pool below. She stood up but shook her head as Alyssa turned to go back to the house.

Alyssa left her standing there, a tiny upright figure in sturdy shoes and a sun-hat, and when she reached the bend of the stream, she heard the splintering crash as the rotten planks of the bridge gave way. When she turned back, there was no sign of her friend.